A CALCULATED DEMISE

THE HYPATIA MURDERS

Robert Spiller

PRESS®

Gold Imprint
Medallion Press, Inc.
Printed in USA

DEDICATION:

My wonderful wife Barbara, who makes all things possible.
My three wonderful daughters Nikki, Laura, and Jenny for
their support and encouragement.

Published 2007 by Medallion Press, Inc.

The MEDALLION PRESS LOGO
is a registered tradmark of Medallion Press, Inc.

Typeset in Adobe Jenson Pro
Printed in the United States of America
10-digit ISBN: 1-9338361-5-6
13-digit ISBN: 978-1933836-15-7

10 9 8 7 6 5 4 3 2 1
First Edition

ACKNOWLEDGEMENTS:

<u>My critiques group:</u>
William Mason, Beth Groundwater, Barb Nickless,
Maria Faulconer, Annette Kohlmeister, and
Shawn Rapjack.

NovelTalk and Author, Author for all their help and
expertise.

Lorig's — for all their help with exotic western wear.

CHAPTER 1

When Bonnie Pinkwater arrived at East Plains Junior/Senior High Wednesday morning, a cow stood in her parking place. To be fair, the cow didn't know it stood in Bonnie's parking place. The spot didn't have her name on it, although what that would have meant to a Guernsey was problematic. Unfortunately, the space represented the last remaining faculty parking place.

Bonnie hung her head out the window. "Give me a break, Ruby. I'm running late."

Ruby gave a look that could be interpreted either as "How you doin'?" or "That's nice, dear, don't bother me." Milk-cow body language being the inexact science it is.

Frustrated, Bonnie exited her car. She snatched up an egg-sized piece of granite. "I'm warning you, Ruby. I've had a bad morning, and I'm in no mood to take any bovine crap." She hefted the stone, feeling its weight and taking a bead on the bony rear end of the cow.

Unfortunately for Bonnie and fortunately for Ruby, one doesn't just toss rocks at a friend's backside even if that friend weighs nine hundred pounds and gives milk for a living. "You are one lucky cow, Ruby. There was a time when I wouldn't have thought twice about pegging your skinny butt with a rock." To drive home her point, Bonnie chucked the stone into the flagpole maybe fifteen meters distant. The resounding clang echoed across the parking lot. She shook her head, conceding the spot to Ruby and parking in the student lot north of the school.

Bonnie glanced at her Mickey Mouse watch.

Damn!

Bonnie swiveled the rearview mirror. She grimaced. Steel-gray hair stuck out like straw from the loose bun she'd tied before leaving home. She tried to coax the errant hairs back into a semblance of order with gentle and not-so-gentle pats, but the rebels would have made Che Guervara proud.

Her lipstick had faded, as well. "Boys and girls, this morning Math Analysis will be taught by the Bride of Frankenstein," she said in disgust.

Bonnie pulled her coat tight about her small, thin frame and trudged through gravel and snow to the side of the blue-steel and gray-brick school. After a struggle, the aluminum door grudgingly opened. Squinting, she peered across the gymnasium.

Neither Harvey Sylvester, nor his seventh-grade

boys' Physical Education class noticed her as she sped across the gym. She exited through the far door into the school's main hallway.

By the time she arrived at her classroom, Bonnie was almost ten minutes late. While not a school record or even a personal best, it was the latest she'd been this school year. "What the hell, anybody can be on time," she murmured.

Matthew Boone, her student aide, held open the door for her. "Good morning, Missus Pinkwater." He dropped the absent-list/lunch-count slip into the wire basket fastened to the back side of the door.

Good God, youngster.

"Thank you, Matt." She squeezed by him into the room, keeping her face neutral, the acrid odor of burnt rubber stinging her eyes.

The Boones were, by far, the poorest family in East Plains and heated their trailers by burning used tires in their woodstoves and fireplaces. They lived in a ramshackle collection of four trailers, only one of which had running water. Matthew came to school two days out of three with a less-than-delicate aroma.

"Glad you could make it, Missus Pinkwater," Wesley Oliheiser said with a smirk.

"Glad to be here, Wes." She turned back to Matt. "Go tell Mister Whittaker Ruby is loose in the parking lot again."

The pungent boy nodded and left. Bonnie went to

her desk at the back of the room and opened her lesson-plan book.

She was writing that night's homework on the front board when a girl's voice asked, "Why were you late this time, Missus Pinkwater?"

Bonnie made sure her face was set with a smile before she turned around. Ordinarily, Vikki Bressler wasn't a problem in class, and she wasn't really a problem now. *But what on God's green earth makes you think I want to share my problems with a sixteen-year-old? Especially after the crappy morning I've had.*

In particular, Bonnie had no intention of telling Vikki how, this morning, she woke and sleepily began to talk to her husband, Ben, then realized he'd been dead these past two months. She certainly wasn't going to tell this teenager that halfway through the feeding of her cat and three dogs she'd broken down and cried for the better part of ten minutes.

"I guess I need a new alarm clock. Now I have a question, Vikki. What can you tell me about De Moivre's Theorem?"

Bonnie gave 60 percent of her attention to the girl's answer. The remaining 40 percent flew the distance to a hospital room in Colorado Springs where Ben had lain for the last two weeks of his life.

Ben Pinkwater, I hope you get an arrow in your butt in those happy hunting grounds of yours, 'cause I'm more than a little miserable being left here on my own.

Then she returned her mind to the task of teaching Monsieur De Moivre's Theorem and how it could be used to find the real and complex roots of a polynomial.

"The kid makes me sick, Lloyd." Luther Devereaux was holding court over the lunch crowd in the teachers' lounge. Fifteen teachers sat around two long tables, and Luther slouched at the far end of the same table as Bonnie. "I have to open every window in my classroom and still his smell makes my eyes smart."

"It's not his fault." Principal Lloyd Whittaker stood in the doorway between the teachers' lounge and the main office. "There're not enough beds out there for all those Boone kids to sleep in, let alone enough showers. Matt's a good boy."

"Tell him, Lloyd." Bonnie gave Luther a why-don't-you-eat-feces-and-die-you-missing-link glare.

"Maybe someone ought to look into how those kids are being raised." Luther removed his thick glasses from his overlarge bald head and stared myopically around the room to see if he had supporters for his suggestion. "Maybe get Social Services involved."

From the dozen-plus candidates, only a few teachers grunted noncommittally.

Bonnie slammed her open palm down on the table. "To what end, Luther? Do we split up a family that loves one another because they're peculiar and not as clean as we'd like? Have you ever watched Matt take care of his little brothers and sisters? Never raises his voice. Always listens when they have questions."

"That's about his capacity." Again, Luther glanced around to see if anyone else agreed with him. "First and second graders are his intellectual peers."

Several of the newer teachers tittered in amused agreement but quickly turned their attention to their food when Bonnie gave them dirty looks.

"Enough." Lloyd cocked his head. His glance implored Bonnie to carry the argument no further. "The boy works hard with what he has. He'll be the first Boone in fifteen years to graduate. I'd say that's quite an accomplishment."

"Some of us are handing it to him on a silver platter, if you ask me." Luther glanced fleetingly at Bonnie before looking away.

"Well, who's asking you?" It was all she could do not to throw her hummus and piñon nut sandwich at him.

Lloyd hooked a finger to invite Bonnie into his office.

She huffed, then rose, crossing the teachers' lounge close enough to slap Luther, but she kept her hands to herself. *I wish I had that rock again.* She strode through the adjoining main office and into Lloyd's tiny room.

He waited at the door and shut it behind her.

Rather than taking the seat in front of Lloyd's worn oak desk, Bonnie wheeled on her friend of twenty years. "I know what you're going to say. I shouldn't let him get to me." That said, she fell into a red overstuffed chair, her arms folded across her narrow chest.

Lloyd smiled, and his weather-beaten face radiated good-natured wrinkles. He sat behind the desk. "Then you also know I'm going to tell you after this year, Luther Devereaux is gone, retired, never to be seen in East Plains again."

Bonnie sighed a defeated sigh. "I know. Just four more months." Though at the moment those four months seemed to stretch out like a number line into positive infinity.

Lloyd spread his hands across his mostly empty desk, then leaned toward her. "He's a good teacher and a great wrestling coach."

Shaking her head, Bonnie frowned. "You mean those in reverse order, don't you?"

Lloyd wrapped gnarled fingers around the golfing trophy on his desk. "Don't be an academic snob, Bon. You know as well as I do the two aren't mutually exclusive. Luther has his contingent of students who think he's the greatest thing since sliced bread."

A grin tickled the corners of Bonnie's mouth. Only Lloyd could get away with such a cliché and make it sound original. She felt her anger slipping away and made a final grab to hold on to it. "Damn it, Lloyd, he's borderline abusive to any student who's different, and Matt Boone *is* different."

A sad cast fell over Lloyd's eyes. He nodded solemnly. "I'll talk to him."

Suddenly, Bonnie felt tired. Her shoulders sagged. She stared down at her tan corduroys and grass-stained running shoes.

"How you holding up?" Lloyd whispered.

Unexpectedly, tears welled in Bonnie's eyes. She worked her jaw muscles and tried to mouth something brave, something casual, but the words wouldn't come.

In a flash, Lloyd was around his desk, kneeling beside her, holding her in his arms.

She buried her face into the shoulder of his Western shirt and let the tears flow in earnest. Every sorrow she'd been keeping safely bottled came pouring out.

"Shit, I hate crying," she said in gasped whispers. She gritted her teeth to get control of herself.

Lloyd patted her back. "I miss that ornery redskin myself."

Bonnie smiled at Lloyd's good-old-boy sensitivity. She God damn well didn't need someone telling her everything would be all right. She knew better. Bonnie lifted her head from Lloyd's shoulder and looked him in the eyes.

"I had a rough morning." She sniffed, struggling to keep her voice even. The peal of the end-of-lunch bell startled her.

Lloyd handed her a tissue. "Why don't you go on home? We'll get someone to cover your last period."

Bonnie shook her head while wiping her eyes with the heels of her hands. "I've already missed too many days this year. I've got too much material to make up." She blew her nose. "Besides, I don't want to sit around that empty old house any more than I have to."

Lloyd stood, then held out a hand. "I'd hardly call your house empty, what with two dogs and a cat."

She pulled herself to her feet. "Three dogs."

They shared the laughter of old friends as he opened his door. Doris, the school secretary, pretended to find something interesting on her computer keyboard even though her monitor screen was blank.

I probably look like I just materialized out of a wind tunnel, Bonnie thought.

Lloyd squeezed her arm. "Take care of yourself."

She hurried from the office, through the now-empty teachers' lounge. She had just one minute to get to class before she was late for the second time that day.

Bonnie sat at her desk in the back of the classroom and watched Matt Boone struggle with a linear equation. Since Matt was her first-block aide, fourth-block Algebra

One was his actual math class. Add to that the number of times Matt came for help at lunch, on break, and after school, and it seemed as if the redolent young man was connected to her at the hip.

She ignored a furtive whisper from the front of the room. Another senior, Greg Hansen, her fourth-period aide and possibly Matt's best buddy, was trying to sneak a hint to his friend.

On the surface, the two young men couldn't have been more different. Where Matt carried himself with a good-natured clumsiness, Greg was self-assured, almost graceful. The latter young man, already student-council president, stood a good chance of being named this year's valedictorian.

Matt would be grateful just to graduate.

Both were wrestlers, but Greg was one of Luther Devereaux's favorites, a champion expected to go to the state tournament next month in March. He'd already received offers from colleges to wrestle.

Matt had yet to win his first match.

Bonnie also knew that below the surface, they had another thing in common.

Like Matt, Greg's family was poor. Unlike Matt's ultrareligious family, however, it was rumored Greg's father and older brother supplemented their income with the growing and selling of marijuana. More than once, Greg had confessed he couldn't wait to get out of East

Plains and off to college. With any luck, he'd do it with a wrestling scholarship.

At the board, Matt grew animated.

Evidently, with Greg's help, Matt saw his equation had variable quantities on both sides of the equal sign. He had to eliminate one or the other.

He looked to where Bonnie sat and announced, "I'll kill the five X with a negative five X." Then he hastily added, "And I'll add a negative five X to the other side, too."

When Bonnie offered him a nod of encouragement, his moon face split into a wide grin. Greg shot him a thumbs-up.

The rest of the problem Matt finished without help. He beamed while going back to his desk. Rather than sitting, he approached Bonnie.

"Missus Pinkwater?" Matt looked embarrassed about whatever he meant to ask.

"Yes, Matt?"

He rubbed his palms on his faded jeans. "Mister Devereaux told me to come see him up in the wrestling loft before the end of the day."

She checked the clock. "Is it really important? We only have thirty minutes more of class."

She needn't have asked. Matt would never miss a moment of class if Devereaux hadn't insisted. Bonnie wondered if the odious science teacher had done it on purpose to torture either Matt or herself.

Red climbed from Matt's grimy neck up into his cheeks.

She waved him still. "Never mind. Of course you can go, but hurry back."

She erased the board and wrote out another linear equation. As she finished, Bonnie heard the voice of the new girl who had transferred in that week from Denver.

"Janice, would you like to tackle this one?"

Janice Flick was short, with sallow skin and oily ringlets of black hair, which hung perpetually in her eyes. "Not really." Her mouth turned down in disgust as if the very thought of doing a math problem on the board was distasteful.

Bonnie adopted the icy smile she reserved for teenagers she wanted to irradiate. "Why is that, dear?"

Janice shrugged an I-haven't-the-energy-for-this-crap shrug. "I've never been very good at math. Maybe I just don't have the math gene."

Bonnie almost snickered until she saw the girl was serious. "The math gene?"

Janice glanced around the room to make sure she had an audience. "You know. Something that makes certain people good at math and other people hate it." She stared up at Bonnie with a smug look on her face. "Math's mostly a guy thing, anyway."

The class drew a collective breath.

"You actually believe mathematics is a guy thing?"

The rest of Bonnie's class refused to make eye contact

with the girl. Several students shook their heads in antipathy.

Janice shrank into her desk.

Normally this show of repentance would have been enough to quell Bonnie's indignation, but since it came at the end of a horrible day, she felt the need to hammer home her point. "Let's put aside the fact that I am both a female and a mathematician."

Bonnie put both silk and iron into her voice. "Have you ever heard of Hypatia?"

Several students groaned, and Bonnie shot them threatening glances.

Janice merely shook her head.

"Hypatia was born around 370 AD in the city of Alexandria, perhaps the greatest center of learning the world has ever known. Her father, Theon, was a professor of mathematics at the university there. He told her, at an early age, *Reserve your right to think, for even to think wrongly is better than not to think at all.*"

Bonnie paused to let the words sink in. When Janice merely sat there, Bonnie asked, "Isn't that a wonderful thing to tell a child?"

The girl folded her arms across her chest and shrugged again—the nonverbal form of *whatever*.

I'll let that pass, you pint-sized curmudgeon. "Hypatia went on to become a famous mathematician and astronomer, even more celebrated than her father. Scholars from

Africa, Europe, and Asia came to Alexandria to hear her dissertations. She wrote mathematics books that became standards for thirteen hundred years."

Janice opened her mouth to speak.

Bonnie cut her off. "I know what you're going to say. What does the life of a woman who lived almost two thousand years ago have to do with you?"

The girl pursed her lips and nodded. "Yeah, I guess that's right. Why should anybody care what she did?"

Bonnie smiled, this time with less ice at the edges. "I'm glad you asked that, Janice. We should remember Hypatia not just for the things she did while she was alive, but for the way she died."

Janice sat up straighter. "How did she die?"

"She was murdered. On the way to teach her class at the university, she was snatched from her chariot by a mob that thought much the same as you. It was unseemly for a woman to possess so much knowledge. They tortured her, cut the flesh from her body with sharpened clam shells, then burned her at the stake."

"Dude," the girl whispered, wide-eyed.

"Dude, indeed. Can you see why I might get upset when you say mathematics is the province of males?"

Janice glanced at Bonnie warily. "I guess so."

Bonnie squatted down in front of Janice's desk until her face was level with the girl's. "Hypatia paid a terrible price so you don't have to take a backseat to any man. She showed us all that mathematics doesn't care about gender."

Bonnie's knees creaked as she stood. "It's our birthright."

"Missus Pinkwater?" Janice tentatively raised a hand.

Bonnie stared down at the girl, thinking she meant to ask something more about Hypatia. "Yes, Janice?"

"Could I go the bathroom?"

Serves you right, Pinkwater, for thinking yourself a fountain of inspiration. She resisted an urge to be petty and refuse the girl. "Why not?"

As Bonnie watched Janice exit the room, the clock caught her eye. She shook her head ruefully. Only six minutes left in class.

Then she remembered Matt. *Damn you, Luther Devereaux.*

She glanced over to Greg. "Go see what's happened to Matthew, would you? He's been gone over twenty minutes."

With a determined look on his face, Greg legged it out the door.

Bonnie had just finished solving Janice's equation when Greg stumbled back into the room, his face chalky, his hands trembling.

"Mister Devereaux, dead, stabbed!" Greg's chest heaved. "I think Matt killed him."

CHAPTER 2

"LET ME PASS, PLEASE." BONNIE SQUEEZED THROUGH the crowd of students jamming the steel and concrete stairs to the wrestling loft. Murmurs of protest surrounded her—animated teenagers rubbernecking around the handrails.

At the top of the stairs, she came face-to-face with Clarence Murphy, vice principal and athletic director. Every wavy blond hair in place, he gave Bonnie his best condescending smile. "There's nothing you can do here, Bonnie. Why don't you just wait downstairs? Let Harvey and I do our jobs."

Not bloody likely, you walking hair-spray ad. She craned her neck and peered past Clarence.

Matthew Boone sat on the yellow mat-covered floor, his back against the cinder-block wall and his face in his hands. Harvey Sylvester, the Physical Education teacher, towered over the boy. Harvey's normally open, full-bearded face was grim. His beefy hands clenched and unclenched at his sides.

Across the loft, the body of Luther Devereaux sprawled, head cocked, eyes blank and wide open. One arm dangled beneath the three-bar railing separating the loft from the gym floor twenty feet below. A pool of dark blood threatened to spill over the edge.

Matthew raised his head and spotted Bonnie. His nose ran. Tears streamed from his red and swollen eyes. "Missus Pinkwater!" he bellowed. His voice echoed off the concrete walls. He struggled to rise.

With a hand on Matthew's shoulder, Harvey shoved him back down.

Bonnie took a step forward, but Clarence barred her way. "Don't even think it."

She glared at the vice principal. Her shaking hand pointed toward Matthew. "That's my student, Clarence."

She knew her voice sounded strained, possibly even hysterical, but at the moment she didn't give a good Goddamn. "Unless you intend to knock me down, let me go to him."

When a chorus of students grumbled for Clarence to let her through, his already florid face flushed a deeper scarlet. He stepped aside. "As usual, you get your way."

"Put a sock in it." *That'll cost me.*

Bonnie swept across the loft to Matthew's side, glancing once at Luther's body.

His lifeless eyes gaped at a large kitchen knife lying within inches of his face.

The metal-sweet aroma of fresh blood tickled Bonnie's nostrils. She winced, then looked away.

Matthew reached out, and she let him take her hand. He tugged at it as if she might drift away if he didn't hold tight. Smears of orange-red stained his tattered gray sweatshirt. Black blood crusted his jeans from his lower thighs to his shins.

In slow arcs, Matthew shook his disheveled head. "I didn't hurt Mister Devereaux."

Bonnie gave Matthew's hand a squeeze. "I know you didn't mean to."

Tears flowed down his grimy cheeks. He wiped them and his runny nose onto his sleeve. "No, Missus Pinkwater. I wouldn't hurt Mister Devereaux. He sent me to get him a cup of water from the coach's office. When I got back, he was lying there."

He pointed his other hand toward the body. "See the cup where I dropped it?"

Sure enough, not three feet from Luther, a puddle of water glistened on the yellow wrestling mat. A conical paper cup lay nearby.

The boy stared up at Harvey. "I told Mister Sylvester, but he don't believe me."

Harvey pursed his lips like something sour filled his mouth and he needed to spit it out. "I heard Boone yell, and came running. He was kneeling beside Luther, the knife in his hand. Nobody, other than Luther and Matthew, came up to the loft all fourth period."

How the hell can you be so certain? "Was Luther dead when you found him?"

Harvey nodded.

For the first time, Bonnie noticed how shook up this bear of a man was.

Sweat stained the front of Harvey's T-shirt. "He's carved up something awful—two stabs in his back, his throat cut."

Bonnie swallowed to keep bile from rising. "Matthew, did you see anyone else?"

He frowned, his lower lip quivering. "I just picked up the knife for a second," he said, mostly to himself.

A commotion caused Bonnie to glance back over her shoulder. Lloyd Whittaker and a tall man in a black cowboy hat and a herringbone Western suit stood at the top of the stairs.

Harvey shook his head in disgust. "What's Lloyd thinking? Trent Hendrickson shouldn't be here," he whispered, almost too low to be heard.

Lloyd pushed past Clarence and nodded to Harvey. "The sheriff and the ambulance from the volunteer fire station should show any minute. The sheriff asks we leave the scene untouched."

Lloyd laid a hand on Bonnie's arm. "This is no place

for you."

A scream came from the stairs. Trent Hendrickson held back a violently writhing woman. Long blond hair whipped about her face as she struggled to break free.

"Luther!" she shrieked. Her low-cut dress askew, she extended a red-nailed hand toward the body.

"Oh my God," Lloyd said. "Missus Devereaux."

Trent Hendrickson turned the woman around. She buried her face in the lapel of his jacket and sobbed. The big man gave Lloyd a look that said he had the situation under control. With an arm around her shoulder, he led her back down the stairs.

Harvey glared at the pair.

Tight-lipped, Lloyd grasped Bonnie's elbow. "You need to leave, too."

He waved Clarence over. "If you want to help, Bon, clear those students off the stairs."

"But Matthew—"

"I've already called his parents." Lloyd handed her over to Clarence, who took her arm and tried to pull her away.

Matthew stared up at her like she might be his last hope.

She yanked her arm free. "Something's wrong here."

Lloyd's face grew hard, his jaw muscles working. "Not now." His voice was cold.

She stared at him open-mouthed and let Clarence lead her toward the steps. His eyes held a smirk he hid from the rest of his face.

The sight of the crowd cleared her head. Paramedics would never be able to get to the loft. "All right," she called. "We need you guys to clear the steps."

Clarence let her go.

Arms outstretched, she herded the students into the larger crowd gathered on the gym floor. Of East Plains's four hundred students, more than half stood packed below her. Even though the stairs were now clear, the most direct route was still jammed.

"Ladies and gentlemen, we need you to move away from the bottom of the steps. Clear a path to the doors." She pointed to the double aluminum crash doors off to her left.

Several students grumbled, but most shifted either farther into the gym or out into the hallway. A shaft of sunlight streamed through an open door across the gym, the very door she'd entered that morning. A pair of men shielded their eyes, preparing to leave. Unless she was mistaken, the men were Barty and Kyle Hansen, her fourth-period aide's father and older brother.

What the hell are they doing here, and where are they heading in such a hurry?

The sky flushed wine-purple before Bonnie left school. Driving Alice, her ancient Subaru, Bonnie's mind filled with a jumbled tessellation of interlocking images. The marijuana leaf printed on the back of Barty Hansen's T-shirt. The pool of blood alongside Luther's body. That last haunted look in Matthew Boone's eyes.

"I wouldn't hurt Mister Devereaux," Matthew had said.

An image came to her mind of Matthew staring up at her, the knees of his pants stained black with blood. He must have knelt in Luther's blood after the stabbing. Would a killer, even one so naïve as Matthew, do such a thing?

She'd known Matthew for most of his life, and one thing had always impressed her about the boy. Unlike most young men of his generation, especially in the testosterone-injected cowboy culture of East Plains, Matthew didn't seem cursed with any violence in his soul. She supposed his gentleness explained the reason he made such a poor wrestler.

This train of thought brought her back to Luther Devereaux. Why had he wanted to see Matthew? If Luther had kicked the boy off the team, would the shame of his rejection trigger an uncharacteristic flare-up of emotion?

She tried to picture the scene: Luther yelling at Matthew, then Matthew pulling the long knife and stabbing the man.

Something about the sequence of events bothered her. She'd always had an excellent memory, photographic some people said. Frame by frame she played back the scene in the loft.

The knife!

When she'd first seen it lying by Luther's face, the knife reminded her of the school's kitchen knives, even down to the EP stamped into the handle.

On impulse, Bonnie pulled her cell phone from her fanny pack, then fumbled through her glove compartment until she found the old copy of the school directory she kept stowed there. Dividing her attention between the road and the two pieces of paper that made up the directory, she fingered the home number of Hattie Caulfield, the head cook.

"It's your dime," a booming woman's voice answered.

Suddenly, Bonnie felt ridiculous, but before she could give in to her urge to hang up, she blurted out, "Hattie, this is Bonnie Pinkwater. I need to ask you a question."

"Missus Pinkwater?" Hattie sounded confused. "What can I help you with, sweetie?"

"This is going to come off strange, but is the kitchen missing one of its large carving knives?"

"Have you found it?"

Bonnie kept her voice calm. "So you are missing a large knife?"

"Since yesterday, my favorite carver. Have you seen it?"

"I think I have."

The kitchen staff began its day at four in the morning and was out of the building soon after they cleaned up lunch. Hattie probably knew nothing about the murder.

Bonnie told her of Luther's death and the knife she had seen lying on the wrestling mat.

The cell phone crackled. Hattie's voice went rough and indistinct. "That's horrible."

"Listen, Hattie. I think I'm getting out of range. I'll talk to you tomorrow."

With another crackle, the phone went dead.

The knife had gone missing on Tuesday? It seemed reasonable to assume if Matthew stabbed Luther with Hattie's knife, he'd had it all this time. That made Luther's death not an act of rage—but premeditated murder.

Bonnie shook her head in disbelief. She had talked to Matthew a half-dozen times since Tuesday. Bless his ingenuous heart. The boy just didn't have it in him to keep a secret for ten minutes, let alone two days. She would have seen it in his eyes, his manner.

Bonnie tugged at her ear. Matthew Boone didn't kill Luther Devereaux. She felt it down to the soles of her feet.

As she opened her front door, a chaotic rumble warned her of her welcoming committee. Claws scraped on the kitchen linoleum, then a cresting wave of animals, four in all, rounded the corner into the living room. Leading the pack, a golden retriever careened into her leg.

In spite of her somber mood, or maybe because of it,

Bonnie laughed. She dug her fingers deep into the dog's fur. "At least let me get into the house before you knock me on my rear end, Hypatia."

The animals crowded around Bonnie's knees and ankles. A black Burmese cat climbed onto the end table and stretched up a paw to her.

Bonnie gathered the cat into her arms and pushed past the throng. She brushed her cheek against the soft fur of the cat. "I love you, too, Euclid."

The kitchen phone rang.

Her fingers ruffled across the backs of the animals as she hurried to the wall phone next to the microwave. She flipped on the ceiling light.

"Pinkwaters'." The inherent untruth of her greeting caused her stomach to tighten.

"Missus Pinkwater? It's Simon Boone." Simon, Matthew's older brother, had a voice like a fingernail scraping across a wet balloon, high yet at the same time rasping. He'd quit school four years earlier just before he was kicked out.

Bonnie gripped Euclid, and he protested. She set the cat on the breakfast island of her country kitchen. "What can I do for you, Simon?"

"Missus Pinkwater, they arrested Matt." Simon sounded like he might be crying.

"I was there. I talked to Matthew."

Simon sniffed into the phone. "You don't think he

did it, do you?"

Bonnie pulled the receiver away from her ear. Something in the young man's voice caused her to hold back her automatic denial and play devil's advocate. "He was found kneeling over Mister Devereaux with the knife in his hand."

A bell rang from Simon's end. He waited until it finished its peal before he continued. "I'm at the county jail, downtown Colorado Springs, just got in to see Matt. Mama and Dad are with him now. Visiting hours end at six o'clock, in about twenty minutes."

Bonnie couldn't think of any tactful way to ask her next question. "Simon, why did you call me?"

The receiver grew quiet. Bonnie pictured Simon with his weasel-face and his hair-trigger temper.

After a long moment, he said, "Matt's been asking for you. Insisted Mom put you on the visiting list."

Before she could respond, he said, "My folks think he's guilty as hell. You know how they are."

And how do you know they're not right? Bonnie kept her voice calm. "Mister Devereaux had been pretty cruel to Matthew."

Simon snorted. "Tell me something I don't know. That son of a bitch has . . . had been riding poor Matt all year, and not just in wrestling. I wanted to kill him myself."

"Did you kill him?" She wished she could see the expression on his face.

He answered without hesitation. "Christ, no! What kind of thing is that to ask?"

Is that panic in your voice? "A reasonable one. If Matthew didn't murder Mister Devereaux, then someone else did. Why not you?"

"First of all, I wasn't even at the school. I was working. Second, a couple of folks at the school wanted Devereaux out of the way more than I did. Matt told me he saw Trent Hendrickson and Missus Devereaux leaving the loft. Hendrickson was holding Missus Devereaux."

What are you getting at? "I don't understand."

"Don't tell me you ain't heard. Good old cattleman Trent's been doing the horizontal with Angelica Devereaux since before Halloween."

A call came just past five a.m.

Sleepily, Bonnie lifted the receiver. "Pinkwaters'."

"Bon, this is Lloyd."

From years of such calls, Bonnie was instantly awake.

This was the Lloyd's phone-tree voice. "We're going to cancel school today."

That was it. No explanation was necessary. They both knew the cause of the closure, and what they needed to do next.

"Bon, about yesterday . . ." The tone of his voice

changed, lower, more subdued.

Bonnie sat up in her waterbed, jostling the cat at her feet. At her elbow the furry muzzle of Hypatia draped across the padded bed railing. Moonlight shone on the dog's golden face. "Don't even go there, Lloyd. It's already forgotten. If two old friends can't snap at each other occasionally, their friendship's much too fragile."

"Just the same, I'm sorry."

Bonnie stroked Hypatia's soft brow. "Apology accepted. Are you going to school today?"

"I have to. The sheriff is coming back around eight. Which reminds me, he wants to speak with you."

"Me?"

Then she realized it made sense. Matthew was out of her class when the murder happened. She swung her legs over the side of the bed, finding a place to hang them between the warm flanks of Hypatia and Hopper, the giant black Labrador.

"Did they say when they were going to contact me?"

"Nope. I figured they'd get in touch with you today since school was closed."

Euclid crawled onto her lap and settled in.

Bonnie raked his sleek back with her fingernails. "You want me to come down to the school?"

Lloyd hesitated.

Bonnie could sense this pause was more her old friend being polite than any real consideration of her offer.

"I'm going to say no," Lloyd said. "I think it will only take a few hours, then I'll be taking the day off my own self. You have a good one. Stay out of trouble."

What do you mean by that?

She decided to let it pass. "See you tomorrow, boss."

Lloyd hung up without another word.

The next five minutes were taken with Bonnie calling the two people under her on the phone tree. She used the phone in the kitchen so she could make coffee and open cat food while she called.

Euclid sprang atop the kitchen island. He butted her with his head and tried to steal a preview morsel before she could empty the small can into his bowl.

Greedy little poop.

She swept him onto the carpeted floor, where he landed with a growl of protest. "Serves you right."

She immediately felt guilty, but knew better than to show Euclid any remorse. The cat would guilt-trip her for days if she gave in.

"You only have yourself to blame. Besides, you don't see Hypatia, Hopper, or Lovelace acting like starving pirates."

She smiled, picturing the skinny Burmese wearing a miniature eye patch. She gathered up the bowl and deposited it on the brick shelf at the base of the living-room fireplace.

Euclid's graceful form streaked toward the food. With a mixture of hauteur and territorial frenzy, he dove in.

The current contingent of Pinkwater animals consisted of one cat and three dogs. Over the years, Bonnie and Ben had had as many as eleven cats and dogs at one time, all named after mathematicians. By chance more than design, this existing group of housemates was divided not only by species, but also by gender, the cat male, the dogs female.

After feeding the dogs, Bonnie dressed, then trudged through the snow the quarter mile up to the service road, where she retrieved her newspaper. Hypatia and Lovelace, the Border collie, accompanied Bonnie. They chased one another back and forth across the beaten path to the road. On the way back, she read the article describing Luther Devereaux's murder.

The killing hadn't garnered the headline. That honor went to an eleven-car pileup on Interstate 25, resulting in the deaths of three people and stalling traffic on the highway for four hours.

The East Plains's homicide did, however, make the bottom of the front page.

TEACHER MURDERED IN EAST PLAINS
Tuesday afternoon, the normally peaceful community of East Plains was the scene of a deadly act of violence. Beloved teacher Luther Devereaux was murdered . . .

The story went on to compare the incident with teacher murders in Kentucky and at Columbine. It quoted Lloyd, saying the murder had left the students and staff stunned. No mention was made of Matthew.

Bonnie folded the paper and tucked it under her arm.

What must Matthew be going through? The boy was barely equipped to function in the bucolic world of East Plains. How could he possibly cope with an upheaval of this magnitude?

She called, and the dogs came to heel, following her into the house. As she shook off the cold, the warm smells of toast and wet dog greeted her. The familiar odors transported her, and she forgot herself.

She whistled the opening bars of "If I Only Had a Brain" from *The Wizard of Oz*, a remote part of her expecting Ben to complete the melody the way he always had.

"Don't be stupid, Bonnie," she said, but the admonishment came too late. Loneliness—like a slow-moving mist—crept toward her from every corner of the house.

She had to get away.

Without a look behind, Bonnie threw in the paper and stepped back through the doorway. She slammed the door.

Instead of turning right toward the road, Bonnie let her feet carry her left, toward the foothills beyond her property. In the distance she could just make out the faint outline of the Bluffs.

If the rugged mesa ever had a name, she and Ben never knew it. To them it had always been just the Bluffs. They'd climbed the escarpment a thousand times in the last thirty years, either together or separately.

In the first years of their marriage, they'd race one another to the Bluffs and make love on Indian blankets. When word of Ben's father's death reached them, she'd found her husband on the mesa. They both wept as the sun set over Pikes Peak.

They fled there when they were angry, at each other or at the world. When an indiscretion had threatened to destroy their marriage, they talked the problem through on the windswept crags of the Bluffs.

Strictly speaking, the mesa lay on public land, but Bonnie had to trespass across two neighbors' property to get there. Thank goodness, neither owned a dog.

The trail seemed particularly steep this morning, and a frosting of snow made the hike treacherous. She had to pull herself up using the thin trunks of the aspens, which grew along the path.

Bonnie trekked across the football-field-sized mesa and stared down onto the plains below and Colorado Springs beyond. Absently, she threw a stone over the edge. She cleared the snow from a flat boulder and sat.

She'd hoped the hike would elevate her spirits, give her some perspective on her loneliness, but if anything, she felt worse. This place, with its stark reminders of happier times, gave her no comfort.

"Benjamin David Pinkwater!" she shouted. "You stink."

She tightened the muscles in her face, refusing to cry. "You promised to grow old along with me. You promised the best was yet to be. You promised . . ." With each accusation her voice grew huskier, a harsh whisper fading to silence. She hugged herself, fiercely blinking back tears.

In the distance, a red-tailed hawk screamed, then plunged like a dagger toward the snow-covered plains. It swooped low, claws extended, then rose laboriously, flapping its wings and gripping something dark in its talons.

The entire episode took no more than a minute, but as she watched the bird leaving with its breakfast, Bonnie felt better.

Ben had once told her the red-tailed hawk was his totem. She laughed out loud, remembering how she had told him he was full of shit.

"You're still full of shit, my love," she whispered.

The weight of loneliness, at least in part, lifted from her shoulders. She knew it would return again and again, but for now she was thankful.

The hawk circled and soared up from the plain to land a hundred feet across the mesa, pinning a chipmunk under deadly talons. The bird eyed her, a burgundy shred of flesh hanging from its beak. Something in its wary gaze reminded her of Ben.

She stared back. "I'm damn tired of missing you."

The bird seemed to shrug, its feathered shoulders lifting in dismissal. Ben Pinkwater's voice came clear into her mind. "Who's asking you to?"

I'm going crazy.

Truth was, she felt remarkably calm. "Easy for you to say, birdbrain. You're dead."

Immediately, she felt foolish. Totems and animal guides were Ben's province. She'd never needed any such nonsense. And she didn't need it now. "Besides, I don't believe in you."

Ben's deep laughter echoed across her synapses. "Are you sure?"

"All right, maybe a little." She swallowed, barely believing the leap of faith she was making. "What in hell am I supposed to do now you're gone?"

"You don't need me to answer that. You already know."

And she did. With crystal clarity, she knew what she had to do to snap out of her funk. "I'm going to go see Matthew at the jail."

The bird raised its head and shrieked.

The wild energy of the sound filled her with a resolve she hadn't felt in months. She yelled, "I'm still mad at you, Benjamin Pinkwater, but enjoy your breakfast!"

CHAPTER 3

"SHERIFF'S OFFICE, DEPUTY WYATT SPEAKING."

The voice that answered at the East Plains's substation sounded like it belonged to a teenage girl, with that squeaky quality at once bored, yet hostile.

Bonnie felt every millisecond of her fifty-three years.

Youngsters must have taken over the world when I wasn't looking.

She cleared her throat. "My name is Bonnie Pinkwater, a teacher at East Plains High School. The officer investigating the murder at the school wants to speak with me."

"Hold, please." The line went dead for a second, then Garth Brooks came on singing "Rodeo."

After a chorus proclaiming the allure of pain and latigo leather, Deputy Wyatt returned. "That would be Deputy Hickman. We expect him back around noon. He's at the crime scene this morning."

Hell, I knew that. Lloyd told me. "Could I touch base with him early this afternoon?"

"I'm sure that would be fine, ma'am. Give me your name and a time, and I'll tell him you called."

Bonnie spelled her name, offered two o'clock that afternoon, and was about to hang up when she remembered Matthew. "Do you know if it would be possible to visit Matthew Boone, the suspect in the murder?"

"You're going to have to call the Municipal Building in Colorado Springs. We don't have the facilities to house long-term prisoners here at the substation. Ask the sheriff's deputies if the prisoner has put you on his visiting list. Also, he may be in arraignment this morning. They'll know that over there, as well."

"Do you have the number?"

The girl hesitated. "One moment, please."

Bonnie heard the rat-a-tat of computer keys.

"The number of the El Paso county jail is 555-2020. Will that be all, ma'am?" She sounded somewhat put out. Probably didn't much like being used as a phone directory.

"Yes, you've been extremely helpful, young lady."

"My pleasure, ma'am." Her tone softened. "You have a nice day."

Bonnie hung up and punched in the number.

The phone rang eight times before someone picked up. "El Paso County Jail," a male voice answered.

She waited, expecting the speaker to identify himself. He didn't.

Maybe I'd be reticent to give out my name, if I stared through prison bars at criminals all day.

"I need some information on a prisoner being held at your jail."

Now she expected the man to sarcastically tell her it wasn't his jail.

Cut it out, Pinkwater. You're getting cynical in your senility.

"Name?" The man managed to make the single word sound as if it had a dozen vowels instead of just two.

Not as forthright, coupled with a definite dearth in the sense-of-humor department. "Matthew Boone. He was brought in yesterday afternoon."

"And what information would you like to know?"

"I'm trying to find out if it's possible to see him sometime today."

"Mister Boone is being arraigned in District Court 11-B at nine thirty this morning. His visiting hours for today are listed from eleven to twelve thirty. Are you a relative?"

"No, I'm his math teacher."

The man coughed, sounding like someone trying not to laugh. Maybe he had a sense of humor after all.

"Well, ma'am, I can't promise you'll be able to get in to see Mister Boone. Usually at this early stage of incarceration, only the family and his lawyer are allowed visitations, and those at specified times."

Bonnie's heart sank. "I've been told I'm on his visiting list. Can you find out?"

Again, computer keys clicking.

"You must be Bonnie Pinkwater."

A sparse contingent of spectators were scattered about Courtroom 11-B.

On either side of a narrow aisle, less than a dozen souls populated the eight rows of polished oak benches. Bonnie took a rear seat. Matthew's parents occupied the first bench on the opposite side of the courtroom.

Frank Boone sat ramrod straight—an Old Testament prophet complete with shaved head and long salt-and-pepper beard. He wore a gray-green Western suit. When he turned his head to stare malevolently, his coat hung open, revealing a string tie.

In all the years she'd known him, Frank Boone had never worn a tie or a smile.

Pansy Boone's head barely came to her husband's shoulder. As usual, the woman's gray hair was woven into two ropy braids, like an aging Heidi. Even though Bonnie couldn't see their paintbrush ends, she knew the braids hung down below Pansy's waist.

Just as Frank Boone had insisted his wife, without complaint, bear him thirteen children, he also demanded she never cut her hair. On more than one occasion, Frank had cited Bible passages defending both positions. On every one of these occasions, Bonnie had had to restrain herself from proclaiming the man a gold-plated ass.

Left of the judge's bench, a door opened.

Standing before the bench, the bailiff, a short, stout policeman with a florid, jowly face, shouted, "All rise!"

A woman judge, leaning heavily on a pair of aluminum canes, entered the court. A full head of obviously dyed, raven-black hair framed a painfully thin, yet intelligent countenance. She stopped, pivoted on one of her canes, and regarded the courtroom. For a full second, her dark eyes held Bonnie's, then moved on. Each person in turn received the judge's brief attention as if she'd come for no other reason than to spend that moment with them.

Nicely done, a real teacher move. Each of us is now connected to whatever you say or do.

Laboriously, the judge climbed to her bench. As she reached the top stair, she nodded to the bailiff.

He disappeared through a door to the right of the bench and emerged a minute later leading a line of orange-clad adolescent prisoners. Their ragged charm bracelets shackled them not only at their hands and feet, but also to one another. Matthew brought up the rear.

A trio of uniformed guards herded them into the dock, a tiered gallery of the same oak benches. One guard efficiently unlocked the chains binding the prisoners one to another. When finished, the trio nodded in unison to the judge. They took up a collective position at the far end of the dock, feet and arms at parade rest.

"Matthew Boone," the judge called. Considering her frail appearance, the judge's voice was surprisingly husky.

Bonnie thought Matthew's father would approve of the boy being called first, perhaps even quote the Bible. *The first shall be last, and the last, first.*

A guard led Matthew to a wooden podium facing the bench. Again resuming parade rest, the officer remained by Matthew's side.

The judge stared down, not unkindly, at Matthew. "Mister Boone, I'm going to read you your rights just to make sure you comprehend them."

Matthew didn't appear to have heard the statement, but the judge continued nonetheless.

"You have the right to an attorney. If you cannot afford one, one will be appointed for you. You have the right to confront and cross-examine witnesses against you. You have the right to a jury trial. Do you understand these rights?"

Matthew hesitated. "I think so."

The judge frowned. "Be very sure, Mister Boone. Your life may depend upon it."

After a protracted moment, Matthew replied, "I understand."

Like hell, you do. Bonnie glared, first at Pansy, then at

Frank. *Say something. Your boy needs you.*

As though stuffed and mounted, neither parent moved.

"You have the right to not incriminate yourself. You have the right to a speedy trial. Now, Mister Boone, listen carefully to what I say next. Since this is a capital case, if you plead guilty, you could be sentenced to death or life in prison without the possibility of parole. On this point, be very sure. Do you understand what I'm saying?"

Matthew's entire body shook. "I didn't do nothing." His voice quavered at the brink of hysteria.

The judge never flinched, perhaps realizing she was dealing with a mentally challenged individual. "That's what we're here to determine, Mister Boone, but first, do you understand the importance of your plea?"

Again and again, Matthew inhaled and exhaled loudly. At the end of each breath, he groaned.

Bonnie thought the judge would lose her patience with Matthew, but she steadily gazed at the boy until he settled down.

"I understand," Matthew said flatly.

The judge nodded. "Good. Now, Mister Boone, do you have counsel with you today to help you decide how to plea?"

"Adam Jarvis, Your Honor. I'll be counsel for these proceedings." A blond man in a gray pin-striped suit rose and made his way to Matthew.

"Mister Boone," the judge continued, "the charge

leveled against you is second-degree murder, in that on Wednesday, February eleventh, you took the life of Luther Devereaux. How do you plead?"

Matthew began to shake again.

His lawyer leaned into the microphone. From the side, he looked almost as nervous as Matthew.

"My client pleads not guilty, Your Honor."

Without comment, the judge indicated the officer return Matthew to the dock. His face glistened with tears.

Bonnie gathered her coat and fanny pack. She didn't need to sit through the arraignments of the rest of the prisoners. The blur of a familiar figure heading for the exit caused her to turn and stare.

Looking like he might be sick, Greg Hansen rushed from the courtroom.

Bonnie ground her teeth to keep her tears at bay.

Led by a monstrously large guard, and wearing the same one-piece orange prison uniform, Matthew Boone shuffled into the stark visitors' room. He wiped his nose on his hairy arm. He'd been crying, his large expressive blue eyes puffy and bloodshot. Matt shuffled to a stop across from where she sat. The guard stepped back and positioned himself at the door.

"Hi, Matt."

Bonnie sat inside a three-sided carrel. Two white ceiling-to-floor walls bordered her and had the matte finish of upended countertops. A sheet of thick, clear Plexiglas with a circular copper vent at face level separated her from Matthew.

She had to move left to see the boy's face.

He looked like a child trying to be brave, but not quite up to the task. He wouldn't meet her gaze. "Thanks for coming, Missus Pinkwater."

Now was no time for Bonnie to be weepy. At the slightest show of sadness, Matthew would break down. She steadied her voice.

"Certainly, Matt. When Simon told me you were asking for me, how could I stay away from my favorite aide?"

Matthew reached his shackled hands toward the glass.

The guard cleared his throat.

Like a shamed dog, Matthew bowed his head, then lowered his arms. "Sorry." His eyes filled with tears.

Bonnie said the first thing that came to mind. "Did you sleep well last night?"

It must have been the right thing to ask because the young man perked up. He nodded enthusiastically. "The beds here are pretty comfortable. I had a cell all to myself. They even have showers."

She remembered rumors the Boone children took turns sleeping on the floor. Not enough beds for all thirteen children. A bed all for yourself might seem a luxury even in these extreme circumstances.

"I met my lawyer this morning at my arrangement." Matthew leaned toward the glass. The edge of his hand shielded his mouth from the guard. "I still don't understand what that was all about. But the judge was nice."

Bonnie didn't see any need to tell him she was at the proceeding. He'd probably forget anyway. "I think your lawyer actually called it an arraignment." She tried to think of an innocuous way to describe the procedure. "It's where formal charges are brought against you and where you make your plea, either guilty or not guilty. What's happening is the state of Colorado is deciding if it wants to prosecute you or not."

"That's what they're doing to me? Deciding if they want to persecute me?" His voice rose on the last two words.

She considered correcting him, but decided against it. *What the hell, he might be right.* "That's basically it."

His lower lip quivered. "I want to go home. I didn't hurt Mister Devereaux. He was my friend."

Luther Devereaux was nobody's friend, least of all yours. The man was a bag of crap in tan corduroys and penny loafers. Which, of course, constituted another random thought she'd be better off keeping to herself.

"Did you tell the police he was your friend?"

Matthew nodded, his moon face sincere and thus less vacant than it normally was. "At the school, a man asked me questions about Mister Devereaux, and why I hated him." Matthew's forehead creased. "I told that man I didn't hate Mister Devereaux at all. Mister Devereaux once bought me dinner when the team was at Punkin Center, and I didn't have any money."

Luther purchased your loyalty for the price of a Big Mac. She kept her face neutral. "What else did the policeman say?"

Matthew chewed on his lower lip, then his face brightened. "He read me my rights."

Bonnie had seen that look before.

Matthew Boone didn't ask a lot from life, or himself. The simple act of discovering he could remember not only something that happened yesterday, but also the correct term for it, was enough to lift his spirits.

"He didn't say much after that." Matt's smile faded. "A policeman put handcuffs on me. He took me out of the loft and put me in the police car."

Could the young man have fooled her all these years? Did he have reserves of cunning she never suspected? Bonnie studied Matthew's face. He looked incapable of lying, let alone committing murder.

"Matthew, why did Mister Devereaux want to speak to you?"

The young man sighed, his eyes darting first one way, then another.

Bonnie couldn't tell if he was having trouble remembering or if the memory troubled him. On almost anyone else, the body language signaled a person getting ready to lie.

"He told me I wouldn't be wrestling for the team this coming Saturday on account of I lost the wrestle-off to Vern Montgomery." Matthew shrugged a that's-the-way-it-goes shrug, then smiled as if in apology. "It was the third time Vern beat me."

Conspiratorially, Matthew leaned closer to the glass. "You know, I'm not a very good wrestler. Mister Devereaux asked me if I wouldn't like to quit and become team manager. Pretty cool, huh?"

Oh yeah, Luther Devereaux was a prince among men. "What did you say to that?"

Matthew's face widened into a broad grin. "I told him I'd do it, and he told me my first duty was to fetch him a cup of water." Matthew nodded his head as though, right that moment, he was agreeing to the job all over again.

Could anyone possibly be this ingenuous? She hated herself for doubting the boy, but her curiosity wouldn't allow her to stop.

In for a penny.

"Matthew, you work in the kitchen, don't you?"

He sat a little straighter. "Uh huh. After lunch I wipe down the tables and run the big pots and pans through the dishwasher."

"Do you remember the knife that was up in the loft?" She tried to make the question seem like idle conversation.

Matthew squirmed uncomfortably. "The one they

think I stabbed Mister Devereaux with?"

She nodded, wanting to reach through the glass and stop the boy from fidgeting. "Had you ever seen that knife before?"

He raked his fingers through his hair. "It's not my knife." His voice rose.

She was sure he was going to cry again. If Matthew was putting her on, he was doing a damn fine job of it.

She tried a different tack. "I'm not saying the knife is yours. All I'm asking is, did it look to you like one of the kitchen carving knives?" She took in all of Matthew, his eyes, his hands, his posture, everything that would indicate he might be deceiving her.

She saw nothing change.

He shook his head, his sad gaze meeting hers. "I didn't really see the knife."

He thumped the heels of his hands hard against his forehead. "Stupid, huh? I picked that knife up, but I didn't see it. Not really."

She reached a hand toward him, then pulled it back. "Not so stupid. I'd bet most people in your place wouldn't have paid attention to the knife." She wasn't sure she was telling the truth, but she needed to tell him something.

Matthew pursed his lips as if considering her comment.

An awkward silence grew that Bonnie didn't feel comfortable breaching.

Finally, Matthew said, "Mister Whittaker told me I

did such a good job in the kitchen he'd ask about hiring me full-time once I graduated. My mom's a cook, and we'd get to work together." Matthew's face clouded over. "He ain't gonna hire me now. Is he, Missus Pinkwater?"

Bonnie had to look away. "One thing at a time, Matthew. Let's first take care of this murder business."

He smiled at her, exposing two widely spaced teeth, badly needing a brushing. "You gonna help me, Missus Pinkwater? You gonna make 'em see I didn't do anything bad?"

She wanted to shake her head, tell him no, walk away before she promised something she couldn't deliver.

But Matthew stared at her with those big eyes. Helpless, innocent eyes. If she left now, she knew she'd find herself back on the Bluffs, giving herself hell for being a coward.

I can nose around, ask a few questions, and satisfy my own curiosity if nothing else.

She'd be talking with the investigator this afternoon. She'd tell him about Barty and Kyle Hansen, about Trent Hendrickson and Angelica Devereaux.

The more Bonnie thought about it, the better she felt. "I'll see what I can do, Matthew." Hell, what could it hurt?

CHAPTER 4

EAST PLAINS'S SUBSTATION LOOKED EVERY CENTIMETER the double-wide trailer it had been when trucked out to the plains two decades earlier.

You know you're getting old when you remember twenty-year-old nonevents like the installing of a trailer substation.

Originally, monochromatic gray-on-gray, it could use a coat of paint, yet the weather-worn building stood its ground with grace. Like most things larger than a coyote out on the plains, the building appeared to have been planted and was now growing, along with the sagebrush and yucca, out of the sandy red dirt. This same red soil lent a faint patina of orange to the gray station, giving it a vaguely pumpkin-like look.

Tumbleweeds huddled like weary winter travelers against the trailer's apron. Even the small rusted sign that announced to the world, albeit humbly, this was Substation 1118 of the El Paso County Sheriff had its refugee tumbleweeds clinging to its twin tubular supports.

Somehow, Alice, Bonnie's ancient Subaru, looked right at home in the sparse field that served as a parking lot. Bonnie checked her face in the rearview mirror. She frowned.

"What the hell. This is as good as it gets."

She grabbed her fanny pack off the passenger seat and braced herself for the prairie wind, which seldom took a vacation. She practically fell through the front door into the foyer of the station.

An unfamiliar face looked up from behind a semi-circular Formica countertop. "May I help you?" blond, blue-eyed Deputy Wyatt asked.

Oh honey, you look even younger than I gave you credit for. "I have an appointment with Deputy Hickman."

A sly smile brightened Wyatt's face. "He's been expecting you." The girl hooked a thumb over her shoulder back toward a short hallway, looking for all the world like she was stifling a giggle. "Last office on the left."

Something in that smile bothered Bonnie. She studied the freckled face, comparing it to the rogue's gallery of students she'd taught over the years. Although the surname Wyatt had belonged to a half dozen, Bonnie felt certain this particular urchin hadn't graced her classroom. Maybe the girl was just touched in the head. The wind out on the plains could do that to a person.

"Thank you, sweetie."

Before Bonnie entered Hickman's office, she spied a tall man, maybe six one, six two, standing behind his desk, back to her, staring out a solitary window. An oval of thinning hair encircled a patch of scalp as freckled as Wyatt's face. His blue-gray uniform sleeves were rolled up past the elbow.

With her first footfall, the man turned. Liquid brown eyes regarded her with no small amount of affection.

Despite the thinning hair, Bonnie recognized him immediately. "Byron?"

The man's baby face colored. "Hello, Missus Pink-water."

She did the mental math that placed Byron Hickman in the year of his graduation, then worked forward, calculating his age. "How long has it been?"

She knew the answer, but perversely found herself testing her former student to see if he also knew.

"Gosh, I haven't seen you in more than fifteen years." His eyes twinkled with recollection. "You came to my graduation party. Gave me a book, *The Prophet* by Kahlil Gibran. I still have that book."

"Have you read it?"

"Sure thing, I read it. Afraid I'd run into you someday, and you'd quiz me."

Hands on hips, Bonnie regarded Byron, and liked what she saw. He'd always been a lanky, awkward boy, a basketball player she remembered, but he'd filled out, grown into an honest, open face. His waist was thicker, his shoulders wider. He looked solid, sturdy.

He pointed to one of two cushioned folding chairs facing the desk. "It's sure good to see you."

As she sat, so did he. Head down, Byron rifled through his desk until he came out with a yellow legal pad and a pen. The top two pages were written on, and Byron folded them under. He laid the pen across the pad, then gave her an up-from-under glance.

A thought flashed through her head of a boy, Byron Hickman not fifteen years old, a shock of brick-red hair. Hands folded atop his desk, he had assumed a look of angelic innocence, but for some reason was working his eyebrows furiously, his forehead wrinkling with the effort. Then, without warning, his hair turned to a fountain of red, a topknot spiking his crown. The rascal had stretched a rubber band beneath his hair and worked the damn thing free, gathering his hair into a manic vertical ponytail. There had been nothing to do but laugh along with the rest of her class at this elaborate prank.

Are you still half-crazy, Byron, or has life squeezed that out of you?

She must have let some of that memory show on her face.

He asked, "What?"

"Nothing."

He squinted at her, and a hint of wily intelligence

glinted in his eyes. It was quickly replaced by a toothy aw-shucks smile.

There's more to you than meets the eye, Mister Hickman, she thought. *I'll bet you use that good-old-boy persona to make people underestimate you. I don't think I will.*

He looked down at his notepad, then back up into her eyes. "You ready for a few questions?"

"Fire away."

He again peered at her from under his strawberry-blond eyebrows. The effect all but eradicated his baby-faced features. "Matthew Boone is in your fourth-block Algebra One class?"

"Yes."

"And yesterday afternoon you released Matthew to speak with Luther Devereaux, his wrestling coach. Do you remember what time that was?" He scribbled something indecipherable on the legal pad.

"Two thirty."

"You're sure?"

The question annoyed her. She'd always prided herself on her excellent memory. Byron should remember that.

"I made a point of noting the time because I thought it rude of Luther to ask to see a student of mine in the middle of class."

Byron cocked his head and regarded Bonnie. "I remember now. You and Mister Devereaux didn't get along very well."

She bristled. Over the years, she'd gone to great pains to keep her opinions of other teachers to herself. Certainly she never aired those views in front of students. "What makes you say that?"

He waved aside her question. "Aw come on, Missus Pinkwater. Everybody knew how you and Mister Devereaux liked to spar."

"Everybody?" Suddenly she felt as if he could see through her clothes.

"Pretty much. Lots of folks heard you guys arguing in the teachers' lounge."

He reached across the desk and wrapped a gentle hand about her wrist. "I wouldn't take it too much to heart. Everyone I knew rooted for you. Mister Devereaux was a hard guy to like."

In spite of her discomfort, his words did make her feel better. *Damn, Byron, you're good at this putting-people-at-ease crap.*

"Do you know if Matthew Boone harbored any ill will toward Mister Devereaux?"

The abrupt question caught her off guard, and she fought down an urge to treat it as an accusation. "I don't think so. When I spoke with Matthew this morning, he seemed genuinely fond of Luther."

Byron leaned back in his chair. "He told me the same thing yesterday. I'm having trouble buying it, based on the other accounts I got." He flipped a written page forward. "Luther thought Matthew was being given preferential treatment. Luther had nothing but contempt for Boone. Luther could often be seen at wrestling matches laying into Matthew."

"It's all true."

"So you admit the boy had reasons for hating Luther Devereaux."

"I do, indeed. Matthew Boone had every reason in the world to despise Luther Devereaux." She poked her index finger at the words on the legal pad. "The thing is, despite what these people say, Matthew thought the world of Luther."

"And you believe the boy?"

Bonnie let the question resonate through her before she answered. She had to admit she still owned some doubt. She weighed this doubt against all she knew about Matthew, all she had learned from years in his company.

"I absolutely believe him."

Byron tapped his pen on the legal pad, staring down but obviously with his thoughts elsewhere. "If someone thought about me and treated me the way these people say Mister Devereaux treated Boone, I'd hate him."

"You're not Matthew Boone."

Byron shook his head and smiled.

It wasn't an unpleasant smile, and Bonnie found herself, once again, admiring the man that Byron Hickman had become.

"It's hard to argue with a statement like that," Byron said, "but do you have any evidence to back up your belief?"

He stood and stretched. His body language indicated he didn't expect her to have any evidence, and that the productive portion of the interview was over.

Bonnie checked her watch. Five minutes after two. "Have you eaten lunch?"

Byron eyed her suspiciously. "As a matter of fact, I haven't. I was going to grab something from the vending machine and eat at my desk."

Bonnie offered her elbow. "How about I take you out to eat? We could talk about old times in East Plains."

She felt kind of silly with her elbow sticking out toward him, would feel even sillier if he didn't take it. "Humor your old math teacher."

Byron stepped around the desk and laced his arm through hers. "I get the feeling I'm being set up."

Bonnie ran her finger along the crust of her sandwich and scooped a large blob of hummus into her mouth. Geraldine's was the only restaurant on the plains that had a decent vegetarian section on its menu. Geraldine Albright had reluctantly added one item after another as Bonnie religiously frequented the little hole-in-the-wall and made suggestions.

"You actually like that stuff?" Byron peered at her over the rim of his enormous hamburger. He wore a look on his face halfway between a grin and a grimace.

She shook the sandwich at him. "You can't fool me. You're dying to be offered a taste."

Byron recoiled as though she waggled a snake. He set down his burger, swallowed, and wiped his mouth with a mauve napkin embossed with a large G. "How about we get back to Angelica Devereaux? How'd you come to know she's having an affair?"

"I got a call last night from Simon Boone."

Bonnie realized how ridiculous this must sound. Heat climbed up her neck and onto her face.

"Boone, Boone?" Byron rolled the word around on his tongue as if it was new to him. "I could swear I've heard that name before."

Bonnie glared at him. "Okay, so he's Matthew's brother. That doesn't mean he wasn't telling the truth."

"Try to see this from my point of view, Missus P." Byron tilted back his red-vinyl dinette chair and spread wide his hands.

He appeared the picture of reasonableness. Bonnie wanted to toss her sandwich at him.

"You get a phone call from the brother of our main, hell, our only suspect." His face went scarlet. "Excuse my language."

She waved away the apology, still irked at him.

He sat erect, obviously embarrassed. "Anyway, Simon Boone not only tells you his brother is innocent, but in the same breath lets loose with this juicy bit of gossip about Missus Devereaux and Trent Hendrickson."

Bonnie opened her mouth to protest, but realized she had nothing to offer.

Byron nodded at her helplessness. "Would it surprise you to know that I'm acquainted with Simon?"

"Not especially." *Knowing Simon the way I do, I wouldn't be surprised if he has a rap sheet as long as a Slip 'n Slide.*

Byron gave her a sidelong glance. "Your source of info has been inside the gray-bar hotel on more than one occasion. Drugs. Stolen property. Unless I'm mistaken, I believe he's currently on probation."

Byron showed nothing of the country bumpkin now. He spoke as a no-nonsense cop with little patience for time-wasting diversions. He must have realized he was leaning on her a bit.

His face relaxed, and his voice softened. "Do you have anything else?"

Bonnie felt reticent to mention Barty and Kyle Hansen, but if she didn't say something, she'd have to just sit quiet, a skill she'd never been particularly good at.

"Yesterday at the school, before you got there, I saw Barty and Kyle Hansen in the gym."

An increment of color drained from Byron's face.

"Go on." His voice carried just a hint of a quiver.

The hair on Bonnie's neck stood on end. *Walk carefully, Pinkwater. There's something weird going on here.* "I was herding students off the loft stairs when I spied Barty and Kyle. They were running out of the gym before they could be spotted."

She ignored the guilty little voice telling her she'd embellished the truth a molecule or two.

Byron stared past her, lost in some private thought. He shook himself free. "Barty Hansen was ahead of me in school, maybe three years. When he was just a sophomore, Barty got Kyle's mama pregnant." Byron's voice was flat. He tossed his napkin onto his plate, his lips pressed in a tight line.

Why are you telling me this?

A vague recollection of a young Barty Hansen draped around a tall, bleached-out blond passed through Bonnie's mind. The girl hadn't been at the school long before she got pregnant and dropped out.

And what in hell has come over Byron? Her former student looked as if he wanted to kill someone.

"Are you all right?" she asked.

At first, he didn't seem to hear, then he returned her gaze, his eyes lifeless. He stood.

"It's nothing."

From his left pocket, he extracted a small wad of bills bound with a gold money clip. He pulled free a ten-dollar bill. His hands shook. "Listen, Missus P, it's been great seeing you, but I've got a load of work back at the station."

What the hell?

Bonnie peered up at him, almost too stunned to speak. "Lunch was on me."

Byron nodded vacantly. Without returning the bill to the clip, he shoved it and the money clip into his pocket.

"Thanks." He turned away and headed toward the door.

"Byron?" she called. "I'll drive you back. It's got to be a half mile back to your office."

He must not have heard. Quickening his pace, Byron crossed the small restaurant, swung wide the glass-and-aluminum door, and stepped into the cold afternoon sun.

In the early winter darkness, Bonnie drove east along Colorado Highway 24 back to her house in Black Forest. A light snow had begun, and luminescent snowflakes swirled in the beams of her headlights. Just out of reach, a nagging memory plagued her.

Sketchy details of Barty Hansen's sophomore year swam in and out of her mind like the snowflakes surrounding her Subaru. She remembered Kyle's mother had been a senior new to East Plains High. Pale and nondescript, she'd floated, barely noticed, through the halls.

Until she hooked up with Barty Hansen.

Even as a sophomore, he was bad news—disruptive, disrespectful. Always in trouble, that type of boy often attracted girls with no real sense of self.

Kyle's mother had been that type of girl. She must have been desperate, taking up with a sophomore like Barty, foulmouthed, no brains, and a good six inches shorter than her.

Bonnie turned onto her long dirt driveway as the snow began to fall in earnest. She pulled into her garage to the sound of barking dogs, killed her ignition, and sat illuminated by the single bulb burning in her garage-door opener.

Why had Byron reacted so bizarrely? If he was right and Barty was three years ahead of him in school, then young Byron Hickman had been a seventh grader when Kyle's mother had dropped out of school. Bonnie hadn't gotten to know Byron Hickman until he showed up in her freshman Algebra One class two years later.

The kitchen phone rang, but before she could gather her things, it stopped. She hurried from her car and heard the final click, then the long whirr of her answering machine. At her feet, Hypatia and company jockeyed for position. The burly shoulders of the black lab, Hopper, impeded Bonnie's progress to the machine.

She hit the replay button, and just as she hoped, she heard Byron's voice. "Missus P, I wanted to catch you at home. Looks like I'll have to settle for leaving you an apology on your machine. I'm sorry for cutting out the way I did. Next time I see you, I'll try to explain and maybe make it up to you. You take care. It was good to see you."

Bonnie stood in her kitchen, staring at the answering machine, before a thought came into her mind. Hurrying as best she could through her canine obstacle course, she made her way into the library. There, filling an entire shelf, sat thirty-three volumes of East Plains's yearbooks, one from every year she'd taught at the school.

She located the right year on her second try and ruffled through the pages until she found the senior pictures. There were only eighteen, three rows of six. On the second row, Bonnie found what she was looking for.

The pale girl stared out of the page like she was embarrassed to have her picture taken. Her blond hair hung limply about her face. Bonnie had forgotten how freckled her face had been. Just like her brother.

The name beneath that pale, freckled face read Cynthia Hickman.

Friday morning, Bonnie woke, half expecting another day off because of the snow. No such luck. Sometime in the night, the snowstorm had petered out, leaving little more than an inch of new frosting.

Alice, the ancient Subaru, had no trouble churning

through the white stuff. Parking place bovine free, Bonnie arrived at school by seven thirty, earlier than most days. This morning she had an agenda.

She wasn't sure she could count on Byron to investigate Trent, Angelica, and especially the Hansens. If Cynthia Hickman was Byron's sister, then Kyle was his nephew; Barty, his brother-in-law.

She meant to find out what the Hansens, Trent Hendrickson, and Angelica Devereaux were doing at school on Wednesday.

Every visitor to the school was supposed to check in at the main office before they went anywhere else. The legacy of the Columbine shootings demanded that no stranger wander a school without the principal knowing why they were there. Surely Lloyd would know about Trent since the two had come to the loft together. Angelica Devereaux was another story. Bonnie refused to believe the woman just happened to be at the school the day her husband got his throat sliced.

But the presence of a school kitchen knife suggested Luther's killer might even be a student.

Because Matthew had actually talked to Luther, whoever killed the wrestling coach needed to be in that loft sometime between two thirty—when Matthew left her class—and two fifty-eight, when Greg Hansen told her of Luther's death.

She discounted the PE teacher's claim that no one

else had been in the loft besides Matthew and Luther.

Hell, I've passed through that gym dozens of times without Harvey or his students noticing me.

If someone really wanted to sneak up to the loft, Bonnie had no doubt they could do it without Harvey knowing.

What she needed was a list of students who were out of class during that crucial half hour. A school as small as East Plains couldn't have more than a handful in the halls at a time.

As she walked through the front doors, her mind focused. *This is my arena. Here I can handle anything. It's only outside these walls that my life turns to caca.*

In the office, chaos reigned. A faux-oak L-shaped counter, with a swinging gate at one end, separated the administrative section of the office from the student waiting area. This morning, parents and students, many of whom were yelling, packed the latter.

Bonnie excused herself through the crowd, narrowly avoiding being smacked in the face by an arm-waving man in overalls.

Lloyd stood behind the long counter. His normally relaxed face looked pinched and tired. "We have counselors ready, if students need to talk," he was explaining to a red-faced mother. "Of course, if you want to take Dale home ..."

Lloyd peered over the woman's head as Bonnie walked by and nodded.

Bonnie squeezed past Mister Overalls and through

the gate. She toyed with the idea of helping Lloyd sort through the concerned parents, but decided against it.

She laid a hand on Doris, the school secretary. "I have an unusual request."

Five minutes later, on her way to class, Bonnie held a pair of computer lists. The first delineated students who'd been called out of class by the principal, vice principal, or counselor. The second told of students who'd supposedly left school during last period. These lists weren't exhaustive by any stretch of the imagination. She would also need to see every teacher who had a fourth-block class and ask them who they had released from two thirty to three o'clock.

When Bonnie reached her classroom, Greg Hansen stood by her door.

CHAPTER 5

A TUG-OF-WAR PLAYED BACK AND FORTH ACROSS BON-
nie's mind.

The lists tucked beneath her arm demanded perusal.
Hell, she could almost hear the damn things whispering,
teasing her with what she'd find if she could sit down for
ten minutes. All the way from the office, she'd avoided
looking just so she could spread the papers out across her
desk and take her time. Now she felt peevish because that
time was being stolen from her, and she resented it.

Here was Greg, standing at her door, obviously upset,
obviously needing to talk. Another time, certainly another day, she'd welcome the chance to play confidante.

*But God damn it. Is it too much to ask for maybe one
day when I don't have to be everybody's Dutch uncle?*

Greg opened his mouth to speak.

Bonnie cut him off with an upraised hand. She felt
a small shred of satisfaction for at least making him wait

until she could lay her fanny pack on her desk.

"Come on in. I don't want to talk in the hall."

Bonnie let them both into the classroom, then crossed the room in long strides that didn't invite conversation. By the time she'd stepped behind her gray metal desk, she composed her expression and settled her mind.

"Okay, Greg, I'll bite. To what do I owe the pleasure of this visit?"

She slapped the lists down on her desk, then noticed Greg eyeing the names. She covered the papers with her fanny pack before she sat.

Greg lifted his eyes from the papers to her. Anger or a reasonable facsimile wriggled onto, then passed from his handsome face. He shrugged, as if to tell her he didn't want to see the stupid papers anyway.

"I saw you in court yesterday morning."

"And I saw you."

Bonnie felt her impatience rising. Why wouldn't the boy come to the point? Then another portion of her brain—a portion she'd come to call her sage-on-the-stage—kicked in its two cents. *Aren't you just the least bit curious what this boy has to say? After all, it was his father and brother you saw making a hasty exit out of the gym.*

She closed her eyes and exhaled. With the release of her breath, she also released her irritation. "I went to see Matthew later that morning."

"I know. I followed you."

Bonnie thought she ought to say something in response to this disturbing revelation, but she never got the chance.

"I didn't actually follow you," Greg said. "I walked over to the City and County Building, hoping to get in to see Matt, but they told me there was no way. I wasn't on his visiting list."

Greg reached behind him and slid a student desk up to his rear end. With a grace that defied gravity and had always seemed the sole province of athletic teenage boys, he one-handedly hoisted himself onto the top.

"When I got about a half block away, I looked back and saw you going in. I figure you were gonna get the same treatment, so I waited." A hint of a smile touched Greg's face. "And waited. And waited. Twenty minutes later, I figured you got in to see Matt, so I caught the bus back to East Plains."

Not for the first time, Bonnie considered Greg Hansen and wondered how he ever got hooked up with Matthew Boone. Here was this teenage Adonis—blond hair, blue eyes, as muscled as any grown man, and intelligent as all get-out. On the other side of this lopsided equation squatted Matthew Boone—short, dirty, with a penchant for tripping over his own feet and an IQ that qualified him for special education. What in hell did the two of them find to talk about?

Then again, maybe that was a magic she'd grown too

old to understand. "You'd like to know how Matthew's holding up."

Greg nodded, the smile gone from his face.

"As well as can be expected. He's scared, doesn't understand everything that's going on around him." She meant to stop there, but her Imp of the Perverse kept her mouth going. "He asked me to help him."

Greg chewed his lower lip. "Help him how?"

And now she knew she'd put her foot in it.

Hell, in for a penny . . .

"I told the deputy in charge I saw your father and brother leaving the gym not a half hour after the murder." She wasn't sure what reaction she was expecting, but a pensive nod didn't fit the bill.

"I saw them, too."

Bonnie struggled to keep from rushing her next question. "Did you ask them why they were there?"

Smooth, Pinkwater. Do you really expect this young man to turn belly-up and choose you over his own blood?

Greg shook his head in a nervous little twitch. "It ain't the sort of thing I can just up and ask, if you know what I mean. To tell the truth, I've pretty much kept out of Pa and Kyle's way for the last two days."

"This isn't going to go away, Greg. I'm surprised the deputy hasn't already been around to question them." Was it really that surprising, though, considering Byron was Kyle Hansen's uncle? For that matter, wasn't he also

Greg's uncle? "I think you know this deputy."

Greg squinted at her, then the slow light of comprehension dawned on his face. "You mean Uncle Byron?"

"The very one." Bonnie felt like the world's biggest jerk. It wasn't her place to lay all this crap on this boy's shoulders, which even as she sat, seemed to have slumped considerably.

Greg's face hardened. "The heck with it. There ain't nothing I can do about Pa or Uncle Byron, but I want to help clear Matt. He's the only real friend I've ever had at this Podunk school."

Greg pointed with his chin toward her fanny pack, which now lay between her elbows. "You got a list there of everybody out of class that afternoon, and you mean to talk to them."

Bright boy. You got all that from a fifteen-second peek. "Something like that."

A rattle in the hall warned Bonnie that her first-period class would soon be storming the gates.

"Let me help."

"I don't think so." She shook her head to emphasize her point.

Her door opened, and Wes Oliheiser poked in his head. "I'm sorry. I didn't expect you to be here, on time I mean." He gifted her with a sly smile.

"Nice, Wes. Come on in. Greg was just leaving."

"Think about what I said." He poked a finger down

on the exposed corner of lists. "These folks'll talk to me before they do you."

Once again her Imp of the Perverse had her speak when she should shut her mouth. "Come back and see me during second block."

Only eleven of Bonnie's twenty-one Math Analysis students made it to class. She couldn't blame the other parents for keeping the children home. Murder had a tendency make some people feel less than secure.

Go figure.

Those students who sat before her fell into two categories. Some of them looked shell-shocked, staring grimly back at her. They would have preferred to have stayed home, but their parents wouldn't allow it. The rest of the class wore their excitement like a party hat. A weird circus atmosphere permeated these students. They might be afraid, but they'd chosen to be there, not wanting to miss anything.

Bonnie went through the motions of teaching, but gave up after ten minutes, her heart simply not in it. "Does anyone want to talk about Wednesday?"

After an awkward pause, Wes Oliheiser raised his hand. "You scared, Missus P?"

The question took Bonnie by surprise and shunted

her thoughts in an unexpected direction. For the first time since the murder, Bonnie realized she was afraid.

"I think I am, Wes."

She let her gaze linger, one by one, on each of her charges. "How about you guys? Anybody frightened?"

No one responded. They peered surreptitiously about the room, unwilling to admit their fear.

In a defiant gesture, Wes raised his hand, his blue eyes daring classmates to join him. "I admit it. All year, I sat next to Boone in Language Arts. When I think of what he did—"

"Yeah." Clarice, a plump Chicano girl with shoulder-length braids culminating in pink ribbons, thrust up her hand. "I saw Mister Devereaux's arm dangling from the loft."

She shuddered, but the gesture seemed feigned, artificial, like something she learned watching teenagers react in murder movies. "I heard Matt opened him up like a can of beans." She dragged a finger across her throat.

Yo, girl! Who knew you kept a pirate deep down in your soul?

Taylor, a normally quiet black boy, raised his hand. "I never liked Matt."

A chorus of voices agreed.

Bonnie could see their commiseration rapidly turning into a Matthew Boone pecking party with everyone taking a stab at the boy. She held up both hands, palms toward the class, her usual signal for attention.

"Does everyone feel that Matthew is definitely guilty? Doesn't anyone think perhaps it's all a big mistake?"

Oh piss, piss, piss. That was dumb, Pinkwater. These are teenagers with imaginations like race cars. They'll take off with this thought. God knows what will be circulating in the rumor mill by the end of the school day.

Before she could even acknowledge him, Wes Oliheiser asked, "Is that what you think, Missus P?"

Sweet Jesus.

She mentally apologized to Lloyd for the phone calls he'd be getting that evening. It didn't matter how she answered. Parents would be saying she stirred the kids up, put a wild idea in their heads when they were already reeling from Luther's murder.

A hint of a smile played at the corners of Wes's mouth.

The little shit knows he's backed me into a corner. Now that she'd hesitated this long, if Bonnie said that wasn't what she thought, the lie would be obvious.

Damned if I do . . . to hell with it. "I suppose it is."

The words burned as they left her mouth. Certainly, they'd come back to burn her derriere before too long.

"Really?" Clarice stared at her incredulously. "But if you're right, that means—"

Wes's grin emerged in earnest. "Somebody else offed Mister Devereaux."

Bonnie waited twenty minutes for Greg Hansen to show, and when he didn't, she snagged her fanny pack and made for the door. A schoolwide ten-minute break followed first block. This led into Bonnie's second-block planning time—an hour and fifteen minutes on the block system. Altogether these two respites gave her almost an hour and a half free to gather her thoughts. She didn't want to waste another minute waiting on a student who had the temerity to stand her up.

The boy could have legitimate reasons for not showing. As a matter of procedure, counselors from all over the area would have set up shop at the school to deal with student trauma. Greg could be sitting with a counselor even as she cooled her heels in her classroom. After all, Luther was his wrestling coach.

Besides, Pinkwater, as Rickie was so fond of telling Lucy Ricardo, "You got some 'splaining to do." She headed for the hallway and Lloyd Whittaker.

Her principal looked weary seated behind his large battered desk—chin resting in his rough hands. Even his fringe of gray-red hair looked tired.

Bonnie hated adding to his troubles, but she couldn't avoid telling him of her lapse in judgment. She marched through the swinging gate, entered the tiny office, and shut the door behind her.

Lloyd held her gaze. "I get the feeling this isn't a social call."

Bonnie plopped into the overstuffed chair. "I blew it."

She had never really mastered the art of shallow chit-chat, so she charged right into what she'd said to Wes Oliheiser. She made no attempt to mitigate her stupidity. "There's an outside chance you might get a few phone calls." She hoped this poor excuse for humor might ease the tension. No such luck.

Lloyd had listened without comment, a hint of sympathy shining in his eyes. It didn't, however, translate into a smile or even a friendly shake of the head.

He rubbed the heels of his hands into his tired eyes. "I think *blew it* just about covers it. I wish you'd consider thinking sometimes before you cut loose with that Imp of the Perverse of yours."

He laced his fingers across the top of his thinning hair. "You're right about those phone calls. One of the disadvantages of living in a town the size of a postage stamp. And being the principal of the only high school."

Lloyd rose, went to the door, opened it a crack, and peered out. When he shut it again, he turned an exhausted face in her direction.

"But you want to know what I think?" He cocked his head and managed a rueful smile. "Right now, I don't give a hairy rat's behind. I get the feeling my phone's going to ring off the hook tonight even if you hadn't pulled such a boneheaded stunt."

"I'm sorry. If there's anything I can do . . ."

"Some of those phone calls will wind up going to the school board, and maybe even to Superintendent Divine."

Bonnie grimaced. She hated Divine and was fairly certain the feeling was mutual. She also suspected the man knew she called him The Divine Pain in the Ass every chance she could.

This could get ugly.

Lloyd shook his head, staring at her as if she might possibly be mentally challenged. "Explain to me what was going through that normally brilliant mind of yours when you made such a suggestion."

Bonnie wondered how many of her thoughts of the past twenty-four hours she should share with him. She waded in slowly. "I went to see Matt yesterday."

Lloyd nodded, but Bonnie could see he expected a lot more by way of explanation. "There's just a lot I think isn't right about Luther's death."

"You mean besides the fact he was murdered in our wrestling loft?"

"You know what I mean."

Lloyd leaned on his desk. "Don't be so sure. Give me a for-instance."

"All right. Did you know Angelica Devereaux and Trent Hendrickson, two people who were at the school yesterday, were having an affair?"

Lloyd rose, his eyes flashing in anger. "Who told you that?"

It's true, and you already knew it! "How long has it been going on, Lloyd?"

"You've got to promise me you'll keep this to yourself."

Bonnie didn't say a word.

He exhaled, puffing out his lips. "It's been over since Christmas. He tried to break it off, but she went crazy. Kept going out to his ranch all hours of the day and night. Saw her there once myself. When Angelica saw me, she spun out of Trent's parking lot in a cloud of dust. Gave me the old middle-finger salute."

Bonnie recognized Lloyd's attempt at humor, but she wasn't buying any of it. "What was this crazy woman doing at the school? For that matter, what was Trent doing here?"

Lloyd waved away the question as if it had no bearing on anything important. "Trent came about his boy. The man takes this single dad thing pretty seriously. Kip's on the wrestling team, and Luther was being hard on him."

You think it might have something to do with the fact that the boy's dad is playing hide-the-bologna with the wrestling coach's wife? "What about Angelica?"

"From what I understand, she came out to the ranch again Wednesday." Lloyd scratched at his salt-and-pepper growth of beard, making a sandpaper noise. "I guess she saw Trent leaving and followed him here."

"With Luther here at the school?"

Lloyd spread his hands. "I told you, she's one crazy lady."

Luther, you poor dumb shit.

Bonnie realized her thoughts had been sidetracked. "Hold it. How do you know all of this?"

"When Trent took her away from the loft, he brought her to my office. After I finished with the police, I came back. I heard them arguing."

"You mean to tell me, with her husband dead only an hour, Angelica was still chasing after Trent?"

Lloyd looked embarrassed.

Bonnie remembered Lloyd was a churchgoing man involved in a distasteful turn of events. His friendship with Trent had most likely been tested to the breaking point in the past half year.

"Do you know when Angelica got to the building?"

Lloyd stared up at her uncomprehendingly. "What do you mean?"

"I mean, how long had she been in the school before we saw her weeping on the loft steps?"

"What are you getting at?"

Are you being purposely obtuse?

She threw up her hands in frustration. "Think about it. First, she follows her lover down to the very school where her husband works. Bold, and not too bright. Then she falls to pieces when that same husband is found murdered."

Comprehension glowed in Lloyd's face. "Then later she's back to throwing herself at Trent."

Bonnie nodded. "Bizarre in a vampirish sort of way."

"Are you saying this makes her a murderer?"

Bonnie fell back into her chair. She glanced at the clock. She had only forty minutes of her planning period left. The thought made her weary.

"I don't know what I'm saying. There's just so much going on."

"I'm afraid to ask what else."

"How about the fact I saw Barty and Kyle Hansen in the gym while Luther's body was lying up in the loft?" She hoped to see a look of shock on Lloyd's face, but was disappointed.

Again he waved away the news like it signified nothing. "They came by the office and told me they needed to speak with Greg."

Bonnie squinted up at Lloyd. "Did they say about what?"

"I didn't ask. They said it would only take a minute, and I had Trent Hendrickson waiting."

As Bonnie hurried back to her classroom, she almost ran headlong into Marcie Englehart, the school nurse.

A tall, spare woman with graying blond hair, Marcie always seemed in a hurry to be somewhere other than where she was. When she did slow down, the woman spewed gossip like an obscene fountain. Over the years, Bonnie had become one of her favorite drainage sites. No amount of discouraging remarks or looks could dissuade the woman from sharing what she knew.

"Excuse me," Marcie said breathlessly. "Are you all right?"

Another annoying habit the woman had was invading space. Right now, her face hovered inches from Bonnie's. Her cigarette breath and perfume made Bonnie wonder how long she could hold her breath.

"I'm fine, but in a bit of a hurry."

Bonnie squeezed by and strode toward her classroom. *Don't look back, Pinkwater. Therein lies madness.*

Never one to take a hint, Marcie fell in beside her. "Isn't it tragic about poor Mister Devereaux?"

Bonnie mumbled noncommittally. Besides, from the excited lilt to Marcie's voice, the nurse thought the news was anything but tragic.

When Bonnie swung wide her door and entered her room, Marcie came right behind.

Busying herself at the front of her desk, Bonnie felt Marcie orbiting at her back, hovering, ready to pounce if even the slightest interest was shown.

"At least the poor man's done suffering," Marcie

whispered.

I'm going to regret this. "Suffering?" Bonnie turned around.

"I really shouldn't say anything." She looked about as if someone might be eavesdropping. "But I guess he can't be hurt anymore."

She pinned Bonnie against her teacher's desk.

"His eyes," Marcie whispered. She made her hands into a pair of makeshift binoculars. "Glaucoma." Her own eyes were down-turned, her lips pursed in mock sympathy.

Bonnie gave up any pretense of disinterest. "Glaucoma? How bad?"

"Bad enough. The disease was one of the reasons he planned to retire. His eyes resisted all forms of traditional treatment." The corners of Marcie's mouth twitched.

You're loving this, aren't you?

Bonnie felt like a ghoul for listening, but she was hooked. "Going blind," she mused and wondered why a fellow as cynical and savvy as Luther Devereaux would trust his secret to a blabbermouth like Marcie.

Marcie nodded frenetically. "About two years ago, when he first started having trouble, Luther came to me and told me his vision was deteriorating. It sounded like glaucoma, so I advised him to have it checked by his ophthalmologist. When he found out I was right, he swore me to secrecy."

A promise I'm sure you're now more than happy to break.

Marcie cupped her hands around her mouth conspiratorially. "It could have been a lot worse than it actually was. If you know what I mean . . ."

Bonnie had the unsettling feeling the woman was preparing to wink at her.

Dear God, no.

"I'm afraid I don't."

Marcie sighed and patted Bonnie's arm. "Bonnie, poor naïve Bonnie. I told you he didn't respond to traditional treatments. He did, however, respond to—how should I say it?—a certain nontraditional treatment."

Bonnie felt thickheaded and wanted to smack Marcie for making her feel that way. The odious woman was all but calling her stupid, and she still didn't know what this gossip-spewing school nurse was talking about. Then the light dawned. "Marijuana?"

"Ganga. Silly smoke. The devil's weed." In one complex expression, Marcie's face conveyed both amusement and feigned horror. "At first he didn't think I knew. He certainly didn't want anyone at the school to know, but the stuff was saving his sight."

Bonnie sidestepped Marcie and peered back at the woman. "Hold it. Luther Devereaux had some sort of medical prescription for marijuana?"

This time, Marcie's shock wasn't feigned. "Are you kidding? In East Plains? Folks out here would eat him alive. Can you imagine what Old Man Boone would do with that piece of breaking news?"

Bonnie could imagine. Once, the ex-husband of a young elementary teacher was arrested for drugs in Colorado Springs. Even though the woman had been divorced for over a year and a half, the school board didn't renew her contract. They said it was because of her performance, but she had received exemplary evaluations up until her ex-husband's arrest. Since she wasn't on tenure, and wasn't in the teacher's union, nothing could be done.

"If Luther didn't get a prescription, how do you know he smoked marijuana?"

"I figured it out." Marcie tapped the side of her head with her index finger. "First of all, I smelled it on him a few times. He denied it, of course, but in a moment of weakness, he owned up."

Luther, you were slipping, you poor horse's ass. "But—"

Marcie held up a hand as if Bonnie meant to dispute her. "I know what you're thinking. What a mistake for Luther to make, but I'll have you know, his secret's been safe with me all this time. Besides, I'm a nurse, and marijuana helped Luther's failing eyesight."

The bell ending second period sounded. Already, Bonnie could hear the slamming of lockers and the rumble of teenagers pounding their way to her end of the hall.

Marcie stood, smoothing her dress. "We both have things to do. Listen, do me a favor?"

Still partially immersed in her reverie, Bonnie took a

moment to register the question. "A favor?"

"Either don't tell anyone what I told you, or if you do, don't tell them how you found out." Gone was any hint of humor. Marcie was honestly concerned. "I could get in trouble for not reporting something like this, if not with the police, then certainly with the good citizens of East Plains."

What the hell?

Bonnie didn't like the woman, but Marcie sure didn't deserve to lose her job. "Your secret's safe with me." It sounded strange to be saying that to Marcie.

She stared at Bonnie for a moment, then exited the room.

Bonnie's third block filed in. She barely heard them.

Her mind was taken up with the thought of Luther Devereaux smoking marijuana. An image floated into her mind: Luther Devereaux as the caterpillar in *Alice in Wonderland*, sitting on a toadstool smoking a hookah. The oversized bug adjusted his thick glasses and asked, "Who are you?"

Never mind who I am, Luther, you big putz. I think I know where you got your supply of devil's weed.

CHAPTER 6

At the end of fourth block, Greg finally showed, huffing and puffing his apologies. Now he stood toe-to-toe with Bonnie just inside her classroom. The halls beyond echoed with the excited voices and heavy footfalls of students slamming their way into a weekend.

"With or without you, Greg, I'm going."

The boy shook his head so violently, Bonnie was sure he'd wrench his neck.

"No way, Missus P. My brother and Pa are bad news. You don't wanna be in their face, 'specially right now."

"Then come with me." She set her jaw to show this huge man-child she meant business. "You said you wanted to help, so help."

She repressed a not-so-still, small voice that accused her of blatant manipulation.

So, sue me.

Just as she was getting ready to add more wood to

her argument, she stopped herself. *Keep your mouth shut, Pinkwater. Let him talk himself into going.*

"This is really nuts, Missus P." Already, his voice carried none of its earlier vehemence. "They're both out of their minds over the death of Mister Devereaux."

She couldn't let this one pass. "Out of their minds? In what way?"

Greg turned both palms up, as if explaining his father and brother to an outsider was a monumental task. "Okay, on Wednesday night, they got drunk and . . ." He rubbed his fingers across his lips.

"And high?"

"And high," he agreed reluctantly. "I could hear them from my room. As they got more and more hammered, they got louder. At first they seemed super unhappy about Mister Devereaux's death—like he was their best friend or something."

Or at least a very good customer.

"But by the end of the night, they were laughing. Once or twice I heard them slapping hands, high-fiving. Screwy, huh?"

"Really screwy." Alarms were going off in Bonnie's head. "Greg, I need to ask you a question. I'll understand if you don't want to answer, but I've got to ask it anyway."

Greg backed away as if giving room for Bonnie's question. "This has to do with Pa and Mister Devereaux, doesn't it?"

"You always were sharp on the uptake. Yeah, I need to know if Luther and your father had a . . ." *come on, Pinkwater, just say it,* ". . . commercial relationship."

"Is that what you want to ask Pa, if he was selling dope to Mister Devereaux?"

"Well, yes." Greg's tone irked Bonnie, made her feel more than a little foolish and old, as if she hadn't a clue about how the world worked, and this teenager needed to school her.

"Did your father sell marijuana to Luther Devereaux?"

"Before I answer that, how much do you know about Mister Devereaux?"

Bonnie's ego demanded she establish she wasn't just some know-nothing old fogey. "He had glaucoma, and he was treating it by smoking weed."

That's right, mister. I can talk the talk.

"Okay, I'll level with you." Greg's eyes opened an increment wider, and a smile teased the corners of his mouth. "I don't really know."

You little bugger.

She intended to give him a supersized piece of her mind, when the boy cut her off.

"But I know Mister Devereaux was toking, and I kinda suspect Pa was the one getting it for him." The words came out in a rush, like air escaping a balloon. "You got to know I went out of my way not to get mixed up in that crap. Pa and Kyle knew how I felt and worked everything so I could stay clean."

"Good for your father."

Greg frowned and shook his head. "It was just easier for the two of them if I was on the outside and not really looking in."

"Easier for you, as well. Someday, when you're off changing the world, you'll look back and see what a favor your father did for you."

She went to her desk, snagged her fanny pack, and slung it over her shoulder. "All right, then. What say we get going?"

He stared at her for a long incredulous moment, then sighed. "This is a real bad idea, but I won't let Kyle or Pa hurt you."

Bonnie resisted the temptation to pump a fist in the air. In the midst of her I'm-going-with-or-without-you bravado, she hadn't allowed herself to ruminate on how much she really wanted Greg to run interference against his father and brother. "I'm glad to see you come to your senses."

He gave her a two-finger salute. "Yes, ma'am, Greg Hansen, Mister Sensible."

Ten miles from the school, a small stand of antelope, a buck with maybe ten does, grazed behind the barbed-wire fence that ran along East Plains Highway. From the mountains to the eastern horizon, stretched that excruciating sapphire sky only wintertime can claim. Jim Croce blared from Bonnie's radio, proclaiming the foolishness of pulling the mask off the old Lone Ranger.

That's me, all right. The happy idiot going to unmask both Barty and Kyle and taking the little brother along as protection.

She turned down the radio and gave Greg a sidelong glance. He hadn't said boo since they'd climbed into the car. "Soooo, where were you second block?"

Greg pushed back the sleeve of his coat, then his shirt. From his wrist to the crook of his elbow, written in black ink, a smeared column of names emerged. "I got kinda busy."

At first Bonnie couldn't see the meaning of the names until she recognized a few of them and their context. "My list. You little outhouse."

He gave her an up-from-under stare as if to say, "Look who's calling who little," then offered a nonchalant shrug. "If you don't want to know what I found out, I understand."

She slapped his arm, stinging her hand against a rock-hard bicep. "Not only an out-house, but a smug one. You know darn well I want to know, but that doesn't mean I approve."

"That makes us even 'cause I don't like this whole trip even a little bit."

"Touché. Now, give over."

Greg tapped the second name down from his hand. "Unice Powell, she thinks she's so tough, her and these two." He pointed to a pair of girls farther down the list.

"They each got out of their classes at two forty. Met in the bathroom." He pretended to take a drag on a cigarette. "To hear Unice talk, they do it just about every day."

"This is all very interesting, but how does it help Matthew?"

"Unice saw Matt come out of the gym holding a paper cup, get some water, then go back in the gym."

Bonnie evaluated how much that piece of news could help Matthew and decided not much. A prosecutor wouldn't argue that Matt never got the water—hell, the cup had been plainly visible on the gym floor. Matt could have killed Luther after returning to the gym.

"Anything else?"

One by one Greg ticked off names. One girl heard Matthew and Luther arguing. Another thought she saw someone besides Matthew go up into the loft but, like she told the cops, she couldn't be sure. When Greg had covered about half the names on the list, he rolled down his sleeve. "An interesting bit came from Josh Kramer, a sevie in Mister Sylvester's PE class."

As far as she knew, the high school and junior-high school's schedules were staggered so the younger children never intersected with their older counterparts—fewer small humans ending up headfirst in trashcans. "How'd you get time to talk to a seventh grader?"

Greg's neck reddened. "Things were royally chaotic today, Missus P. Kids going to counselors, roaming the halls. Teachers not even bothering with roll. Just dumping their classes in the gym or the library. I sat in the gym bleachers all morning and talked to whoever."

Bonnie couldn't decide whether she disliked this news because order had broken down, or because she didn't get in on an easy day. "What about this Kramer kid?"

Greg gave the slow nod of someone with a juicy story to share. "Okay, this guy's in Mister Sylvester's last-block PE class. A half hour to go, and Mister Sylvester hands out Nerf dodge balls, then leaves class to go into the coach's office—the one under the wrestling loft. He's gone for over ten minutes."

Holy crap, Harvey. What were you thinking? Your ass and your liability were way out in the breeze. "Was this child positive?"

"Oh yeah. And you know how crazy those dodgeball games get, twenty sevies screaming, chasing, beaning one another. They get about ten of those Nerfs going."

"This is amazing."

"There's more."

Bonnie couldn't think what else Harvey could do wrong. "Uh huh?"

"Josh gets himself smeared and sits out for a minute. He swears he heard a woman's voice coming from the coach's office. A couple of other sevies told me they heard her, too."

Bonnie slapped the steering wheel. *You big shit-head, Harvey. What in hell were you up to?*

She turned off East Plains onto Billings, the rutted dirt road that led to the Hansen ranch, such as it was. It sat in desolate isolation by at least a quarter mile in every direction.

"Greg, I need to ask you something."

The boy eyed her suspiciously. "What?"

"Mister Whittaker told me your father and brother came to the school on Wednesday to speak with you. Were they telling the truth?"

"No." Greg spoke without hesitation, his voice hard. "The first time I saw them was in the gym after Mister Devereaux's death. They saw me, too, and didn't say squat to me."

"Did they later tell you what they were doing at the school?"

"Like I said, I've pretty much kept out of their way for the last day and a half." With his chin, Greg pointed up ahead. "Looks like someone's at the house."

No doubt, Greg's eyes were better than hers. The Hansen place was still several hundred yards up Billings.

Then she saw what he meant. Next to a faded red barn sat a car, most of it obscured by a white double-wide trailer.

"Slow down," Greg said. "Something doesn't feel right."

Without hesitation, Bonnie did as he instructed, creeping up to the driveway entrance, then stopping. "Do you recognize the car?"

Greg nodded. "It's Old Man Boone's Studebaker."

Bonnie craned her neck over the steering wheel. The massive barn hulked at the end of the dirt drive, past the double-wide. Parked in the high weeds in the shadow of the barn, the Studebaker sat with its trunk open.

When Greg popped open his door, Bonnie's heart gave a double beat.

"I got to see what's going on," he whispered.

Before she could voice her objection, Greg was out. Against her better judgment, Bonnie hurried to join him. Before they'd gotten halfway up the drive, the upper door of the barn swung open.

Twenty feet above the ground, Simon Boone stood framed in the tiny opening. He held a black garbage sack. Without prelude, he dropped the sack into the Studebaker's open trunk.

Every molecule in Bonnie's being demanded she hide. Perversely, she and Greg stood paralyzed, staring up at Simon.

His task complete, Simon peered down the drive. His eyes went wide the moment he spotted them. From beneath his shirt, Simon produced a pistol. Awkwardly, he shifted in the window and took aim.

"Holy shit!" Greg grabbed Bonnie's hand and jerked her toward the trailer.

Simon's first shot kicked up a plume of dust not three feet from where they had stood.

As they dove behind a trio of steps leading to the trailer's side door, a second shot rang out.

Bonnie peered over the steps. Simon had disappeared from the upper window.

"He's coming down to get us," Greg whispered. "We gotta get out of here."

As if to belie that intention, Greg opened the trailer's screen door, then slammed it shut.

Bonnie didn't need any explanation. Hopefully, Simon would think they'd entered the house.

On all fours, she and Greg scrambled along the skirt of the trailer and around the front. Bonnie chanced a look back.

Simon emerged from the barn's sliding door. "I'm sorry, you guys!" he shouted. "You scared me. I thought you were the cops." Simon crept toward the trailer, gun held high.

Bonnie pulled back and held her breath.

"Come on, you guys." Simon climbed the steps and swung open the screen door.

When she didn't hear the scrape of the inner door, Bonnie knew Simon was just standing on the top step, staring around, probably debating whether to enter.

Just go in, you homicidal dwarf.

After what seemed like God's own eternity, she heard the inner door. She almost screamed when Greg tapped her on the shoulder.

"Let's get in the car," he whispered.

She shook her head in a short nervous jerk. No way was she trusting her life to a car that only started about 78 percent of the time. She could just picture her and Greg sitting in Alice's front seat, the ancient engine churning like a cement mixer. Then Simon strolls up and blows the two of them away.

Greg must have read her mind because he grabbed her hand. "I know where to go." He led her around the back side of the trailer.

They hadn't gone a hundred feet when one of the windows of the trailer exploded.

"Run!" Greg bellowed.

He didn't need to tell her twice. She was hot on his heels, fully expecting Simon to shoot her in the head.

Greg stopped at a sun-bleached pair of doors that seemed the remnant of a house that had been sucked into the ground. "Help me." He grabbed one door and tugged.

Even as Bonnie reached for the other, she heard the trailer's screen door slam. She pulled. Rusting hinges protested, but the pair of doors swung open. Bonnie and Greg dove into the dark opening. A gunshot sounded just as the doors slammed shut. The darkness that enveloped

Bonnie was complete.

"We need to find something to bolt it from the inside." Greg's disembodied voice whispered into her ear.

Bonnie fell to her knees. When the doors were open, she'd caught a glimpse of a trash heap at the back of the tiny room. Now she rummaged through the pile, frustrated because she couldn't make out what she was touching. After an eternity, her fingers closed around something metal with a cord tied to one end. "It feels like a transom rod."

Greg took the rod from her hand.

Bonnie heard the sound of metal sliding across wood.

Simon's running footsteps stopped just beyond the doors. For a moment, there was silence, then the doors began to creak. A widening line of light pierced the darkness. When the curtain rod caught, Simon shook the doors, slamming them up and down.

"To the side." Greg pushed her.

The words weren't two seconds out of Greg's mouth before a shot rang out. The wood of the left door splintered. A circle of sunlight appeared on the dirt floor.

In the new light, Bonnie could see the small room in which she seemed destined to die. Maybe ten by ten, she recognized the room for what it was—a storm shelter. From the looks of it, the shelter had been turned into a junk pit—rusted picture frames, broken flowerpots, old phone books, an ancient typewriter—nothing could be used to strengthen the transom slide bolt.

Above, Simon grew strangely quiet. Bonnie could imagine the little weasel standing in the winter sunlight, seething with fury. Sooner or later he'd lose it and go nuts on the doors again. The curtain rod wouldn't take much more abuse before it bent enough to let Simon look in and draw a bead on them.

Bonnie rubbed her sweating palms on her pants. Her fingers brushed across a rectangle—her cell phone. Shaking, she pulled it from her pocket and flipped it open. It offered scant illumination and even less hope. She'd never be able to get a signal from out here in the boonies and certainly not down in this hole.

But it didn't matter.

"Hey, Boone!" she shouted.

"What are you doing?" Greg whispered.

"Trust me," she mouthed, hoping he could see her lips in the gloom.

"Hey, Boone, I'm talking to you."

"I hear ya." Simon's voice sounded close, like he was lying against the doors.

"Then hear this." She tapped the phone against the door. "That's my cell phone, you refugee from the circus."

She opened the phone and pressed buttons at random. The beeps echoed in the small room. "Yes, Officer, I'd like to report a maniac."

"You bitch!" Simon screamed. He fired once, then

again. The wood splintered, and more light poured into the tiny room.

Bonnie threw herself against some bookshelves.

The doors rattled violently. The rod looked as if it meant to break in half. With each wrench, Simon cursed like a child throwing a tantrum. "I'll kill you! I'll kill you!"

Then nothing.

Eyes wide, Bonnie and Greg stared at one another across the tiny room.

When two minutes, then five, had passed, Greg whispered, "Think he's gone?"

Bonnie shrugged. "I thought I heard footfalls leaving, but that could have been my heart pounding."

"I know what you mean. I think I'm going to need new underwear."

"That's an image I could have done without."

Again Bonnie waited in silence, straining to hear anything outside their sanctuary. Eventually, she said, "No matter how long we wait, it's never going to seem like enough. I think he left."

Greg didn't look so sure, but he nodded. Slowly, he pulled the rod through the handles. Then he set his back against the right door and lifted.

He peered out. "I can see the barn. The Studebaker is gone."

Bonnie held her breath and followed Greg into the sunlight.

Once she was clear, Greg let the door slam down. "Pa! Kyle!" he shouted. He waited no more than three seconds before he shouted again, this time running.

Bonnie wanted to stop him. Hell, Simon could be parked just the other side of the double-wide. She ran to keep up.

Greg crashed through the trailer doors, shouting for his father and brother.

Just as Bonnie began to climb the steps, Greg emerged from the trailer.

"They're not in here." He bounded past her, heading for the barn.

"Pa's truck is still here!" he shouted back and disappeared into the barn.

Even with the door open, the setting sun didn't illuminate the interior significantly. Bonnie barely made out the front end of the truck.

"Pa!"

Greg's scream shook Bonnie to her marrow. She found the boy standing at the rear of the truck, staring down at something on the dirt floor.

Her eyes adjusted to the gloom.

Barty and Kyle Hansen lay faceup, their shirts dark with blood.

The sun had set by the time Deputy Hickman's cruiser and a single state patrol car came to an abrupt halt in the drive. Lights and sirens died in tandem, leaving a vacuum that rang in Bonnie's ears.

Standing in the barn's doorway, she gave a wave to her former student and walked around the truck to check on Greg.

The boy was kneeling where she'd left him. His lips were moving, but Bonnie only caught the random whispered word. "Stupid . . . assholes."

She laid a hand on his shoulder. "We should get away from the crime scene."

Greg nodded and stood shakily. His eyes were dry. "Dumb asses," he said in flat monotone, "thinking they could make big money growing weed. Now look at them."

Bonnie led him around the truck where Hickman and a deputy she recognized as Lloyd's friend, Fishbach, stood in the doorway. Greg kept walking past the two officers.

"Stay with the boy." Hickman pointed with his chin, and Fishbach fell in behind Greg.

"The bodies are behind the truck," Bonnie said. "I checked them. Both are dead. Shot in the chest."

"I wish you hadn't."

Bonnie felt her face grow hot. This man had no idea how hard it had been to touch the clammy skin, to unbutton the blood-soaked shirts. How long she'd washed her hands afterward. "I had to make sure. What if they were still alive?"

His face unreadable, Hickman nodded. "What's done is done."

He gave the truck wide berth.

Bonnie stood an arm's length away.

He fished a penlight from his pocket and brought it to bear first on Kyle, then Barty. Their shirts were still open from when Bonnie had checked the wounds.

Hickman focused the beam on Barty. "Looks like one shot each, left side, entry wound in the front."

Until Hickman turned to look at her, Bonnie couldn't tell if he had been talking to her or just to himself. "I didn't find any more."

"Someone knew what he was doing. You said on the phone the shooter was Simon Boone?"

"That's right. He shot at us." A part of Bonnie marveled at how composed this former student was. After all, the two corpses in question were his brother-in-law and nephew.

Hickman led her out of the barn. "Another state trooper was sent to the Boone house, but I don't expect to find Simon there. The good thing is that there aren't too many Studebakers left on the road. We'll get him."

Greg and Deputy Fishbach leaned against the sheriff's cruiser. Evidently, Fishbach had given the boy a stick of gum. Greg was vacantly chewing while staring at his feet.

Neither appeared to have anything to say to the other.

A pair of troopers approached. One male, one female, both blue-eyed, both surfer blond.

Did they always look alike or, like an old married couple, did they morph into twins?

The male trooper, Jubb according to his nametag, stepped past Byron into the barn. Bonnie heard the sound of boots knocking against the rungs of a wooden ladder.

"There's a regular nursery up here," the trooper shouted. After a moment, he reappeared at the barn door. He nodded toward Greg. "That one live here?"

Byron nodded. "Youngest son."

"You want to take him in, or should we?"

"You're kidding, right?" The words were out of Bonnie's mouth before she realized she had said them. "That boy's father and brother are lying dead in this barn, and you're suggesting he be arrested?"

Hickman laid a hand on her arm. "Take it easy, Missus P. Officer Jubb is only doing his job."

Before Bonnie could give free rein to her Imp of the Perverse, Hickman stepped forward and took Jubb by his well-muscled bicep.

"Can I talk to you?"

The two men moved along the front of the barn, stopping about ten feet distant.

Bonnie strained to listen, but couldn't make out anything meaningful. She felt awkward cooling her heels in the company of the female officer, until she caught the woman also inclining her head in the direction of the men.

Jubb leaned into Hickman. For a tense moment, Bonnie thought the two men might come to blows.

Then a stony-faced Jubb strode away from the conversation and back to his partner. "We're out of here."

The woman gave him a questioning stare.

"I'll tell you in the car." Without another word, Jubb walked toward his vehicle, leaving his partner with no choice but to catch up.

Hickman stood apart until the troopers had left the drive, then he called Greg over. "You can't stay here tonight. All the buildings are crime scenes. Once the CSI fellas get here, we're leaving."

"I don't understand."

Greg couldn't have looked more confused if he had been told he'd been sold to a circus.

"You're a minor, Greg, and you've got no place to stay. For all we know, Simon Boone may return."

"So where will he go?" Bonnie asked.

"I'm probably going to be handed my ass on a platter, but I'm taking him home with me."

CHAPTER 7

JUST PAST SEVEN, BONNIE TURNED DOWN JIMMY BUF-
fett in midlament as he proclaimed the medicinal value
of tequila. She stopped Alice, The-Little Subaru-That-
Could, at the crest of her long driveway.

"What the hell?"

Beyond the garage, beyond the house, the back end of
a vehicle protruded from a snowy stand of scrub oak. The
car's rear lights cast a red glow onto the snow as if someone had sprayed the drive with Hawaiian Punch.

She rolled down her window. The distant blare of a
car horn mixed discordantly with the intermittent barking of dogs.

Bonnie eased the Subaru down the drive. The last
thing she needed was to follow this schmuck's lead and
slide headlong into the scrub oaks, or worse still, into the
car. She hadn't gone halfway before she recognized the
vehicle—Trent Hendrickson's Avalanche. Her stomach

flip-flopped. "What are you doing here, you son of a bitch?"

She pulled up behind the Chevy. The horn was deafening.

Bonnie climbed out of her Subaru and, hands clasped over her ears, trudged up to the driver's window.

Trent sprawled across the steering wheel. He wasn't moving.

When she popped open the door, an empty fifth of Johnny Walker Red toppled onto the snow. The smell of hard liquor greeted her nostrils.

Trent stirred, first smacking his lips, then groaning. He lifted his head, and for a blessed moment, the blaring horn was silent. Then with a thud, his chest reconnected with the wheel. The honking resumed with a vengeance.

"Oh no, you don't." Bonnie grabbed the big man by his blond hair and yanked him backward.

He flopped bonelessly against the seat back and opened one eye to peer at her. "Binnie! I came to see you."

The man's breath was a sour mixture of cigarettes and whiskey.

"Yes, you did, you big horse's ass."

Evidently, Trent found the appellation hilarious. Laughing, he slapped the steering wheel. "Horse's ass."

Trent swung his long legs out of the truck and pushed up, almost toppling forward in the process. Unsteadily, he righted himself. His face went as sour as his breath.

"I'm mad at you." His lower lip protruded like a child in full sulk.

Bonnie stepped back. Since an isolated evening a decade and a half ago, he'd always been a gentleman, but then again, he was drunk. And there was that business with Missus Devereaux.

I should just leave your drunken rear end sitting here to sober up.

Odds were, he'd fall down trying to get from the truck to the house. He might even pass out and freeze to death.

Oh hell.

"Why don't you tell me all about it?" She offered her arm.

Sipping a cup of black coffee, Trent slumped at the breakfast island. Getting the big man from his truck into the house had been an ordeal. They'd fallen once in the snowy driveway, him laughing, her cursing.

Bonnie sat across from him, nursing her own cup and a growing uneasiness. Her thoughts took her back fifteen years. Back to a time she'd just as soon forget.

She and Ben had been going through a rough patch. He'd left for his family's reservation. The telling thing was that she hadn't been invited, and he'd be gone for over a week.

Two nights after Ben left, she invited Trent over. She had hoped to talk, get some insight into what was bothering her husband.

The invitation had been a mistake. Hurt and loneliness got the better of her. Trent ended up spending the night. In the morning, she felt wretched. She told him she loved her husband, begged him to forget what had happened.

Evidently, it hadn't meant that much to Trent. He went on to a string of affairs that now included Luther Devereaux's wife, Angelica.

Bastard. "You going to tell me what you're angry about, or do I throw you back out into the snow?"

He raised his head like it weighed a ton and fixed her with red-rimmed eyes. "Deputy Hickman came to see me today. You put him up to it?"

From the look on Trent's face, he already knew the answer to that question. Besides, she didn't owe him anything. "Yes, I did. I told him I saw you with Angelica Devereaux. I also told him what's going on between the two of you."

A half smile tried its best to creep onto Trent's face, with limited success. He seemed to settle for a sardonic shake of the head. "And what, Little Miss Righteous, do you think is going on?"

"That you've been having an affair since October. I

know it's true, so don't try to deny it." Bonnie couldn't believe how prissy she sounded.

This is about Matthew, Bonnie, not about some evening fifteen years ago.

"I do deny it. We're through." Trent said the words with enough vehemence that Hypatia, who'd been lying at Bonnie's feet, growled.

"Good puppy." Bonnie leaned down and stroked the dog's head. "You know what just occurred to me, Trent? You're the one who came to see me. So if you want to play the accusing game and then lie, I've got better things to do with my night."

The big man's face went red, and his jaw began to work. After a long moment he sighed. "I thought we were friends, maybe more than friends."

Bonnie made no effort to keep the contempt from her face. "Where in hell did you ever get that idea? For that matter, don't you dare even go there."

"For Pete's sake, I was a pallbearer at Ben's funeral."

"You were Ben's friend, never mine. And now that you're playing house with another man's wife, you're even less so."

Trent sat up straight. "God damn woman, you don't pull any punches, do you?"

"God damn, yourself. You don't deserve any pity." She was too tired for this bullshit. "You wanted to talk about Byron Hickman?"

Trent nodded, looking almost relieved to be changing the subject. "Came out to the ranch. Had all sorts of questions about me and . . . Angelica."

"What sort of questions?"

"He wanted to know what Angelica and I were doing at the school."

"What were you doing?"

"*We* weren't doing anything, not together, anyway." Trent scowled at her. "I came down to have words with Lloyd about Luther's treatment of my boy, Kip. That's all. I came alone."

"And Angelica followed you."

Trent puffed out his cheeks and released a breath. "You've been talking to Lloyd."

"We've talked. What of it?"

He leaned in close. "Can you keep a secret?" Trent didn't wait for her to answer. "Lloyd thinks I broke it off with Angelica, that I—how do the kids put it—dumped her. Truth is, she got tired of me."

"Why would Lloyd think you dumped her?"

"It's what I told him. Didn't want him feeling sorry for me. Didn't want to look any more the fool than I already felt." His words slurred like he was talking around a mouth full of grapes.

He reached across the table and latched onto her arm. "She found someone younger, more fun." He laughed mirthlessly. "Someone better."

Bonnie wasn't sure how much of this she believed. "So she didn't try to win you back?"

"Win me back?" Trent snorted. "The last time we spoke, she said I wasn't even worth disliking. Just a boring old fart."

His grip tightened on her arm. "But here's what's weird: Luther knew about the affair."

"I don't understand."

"Everything was a big game she and Luther played. Played it a half-dozen times before me. She'd go home and tell that sick shit everything . . ." His voice trailed off into something sloppy and wet.

Bonnie peeled Trent's fingers from her arm. "But Lloyd heard her arguing with you in his office, heard her pleading with you."

A calloused thumb swiped at a tear. "I tried to comfort her. Told her I would take care of her now Luther was gone."

Trent's eyes blazed. "She laughed at me."

He tightened his fist. "Bitch." Angelica was right there in his hand, and he was squeezing the life out of her. "If Lloyd heard her pleading, it was for me to leave her alone."

Bonnie had no intention of being sucked into this cow-town soap opera. If shit blew up in Trent's face, it was no less than he deserved.

One thing did bother her. "Then why did Angelica

come to the school?"

"To meet her new lover."

"At the school?"

He nodded, a look of angry acceptance hardening his fleshy face.

"How can you be so sure?" Bonnie asked.

"She told me in Lloyd's office."

"Did she say who?"

Trent shook his head. "Nope. And I got no idea."

Like it was too heavy to hold up a moment longer, Trent lowered his head onto his arms. His breathing became regular.

"Trent?"

She couldn't believe it. The man had fallen asleep.

Bonnie downed the last of her coffee, left the kitchen for her bedroom. She wanted to push her face into a pillow and scream.

God damn you, Trent.

She couldn't send the man home in his present condition. Even if his car would drive, he'd never make it up the hill, let alone navigate the roads of Black Forest. The thought of this drunken Lothario spending the night made her want to kick something, or better yet, someone.

And yet this same knucklehead had been the lover of a woman twenty years his junior. What a piece of work Angelica Devereaux must be. Beautiful in a slutty sort of way, not only did she have an affair with Trent—the thought of it and the memories it engendered made Bonnie shudder—but if he was telling the truth, Trent was just the penultimate in a line that included a half-dozen others.

Then Angelica went home and shared her erotic adventures with her half-blind, pot-smoking, kinky, and now recently deceased husband. And she was currently involved with some new horse's patoot, who, according to Trent, was at the school the day of this same husband's murder.

Toto, I don't think we're in Kansas anymore.

Just as Bonnie was trying to wrap her mind around who this new lover might be, a random memory flitted across her synapses—something Greg Hansen had told her.

Bonnie had just managed to get Trent ensconced in the guest bedroom when the phone rang. The big man snorted, then rolled over. Bonnie hadn't gotten his boots off and frowned at the mess they were making of her comforter. She left the room, promising herself she'd return and slap Trent once just for her own peace of mind.

She picked up the phone on the fourth ring. "Pinkwaters."

"Bon, it's Lloyd."

She didn't like the tone in Lloyd's voice. "What's going on?" She braced herself for bad news.

"Those calls you thought I'd be getting from the community, most of them didn't come to me." He hesitated, breathing heavily. "A raft of them went to the school board, a second bunch to the superintendent. I just got off the horn with him."

Bonnie winced at the mention of Superintendent Xavier Divine, who forever would be The Divine Pain in the Ass as far as she was concerned.

"I take my bad news straight up, boss. What does our fearless leader want?"

"Superintendent Divine wants you to come in to see him on Monday. I got a not-so-good feeling about this, Bon. The man called it damage control."

It did sound awful. Divine's idea of damage control would be to distance himself and the district from Bonnie's lapse of judgment. If he could, he'd throw her to the wolves, probably at some open forum board meeting where members of the East Plains community could take potshots at her. She could almost picture Divine rubbing his hands together, relishing this opportunity to twist a knife into her side.

Screw him.

"Thanks for the warning, Lloyd. Anything else?"

"Just that you keep your head down. If I were you, I'd lead off with an apology to Divine, then go into a song and dance about how you were only suggesting that everyone, including Matthew Boone, is innocent until proven guilty."

Her gut tightened at the thought of apologizing to Divine. She bit back her anger. "Sound advice, boss man. I'll take it to heart."

For a long moment Lloyd said nothing. "I know you, Bon. And I know how you think, especially when you go all cooperative on me. Don't do anything stupid."

"Lloyd Whittaker, if we weren't friends for these last twenty-two years, I'd take offense. I am nothing if not tactful. I will show Superintendent Divine the deference his position of authority warrants and extricate myself from this dilemma with remorse and dignity."

Lloyd chuckled. "Woman, how you talk. But I'm going to hold you to it. No Imp of the Perverse."

"He won't even rear his ugly little head."

"Then I'll meet you in Divine's office at seven thirty Monday morning."

"I was thinking more like ten."

"Bonnie!"

"Just teasing. Seven thirty sounds like a perfect time to mend fences."

"Call me if you need anything." He hung up.

Bonnie stared at the phone in her hand. God damn that Divine. Even from the first, he'd been like oil to her water. And here she was again, about to be under his plump little thumb. She blew out a frustrated breath of air.

"What the hell. With any luck, we'll have a thermonuclear war before Monday."

Bonnie resisted the temptation to slam down the receiver. The red light from the coffee urn caught her eye, and she grabbed her cup. Something in her pocket crinkled. She brought it out. A slip of paper held Byron's phone number. He'd given it to her just before leaving with Greg in tow. She checked the clock on the microwave—eight twenty. Not too late to check on Greg.

No matter how bad a time she was having, it was nothing compared to what that boy must be going through. She punched in the number.

Byron picked up on the first ring, like he was standing right by the phone. "Yeah." His voice sounded rough and impatient.

"Byron, it's Missus Pinkwater. How are things?"

Byron sighed. "They've been better."

Bonnie waited for him to elaborate. Greg's voice in the background asked who was calling. The phone went silent, and Bonnie assumed Byron had placed his hand over the receiver.

"Missus Pinkwater?" Greg's voice, all anxious and excited, came on the line. "Am I ever glad you called."

As much as she liked the fact that the boy was happy to hear from her, Bonnie was taken aback by his energy. Greg Hansen had to be reeling from the events of the day.

"How are you doing, Greg?"

"I pretty much feel like crap. I still can't believe Pa

and Kyle are dead. It's like I wished them to death."

She didn't care for the direction this conversation was taking. "Stop that bull pucky this instant!"

He inhaled sharply. "What?"

"You heard me. For good or ill, they were your family. Of course, you had mixed feelings about them. That's what it means to be in a family. But by no stretch of the imagination was any of this your fault."

His breath blew ragged across the receiver. He sniffled. "You mad at me?"

Bonnie made a conscious effort to soften her tone. "Gregory Hansen, why in the world would I be mad at you?"

"I'm glad you're not mad 'cause Uncle Byron and I . . ." his voice went to a whisper, ". . . we're not getting along. He's got something going in East Plains, but he said he'd drop me off at your place, if it was okay with you. Could you and me talk?"

The boy tried to keep the question casual, but Bonnie heard the need in his voice.

"Any particular subject?"

He hesitated. "If it's a problem . . ."

"Cut it out, Greg. There's no problem. I've got an errand to run in the morning, but I should be back before noon. I'll make us lunch."

"Sounds great." He couldn't disguise the relief in his voice. "Listen, Missus P, Uncle Byron wants to talk with you. I'll see you tomorrow."

"It's a date."

When Greg handed off the phone, Byron began without prelude. "I really appreciate you taking him off my hands for a couple of hours."

"What's this about a fight?"

"I'll tell you about it someday. Let's just say, Greg and I have a bit of history."

"I'll hold you to it. So, are you going to tell me about your business in East Plains?"

"I hadn't planned on it."

Bonnie wanted to reach through the receiver and wring a straight answer from this closemouthed former student. She had to remind herself he no longer was her student, and she had no right to expect him to supply her with answers.

"At least tell me what's going on with Simon."

"He's fallen through a crack in the earth. No sign of him anywhere. What a lot of folks don't realize is that East Plains covers an area bigger than Colorado Springs and Denver put together. The only chance we got is finding that Studebaker. And that's all you're going to get from me."

Bonnie expected to hit a brick wall if she kept pressing, but promised herself she'd get more out of Byron tomorrow. "Fair enough. Well, I can't say it's been pleasant or especially informative talking with you, but I look forward to seeing you on the morrow."

Byron grunted. "See you around noon."

She hung up and reached for the notepad she kept hanging by the phone. Saturday promised to be a busy day, and busy days warranted to-do lists.

Since she was a little girl, Bonnie had always delighted in organized lists. This tendency probably had a lot to do with her choosing mathematics as a vocation. Two-column proofs had been her meat in high school and college. The organization of theorems, postulates, and corollaries demanded list structures, and she was never closer to heaven than when she was cataloguing items and symbols.

She wrote *Saturday* at the top of the page, and underlined the word twice. Certainly, she'd have to plan a meal for herself and Greg and maybe even Byron if he could spare the time. She wrote *grilled cheese* in the middle of the page.

She groaned.

Trent Hendrickson had to be dealt with as part of any plans she had for Saturday. The man would just have to be shown the door long before Greg and Byron arrived. She wrote *Trent gone before eight o'clock* just beneath the double underlined *Saturday*.

What was left was a window of time between eight thirty and noon. On the paper this was represented by an empty rectangle of space. Into this space, she wrote, *Go see Harvey Sylvester.*

CHAPTER 8

BONNIE AWOKE SATURDAY MORNING UNABLE TO breathe. She pushed Euclid's furry rear end off her face. "One of these days, buster, I'm going to throw you out a window."

Euclid gave a you-talking-to-me? look and stretched, his black fur almost blue in the early-morning light. Seeming to defy gravity, the cat leapt gracefully from the waterbed.

Bonnie blinked, checking the clock on her night-stand—seven forty. The smell of coffee came at her in the same instant she heard the whistling. It took her a moment to recognize "Oh, What a Beautiful Morning."

Good God, couldn't the man have the decency to be hung over and miserable? What next, a chorus of "Oklahoma" while he made omelets?

Fifteen years faded away in a heartbeat. Trent had made omelets and coffee that morning, as well. She shuddered, feeling uncomfortable on so many levels she didn't want to get out of bed. Conversely, she wanted to storm into the kitchen and punch the big rancher in the stomach.

Get a grip, Pinkwater. So the man saw you au naturel fifteen years ago. He's not worth getting your panties all in a bunch.

Mustering a reluctant trickle of energy, Bonnie sat up and tossed aside her duvet. She dressed methodically, choosing panties, a sports bra, a Michigan State sweatshirt, and blue jeans. She clumped into her tiny master bathroom, a trio of dogs crowding her steps.

"Do you mind?" She gave Hypatia the evil eye.

"Did you say something?" asked Trent's voice from just beyond the bedroom door.

"I was talking to the dogs."

"What?"

"I said . . . Just forget it," she called.

Bonnie considered her reflection in the medicine-cabinet mirror, and even that simple act made her angry. Any other Saturday morning, she would have scrubbed a brush across her teeth and another one across her scalp and been good to go. What really pissed her off was the new variable in this morning's equation, besides the fact one of her colleagues had been murdered, consisted of the company in the kitchen. Trent shouldn't be having this effect on her.

She was fifty-three years old for pity's sake, not some

teenager who gave a hamster pellet what a former beau thought.

And there it was.

Some part of her still considered Trent Hendrickson a beau. For a brief and regrettable moment, this man had held her close, had touched her. Forget the fact many teenagers were more mature than Trent Hendrickson. Set aside the knowledge the man had bedded half the women in East Plains, and a great number of them while still married to his now-dead wife. Evidently, the stupid asshole had taken up residence in some forgotten corner of Bonnie's heart, and in fifteen years no amount of reasoning had evicted him.

Let's get down to brass tacks, Pinkwater. A part of you wonders how you compare with his other conquests. With Angelica Devereaux.

Bonnie frowned as she studied her face and her riot of gray hair.

"When did I get old?" she asked Hypatia.

The dog stared up with a look that might have implied—"You're not so old. I think you're beautiful." Of course, the look had an equal chance of meaning—" Get over yourself. I'm hungry."

Bonnie stroked the dog's golden fur and laughed. "Thanks for reminding me what's really important. Screw the son of a bitch." She laughed again, thinking that's exactly what she had done fifteen years ago.

Nothing less and certainly nothing more.

"Trent!" she bellowed. "You better have omelets ready by the time I get out there."

Bonnie doused her cheese omelet with tabasco sauce and peered across the breakfast island at Trent. "How much of what you told me did you give to Deputy Hickman?"

He fisted an eye and yawned. "That depends on what poured out of my inebriated piehole. I wasn't in the best of shape last night."

Bonnie recapped their conversation ending with the revelation Angelica Devereaux had been at the school to see her new lover.

"Thank you so much for bringing that up. I got a few paper cuts you might want to pour lemon juice on." Trent scratched at his facial stubble and sighed. "After our talk, Hickman seemed particularly interested in Angelica. I got the feeling he wanted to talk to her but either hadn't got around to it or couldn't track her down."

"What makes you say that?"

"He asked me if I knew of anyplace else, besides her home, she might be."

"What did you tell him?"

"Pretty much the same thing I told you. Angelica Devereaux is the bride of Satan and no longer a problem of mine." He downed the last of his coffee, then stood. "I need to get on the road. Kip will be wondering where his old man spent the night."

Trent winked. "Imagine what he and most of East Plains would think if they knew I spent it with you?"

Ah yes, Asshole Junction revisited. Thanks for reminding me, Trent. "Imagine what most of East Plains would think if they knew Angelica Devereaux considered you a boring old fart and dumped your useless carcass?"

His face darkened. "I told you that in confidence."

"Seems we both have things we should keep to ourselves."

The hint of a smile played at the corner of Trent's lips. "You're a pistol. You know, neither of us is attached now. There's no reason we couldn't get together."

Bonnie's hand tightened on her coffee cup. "I'd more welcome genital herpes. For that matter, considering your proclivities, I probably could catch it from you."

"Don't sugarcoat your feelings, Bonnie. You'll hurt yourself." He shook his head and made for the door.

Twenty minutes later, with Bonnie at the wheel and Trent pushing from the front, they extricated the Avalanche from the snow and scrub oaks.

The truck now fishtailing up the long icy drive, Bonnie knelt and wrapped an arm around Hypatia's neck. "If you tell anyone this, I'll start feeding you cat food, but for a boring old fart, Trent Hendrickson's still a damn attractive man."

The golden retriever licked her face.

Bonnie scrubbed a mitten across Hypatia's head. "Don't worry, fur face. I still like you better."

Bonnie stood, and the dog followed her into the house. In a few minutes she finished the last of her cold eggs and stowed the dishes in the dishwasher. Then she made for the guest bedroom.

The lower half of the comforter was coated in mud.

Men—they're like bears in cowboy boots.

She tugged the soiled comforter from the bed. A brown rectangle rolled from beneath the folds, falling at her feet. She stooped to pick up a man's wallet.

No doubt the damn thing belonged to Trent, which meant she'd have to endure still another visit when he came to retrieve it.

Did the son of a bitch leave it on purpose?

Harvey Sylvester lived at the outskirts of Black Forest. Although never on a social occasion, Bonnie had been to his house at least a dozen times. Whenever either of them was sick or needed to take a day off, the other would deliver substitute lesson plans to the school.

He occupied a rough-hewn redwood cabin on ten acres of pine and aspen. All week Harvey might be a middle-school Physical Education instructor, but on weekends he fancied himself a mountain man. Four to five times a year he donned buckskin, threw muzzleloaders into his Jeep, and hobnobbed with his fellow throwbacks.

Rendezvous, they called them.

Hopefully, this weekend he'd be home.

Bonnie considered warning him, calling him on her cell phone. She dismissed the idea as inappropriately polite.

I need to surprise Harvey, even if it makes him angry.

She turned off the highway and passed under a massive pine lintel on which hung a redwood plank. Burnt letters in the plank announced *The Huevos Ranch*. Hand-painted, sunny-side up eggs bracketed the letters. Considering Harvey raised neither cattle nor sheep, in fact, not even poultry, the title "ranch" hardly fit. She suspected Harvey just wanted an opportunity to proclaim he came equipped with his own set of huevos.

As she neared the cabin, Bonnie stifled a desire to whoop. Behind Harvey's Jeep sat a white Cadillac convertible. A sticker on the rear bumper told the world its owner could go from sweetheart to bitch in less than six seconds.

Bonnie pulled up close behind the Cadillac, effectively blocking it in. She slammed her car door, clomped loudly across Harvey's wooden stoop, and rapped on his roughhewn door.

Immediately, she heard stirring and hushed voices within.

"Harvey, it's Bonnie Pinkwater," she called out.

The house fell silent, except for light footfalls.

"Bonnie?"

"In the flesh." She expected someone would at least open the door a crack. No one did. "I need to talk to you."

"What time is it?"

Not sure if the question was meant for her, Bonnie answered anyway. "Eight fifty. Listen, Harvey, I know you have company. I'll be out of your hair in a matter of minutes."

The curtains on the front window rustled, and a blue eye peered out, first at Bonnie, then at the parked cars. "Oh, for Christ's sake, let her in. She's already seen the Caddie."

A deadbolt shot back, and the door swung open. Harvey Sylvester, wearing a white silk kimono embroidered with an emerald dragon, filled the doorway. His hairy legs stuck out the bottom of the robe like a pair of tree trunks.

He stepped aside to let her enter, then shut the door a little too loudly. "This better be good, Bon."

Bonnie hoped it would be good, indeed.

Angelica sat on a rawhide-and-antler love seat, red toenailed bare feet propped on a matching ottoman. Her kimono was identical to Harvey's, except her ample breasts looked as though they might, at any moment, burst through the thin fabric and say, "Howdy."

My, my, already to the matching-clothing stage. This

must be true love. Do they also own a pair of I'm-with-Stu-pid T-shirts?

Bonnie had once guessed Angelica's age at about thirty. Seeing her in the harsh glare of the overhead light, Bonnie reassessed her estimate to thirty-five, but grudgingly admitted the woman could pass for someone in her late twenties. What had she ever seen in bald-headed, half-blind Luther?

As Bonnie approached the love seat, she caught the unmistakable scent of recent sex. Before she could stop herself, Bonnie wrinkled her nose.

Angelica smiled, then tapped her pinkie on her blood-red lips. "That's right, I screwed his brains out."

Bonnie turned back to Harvey. With measured steps, she circumnavigated the man, staring up at him the entire time. "By God, it appears she has."

"Enough of this shit, both of you." Harvey glared first at Angelica, then fixed his gaze on Bonnie. "What the hell are you doing here?"

"Forget that for a moment. I would think your first order of business would be how I knew Angelica was here and who else knows."

"She's bluffing." Angelica waved a hand as if dismissing Bonnie as no one of consequence. "How could she possibly know?"

"Less than an hour ago, I parted company with Trent Hendrickson."

Angelica stood, her arms folded across her bosom. She gave Bonnie a knowing look. "I trust you served him breakfast."

The inference smacked Bonnie in the face. *God damn it, Trent, promise me in some drunken moment you didn't tell this odious harpy about us?*

Bonnie returned Angelica's Cheshire grin. "As a matter of fact, he made omelets for me." *Stick that in your corncob and smoke it.*

"He always did give good omelet." Angelica stood, crossed the room, and linked her arm into Harvey's.

For his part, Harvey couldn't have looked more dumbfounded if he'd just discovered the pope was a closet Southern Baptist.

Bonnie considered telling the giant PE teacher that Trent slept in the guest bedroom, and the only thing she shared with him was conversation. The problem was, that would mean telling Angelica, as well.

I'll be God-damned if I give this women the chance to disbelieve me.

"Just hold on." Color rose from Harvey's neck, reappearing above his beard. "How does Trent know about us?"

The big man glared down at Angelica.

"He doesn't, sweetie."

Bonnie felt obliged to come to Angelica's aid, if for no other reason than to blindside her from another direction. "She's right. Trent has yet to put two and two together and come up with Harvey Sylvester."

Bonnie let that statement hang in the air a moment longer before she said, "However . . ."

"However, nothing." Angelica pointed a long red fingernail at Bonnie. "Luther was right about you. You are one nasty little so-and-so."

Bonnie resisted the urge to curtsy. "However . . . I don't think Deputy Hickman will have the same trouble doing the math."

She recounted the seventh grader's report of Harvey disappearing for over ten minutes, then hearing a woman's voice coming from the coach's office.

"Put that together with what Trent has already told Hickman." She met Angelica's eyes. "You know, that business in Lloyd's office where you told Trent you'd come to the school to meet your new lover."

Harvey slowly shook his head. "I'm screwed," he whispered.

I would imagine that's true in every sense.

Angelica squeezed the big man's arm. "Baby, so what if people find out about us? They would have eventually."

"You still don't get it." Bonnie caught a look of panic on Harvey's face. "But you do, don't you?"

"What?" Angelica asked, frustration and impatience straining her voice.

Bonnie pointed to Harvey with her chin. "He lied."

"I never!" Harvey took a menacing step toward Bonnie.

"Back off, King Kong." Bonnie rose up to her full five foot three, putting her level with Harvey's collarbone. "You told Hickman no one except Matthew Boone went up into the wrestling loft during that crucial time from two thirty to three o'clock."

"No one had."

"Have I ever mentioned how much I hate it when people split hairs?" Bonnie swept her hand toward Angelica. "You two were cozied up in the coach's office for over ten minutes during that time. God Himself could have marched up to the loft wearing waders and a propeller beanie, and you never would have known."

"Bon, I couldn't tell Lloyd I'd left my class unattended."

Bonnie's hands trembled with the urge to slap Harvey. "So you put Matthew in a box to save your own sorry ass."

"Now wait just a minute. I found the boy kneeling over the body, knife in his hand."

She waved away the rationalization. "So, what the hell, what's one more nail in his coffin? Is that the way you see it, Sylvester?"

"I didn't say that."

"School me, Harvey. What are you saying?"

The man seemed to deflate right before Bonnie's eyes. "I'll be fired."

"I can't promise you anything, but the truth is bound to get out. Even as we speak, Hickman is trying to get ahold of your girlfriend here. Hell, he'd have already, if she hadn't been holed up here."

"Can we expect him knocking at the door in the next ten minutes?" Angelica asked.

Bonnie shook her head. "Hard to say. But that's not really important. Harvey's going to tell all, because that's the right thing to do."

Angelica looked for a moment as if she meant to laugh. A smile died on her face.

Harvey was nodding. "I have to, baby."

"Why?"

Bonnie stared at the woman, trying to decide if she was really as dense as she seemed. "What do you say we make a logic problem out of it and consider cases?" She splayed the fingers of her left hand and ticked off the thumb.

"Case One, let's call it the George Washington Scenario. Deputy Hickman questions you about those crucial ten minutes. And make no mistake, he will question you. In this scenario, you tell Hickman the truth."

"Why would I do that?" Angelica asked.

"Let's suppose between now and then you get religion. In any event, you tell the truth, just like George and the cherry tree. Then there'll be no need for lover boy here to unburden himself. You'll have done it for him."

"And if I lie."

Bonnie pursed her lips in mock sympathy as if Angelica had answered wrong on *Jeopardy*. She ticked off her index finger. "Which bring us to Case Two. For want of a better name, let's call it the Dumb-Ass Scenario."

Angelica shot daggers at Bonnie.

"Hickman probably has already had a talk with that little seventh grader who heard the two of you making whoopee in the coach's office. If the good deputy hasn't, it's got to be on his to-do list. Then you come along and tell an untruth. Now the bright young Mister Hickman is wondering what's up and is thinking maybe the philandering wife killed off her cuckold of a husband."

"Enough, Bonnie," Harvey said.

"Not by half, Harvey. She needs to see the truth, warts and all. Which, of course, brings up the real question of the day. Did you kill your husband?"

"Hell, no."

Bonnie shrugged as if the truth of Angelica's statement was completely beside the point. "If I'm skeptical, you've got to see that Hickman will have trouble putting aside his suspicions. Which bring us to Case Three." She ticked off her middle finger.

"Harvey decides to lie. This one is a variation on the Dumb-Ass Scenario, with pretty much the same result."

When Bonnie made to tick off her ring finger, Harvey gently took both her hands in his. "Which bring us to Case Four, where I call up Hickman and tell him everything."

Bonnie stared up into Harvey's eyes and offered a sympathetic half smile. "It's for the best."

The big man nodded. "I think it's time for you to leave."

"Don't put it off, Harvey. Call him right away."

"Leave, bitch," Angelica said. "Get out of here before I scratch your eyes out."

This time Bonnie did curtsy.

Bonnie had intended to swing wide of Black Forest, head into Colorado Springs to see Matthew, but her stomach demanded attention. She was feeling light-headed. A tub of garlic hummus called to her, so she aimed Alice for home. A quick hummus and piñon nut sandwich would fortify her for the trip into Colorado Springs.

As Bonnie turned into her long driveway, she reached for the garage-door remote, then shook her head in disgust. When she left for Harvey's that morning, she'd tested the damn thing because it had been threatening to give up the ghost. Although she'd managed to get the door to rise, the remote had proved useless for the task of lowering it again. She should have left her car, trudged the half-dozen steps to the garage, and used the internal switch to get the job done.

But she hadn't.

She'd been too eager to see Harvey. Besides it was a good eighth of a mile up to Burgess Road. Nobody was going to make that trek in the short time she'd be gone.

"Face it, Pinkwater. You were just too lazy."

Bonnie pulled into the garage and got out of her car, thinking how good that hummus sandwich was going to taste. When she tested the door from the garage to the house, she found it unlocked. This wasn't unusual. She rarely locked it since the garage door automatically locked when it touched down.

As she entered the foyer, Bonnie heard a whimpering dog. Quickly, she flicked on the panel of house lights. Hypatia lay in the hallway arch between the foyer and the living room, a bloody red crease marking her brow. Another bloody patch stained her golden fur at the hip. The dog took a labored breath and turned a pained eye in Bonnie's direction.

Simon Boone came around the corner from living room. In his right hand, he held a pistol.

CHAPTER 9

"GET YOUR ASS UP. GOD DAMN DOG'LL BE OKAY." SIMON leveled the pistol at Bonnie's face.

From out in the run, the manic sound of barking dogs filled the hall.

Simon didn't seem to notice. He waved the gun at a hole in the wall. "Only creased the bitch's head."

Bonnie felt along Hypatia's brow. The bullet had sliced a shallow divot just above her right eye. The wound had bled quite a bit, even staining the dog's flank. "She's still hurt, maybe in shock. Let me at least get a blanket and something to clean the wound."

Simon grabbed Bonnie's arm, jerking her to her feet. "I said, get your ass up."

He brought his pockmarked face within inches of hers, his breath sour, smelling of cigarettes. "Don't fuck with me, Pinkwater. You thought you were so smart— you and that pissant, Greg. You're not so fucking smart now, are you?" His voice shook, high-pitched, squeaky, which, if anything, added menace to the question.

Don't say anything stupid, Pinkwater. You won't help Hypatia or yourself. "No, Simon, I'm not so smart now. What do you want?"

He released her arm, then swiped a hand under his pointed nose. "You owe me, lady. Because of you and that God damn Greg, I got every cop in the world after me. You're going to get me a car and something to eat. A turkey or ham sandwich sounds good."

Oh piss. "I'm a vegetarian, but I have cheese."

Simon's face twitched, bloodshot eyes glaring at her. "Get to it."

Bonnie stepped backward, afraid to take her eyes off Simon. His face was drawn and pale.

You look exhausted, you little son-of-a-bitch psychopath. I'll bet you haven't slept since you killed Barty and Kyle. Somehow the fact that Simon wasn't operating on all burners didn't comfort her.

"If I get you something to eat, will you let me tend to my dog?"

"Why the hell should I?" He sawed the gun back and forth along the side of his head until blood stained his greasy blond hair.

Bonnie backed away, feeling along the wall. "I'll get you your sandwich." She gave a last look at Hypatia, hoping Simon would change his mind once he had food in him.

His eyes squeezed shut, Simon nodded. "After the sandwich, make coffee. We got some things to talk about."

Bonnie checked the clock on the microwave—ten thirty. *Shit, Byron won't be coming for an hour and half.*

Panic rose like gorge. Simon was one foot from crazy and was staring over the threshold. How in hell could she keep him from losing it until noon? And even if she could, when Byron showed up, he'd be a sitting duck.

Settle down, Pinkwater. You're not dead yet. Just take it one minute at a time.

She circled the breakfast island to the refrigerator. "You want mustard on that sandwich?"

Simon strode into the kitchen, a streak of blood trickling down the side of his face. He stared first at one appliance, then another as if he'd never seen the like. He bared his yellow teeth, licking at them with a tongue that appeared swollen.

"Nice digs."

Nice face, you pint-sized maniac. Bonnie perversely held Simon's stare.

Never taking his eyes off her, Simon slowly raised the gun over his head and fired.

The explosion was deafening. Bonnie jumped, stumbling against the refrigerator and dislodging a ceramic pig. The pig shattered into a dozen pieces.

"Bang. Not so nice now." Simon laughed. "You

should have seen your face. I swear. You looked like you were ready to meet your Maker." He plopped down on a stool. "As a matter of fact, I would like mustard. While you're at it, put some mayo and maybe lettuce and tomato on that bad boy."

Her heart racing, Bonnie stared at the broken pig. Ben had given her the little statuette the year before he died. She fought down tears, telling herself she'd see this little asshole in hell before he'd see her cry. She kicked aside the shards as if they meant nothing to her.

Yawning, Simon laid the gun on the island's Formica top. He cracked his knuckles and stretched.

Bonnie couldn't take her eyes off the weapon. If she just reached out, she'd be only inches from the gun. Her Imp of the Perverse screamed for her to do it. Lunge for the God damn thing. Blow this nut job off that stool and take back the house. Shit, empty the gun into him.

The moment passed.

Simon laid his right hand on the pistol. He gave her a grin as if he knew what she'd been thinking.

Bonnie promised herself if the opportunity presented itself again, she wouldn't hesitate.

In rapid succession, she brought out bread, lettuce, a huge block of cheddar, a tomato, mustard, and mayo from the refrigerator and set them on the countertop. She unhooked a cutting board from the end of the island.

"I'll need a knife."

"I'll bet you will." He pointed at her with the gun. "Don't do anything stupid."

Opening the cutlery drawer, Bonnie pictured whirling on her captor and hurling a knife. The blade would sink deep into his chest, severing his aorta.

As he bubbled up and died, Simon might say something pithy like, "You got me."

She, in turn, would snatch the gun away before he could exact revenge. Maybe even twirl it for good measure.

None of this happened. She laid the tomato on the cutting board and went to work.

Simon sat across from her, sullen and watchful.

Periodically she'd snatch a glance at him. When the sandwich was complete, Bonnie peered past Simon into the family room. Between the wall of the family room and the fireplace, she could see a few panes of the front window. Snow had started to fall.

She passed the finished sandwich across. "Here you go. How about letting me see to Hypatia?"

Simon slid the knife away from her. He took a bite of sandwich. "Hyper what? What kind of stupid name is that for a dog?" Food sprayed from his mouth.

Bonnie didn't think Simon really wanted an answer to his question, but she gave him one anyway. "Hypatia was a fourth-century female mathematician. She was . . ." Bonnie couldn't believe she was about to mention murder to this psycho.

"She was what?" he asked, impatiently.

"She was the greatest female mathematician of her time." *Nice, Pinkwater. You didn't miss a beat.*

"Big fuckin' whoop." Simon regarded Bonnie through eyes more red than anything else. He frowned, then nodded. "Make the coffee, then we'll talk about math dog."

"You told me I could tend to Hypatia if I made a sandwich. The sandwich is made, Simon. I'm going to see to my dog." She came around the breakfast island.

Simon picked up the gun. "You take another God damn step, I'm going to burn you down where you stand. Then just for grins I'm going blow away your stupid mutt."

Bonnie froze, staring at a twitch that had started under Simon's left eye.

He licked his lips. "We understand one another?"

Bonnie didn't think she could move, but she managed to nod. "I understand."

"Good, now make the God damn coffee."

Bonnie's hands shook as she filled the carafe. Her heart was thrumming in her chest. *Just relax, Bonnie. Think of anything but that gun in his hand.* She took a long breath and released it.

She speculated on why Simon had chosen her house and how he had gotten there. She'd seen no evidence of the Studebaker. Maybe he'd either parked it in Black Forest—in which case, the little bastard had gone out of his way to come here. She didn't want to think what must have been going on in his whack-a-mole mind as he trudged down her long driveway.

Another possibility was that the old vehicle had simply broken down. In this scenario, a panicked Simon Boone would be abandoning his only means of transportation and looking for another. With any luck, the car would be immobile along some Black Forest road. The cops would find it and be scouring the area for Simon.

So, how did he know to come here?

The answer presented itself immediately. Daniel. Last spring she'd had Daniel, along with a few of the other special-needs children, to her home for a party. Simon had dropped off Daniel. She remembered thinking at the time she didn't relish the idea of a thief like Simon knowing her address, but the damage was already done. That was one good deed that had come back to bite her on the derriere.

She turned on the coffeemaker. "Why did you come here, Simon?"

"Funny you should ask. That's the conversation we need to have. You're not going to believe this, and frankly I don't give a shit. Thing is, I didn't kill Barty or Kyle."

Bonnie stared at Simon, unsure how to respond. Simon was right. She didn't believe him for a moment.

But he seems to believe it. Given his mental state, he might believe anything.

"Go on."

"Well, Barty calls me up, see? He's got something for me."

"Drugs."

Simon frowned at her again, probably more for interrupting than the mention of drugs. "Yeah, weed. Anyways, I jump in the old man's Studebaker. He's sleeping. I figure I'll be back before he notices it's gone."

"Speaking of the Studebaker, where is it?"

Simon slapped the table. "You gonna keep interrupting? Damn piece of shit broke down a couple of miles from here. Where was I?"

"You went over to the Hansens' place to make a deal."

"Yeah. When I got there, I couldn't find Barty or Kyle anywhere. I knocked on the trailer, yelled for 'em. Finally, I went into the barn."

"You found their bodies."

"They was already dead. The gun was lying there in the dirt."

Bonnie nodded toward the pistol in Simon's hand. "This gun?"

She knew Simon was no rocket scientist, but to pick up a murder weapon, put your fingerprints all over it—the boy was just plain dumb. That same instant, she realized she was reacting as if Simon were telling the truth.

"It's a good gun," he said. "They didn't have any use for it."

"So, you know for certain the pistol belongs to Barty

or Kyle?"

The question obviously confused Simon. He slowly shook his head. "Not for certain. Who else?"

"How about the killer?"

"Oh shit. You're probably right." He started rubbing the gun along his head again, reopening his earlier wound.

Bonnie's first inclination was to reach across the island and stop Simon from hurting himself. *Screw that. The little creep shot my dog and is now holding me hostage. Give yourself a lobotomy, Mister Boone.*

"When I saw you, you were tossing something down from the barn's loft."

"Keys of weed. I never knew Barty had a garden up in the loft—false wall, grow lights, automatic misters, plants as tall as me with tents of aluminum foil over each one." Simon nodded appreciatively. "Sweet."

"Uh huh. So, how did you find the garden this time?"

"Barty and Kyle must have left it open, then got themselves killed. Shit, I don't know. I just saw a light up above and went to take a look. Found a dozen keys stacked in a corner."

"And, like the gun, Kyle and Barty didn't have any use for them."

If Simon heard the sarcasm in her voice, he didn't show it. "Exactly. I wasn't gonna take them all. I had just pulled the Studebaker around to the side of the barn—

you know, under that swing-out upper door."

"And Greg and I showed up."

"You caught me. Bad fucking luck."

"Yeah. Bad luck all around, especially for Barty and Kyle."

"Screw you. I'm telling the truth. I might have thought about killing them once or twice. I mean, who wouldn't? These guys always had righteous weed, and lots of it."

"Simon, I got a problem with this story. Why did you try to shoot Greg and me?"

Simon spread wide his hands, an effect ruined by the gun. "I panicked. I figured you'd tell the cops. With my record, they'd think I offed Barty and Kyle."

She had to admit, it made a warped kind of sense. She was getting ready to reply when someone flashed by the family-room window and entered the garage.

Her heart hammering, Bonnie quickly returned her gaze to Simon. "So, you've been running ever since?"

"Shit, yeah! Barty's got kin who's a cop. I figure, he'll just shoot me and ask questions later. Then my God damn car breaks down."

Footfalls sounded in the hall leading from the garage.

Simon's eyes widened. Gun in hand, he swung around on his stool.

A thunderous shot rang out from the family room. Simon jerked once, his body doubling. Still clutching the pistol, Simon tried to rise. Another shot sounded. The pistol clattered across the tiles as Simon toppled from the stool.

Bonnie stared at the place where Simon had sat just moments before. Her ears rang from the gunshots.

A rifle to his shoulder, Trent Hendrickson strode into the kitchen.

Forty-five minutes and two phone calls later, Bonnie sat on her family-room floor, Hypatia's head on her lap. The ringing in her ears had yet to subside, lending a surreal aura to her surroundings.

A sheriff's vehicle and an ambulance were parked in her horseshoe drive. In her kitchen, a pair of medics who looked as if they were barely out of high school attended to Simon Boone. One was pumping a bellows-like device that covered almost all of Simon's face. The other worked on Simon's blood-soaked chest, had been, in fact, for the better part of ten minutes. She had to admire their persistence, but she also knew they were wasting their time.

Simon Boone, as he had so aptly put it, had gone to meet his Maker. And he didn't purchase a return ticket. Not for a moment did she consider herself cold for being glad Simon was dead. Given the chance, she would have assisted Simon in shuffling off his diminutive mortal coil.

Trent Hendrickson, standing by her front door, towered over Deputy Wyatt. For what seemed like the hundredth time, he was relating the tale of how he looked through the window and saw Simon Boone, gun in hand, seated at the breakfast island. He then retrieved his hunting rifle from his truck. Yes, he shot Simon, then shot him again. By God, the boy was turning toward him with a pistol in his hand. What was he supposed to do?

As far back as her considerable memory would take her, Bonnie couldn't remember ever appreciating the fact that most of the male population of East Plains sported rifle racks. For that matter, so did a significant fraction of the females.

Hypatia stirred, and Bonnie stroked the dog. "Hush, baby. We'll get you to the vet as soon we clear up this mess."

Bonnie had cleaned the wound and sprayed it with a clear chemical bandage that reminded her of superglue. Still, she had put in a call to the vet, made her promise to treat Hypatia as soon as Bonnie could get the dog there.

Bonnie bent down and kissed Hypatia on her nose. "Your mommy can be very persuasive when she needs to be."

Byron Hickman's voice sounded from the direction of the garage. He strode down the hall, Greg Hansen in tow.

Byron laid a hand on Bonnie's shoulder. "Good God, Missus P. Are you all right?"

Bonnie considered the question before answering.

She took a quick inventory of her house. Her kitchen and her family room had both been decorated with bullet holes. Her dog would probably need stitches. A madman had held her hostage for the better part of an hour. He, in turn, had been shot to death not three feet from where she sat, after having consumed a sandwich of her making. All in all, she felt fine.

"I'm okay."

Wide-eyed, Greg Hansen stared at the bloody corpse of Simon Boone. "Shit."

"Shit, indeed. Greg, would you get me a pillow off the couch?"

When the boy returned, Bonnie gently laid Hypatia's head on the cushion and offered her hand to Byron. As she stood, she said, "I'm glad you're here. I've given a statement to your deputies. I need to get my dog to the vet."

"I'm going to need to talk with you later today, but for now, you can go. I'm thinking just about everybody here will clear out in the next few minutes. Wyatt will need to hang around to give the crime-scene guys access. You okay with that?"

"No problem." She turned to Greg. "I guess it's you and me. You up for a drive into Colorado Springs?"

Still looking like he was in shock, the boy nodded.

"We'll take off in a minute. There's one thing I have to do before we go."

Bonnie crossed the distance to Trent.

He offered a half smile at her approach. "How you holding up?"

"I'm holding. Listen ..."

He took her shoulders in his huge hands. "You already thanked me."

She stared up into his face. "Well, I need to do it again. It's not every day somebody saves your life."

Trent pursed his lips. "I ain't going to let you ... unless you thank me over dinner." He flashed her a smile.

"It's a deal. My treat."

"Damn right, it's your treat. I couldn't pay if I wanted to. You got my damn wallet back there in your bedroom."

Wyatt looked away, but not before her face reddened.

God damn you, Trent. Even when you save my life, you embarrass me. No doubt, Bonnie Pinkwater and her libidinous ways will be the after-church topic of discussion tomorrow morning.

"Your wallet's still lying on the bed, in the *guest* bedroom. You know, the one that's on the other side of the house from mine."

"I'm familiar with it."

"Good. Should we say tomorrow night for that thank-you dinner?" Bonnie tried to make her voice flat and unemotional as if she were negotiating with a salesman.

"Sounds good."

From the look on Wyatt's face, she wasn't buying any of it.

Screw it. "I got to go."

She turned back and took a long look at a bloody Simon Boone. Suddenly, the probable stain on her reputation seemed minor.

Byron was at her elbow. "Listen, I'll be back to pick up Greg about five o'clock. I got some business in East Plains that's going to use up my afternoon."

"I'll make us dinner."

"I owe you a meal. I'll take the three of us out when I get back."

"It's a date."

From the corner of her eye, Bonnie caught Wyatt staring at her.

Oh please, woman. I'm old enough to be his mother.

She grabbed Greg by the elbow. "Let's get out of here."

While a silent snow fell around them, Greg and Bonnie gingerly loaded Hypatia onto Alice's backseat. The snow made the long driveway treacherous. The Subaru fishtailed up to the road, jerking onto the asphalt with a start. Bonnie turned the car's nose toward Colorado Springs.

When it became apparent that Greg had no intention of speaking, Bonnie said, "Simon told me something before he died."

She gave him the entire story of how Simon found Barty's and Kyle's bodies and how they were already dead.

"Do you believe him?" Greg asked.

She thought long before she answered. "Don't ask

me why, but a part of me does."

"I think he's a lying son of a bitch, and I'm glad he's dead."

Bonnie bit back the question of why Simon would lie to her about his involvement. There had to be a number of reasons, not the least of which was that Simon Boone was out of his mind. But from the look on Greg's face, he didn't want to entertain any notion of Simon's innocence.

"Soooo, we have an afternoon. It seems your uncle won't be back for some time."

Greg stared out the side window before answering. When he turned back, he said, "There's something really weird going on with Uncle Byron. He got this call this morning. He thought I was taking a bath, so he didn't even bother to whisper. I think there's been another death in East Plains."

CHAPTER 10

BONNIE GAVE GREG A HARD STARE BEFORE SHE RE-turned her attention to the road. Understandably, the boy had death on the brain. The murder of his family followed on the heels of the brutal slaying of his wrestling coach.

"A death, are you sure?"

Greg chewed his lip. "I think so."

Bonnie wanted to go slow, but her Imp of the Per-verse nudged her to find out as much as she could and find it out now. "Tell me everything. Start with the phone call."

"Actually, there were two phone calls."

"Okay, the first."

Greg nodded as if Bonnie's prodding was all he needed to get his mind focused. "About ten Uncle Byron gets that call. Someone from his station. Anyway, Uncle Byron says he'll be at the scene as quick as he can." Greg pursed his lips as if annoyed. "He starts explaining that he's got yours truly, and has to figure out what to do with me."

"Have I missed something? What did your uncle say that made you think there'd been a death?"

"Just some stuff he'd asked: How long had she been there? Who found her? Stuff like that."

A she. "Did he mention any names?"

Greg shook his head. "No. About that time, I could tell he was getting ready to finish talking, so I had to sneak back to the bathroom. He wouldn't have appreciated me eavesdropping. Not after the argument we had last night."

Bonnie could tell Greg wanted to talk about the argument, but she'd have to get back to it. If there was anything more the boy knew, she had to pick his brain while the memories were still fresh. "What about where? Where did this death happen?"

Greg spread wide his hands. "He never said."

"Fair enough. And the second call?"

"The second call was about you, but that came later. Uncle Byron knocked on the door. He apologized, saying something had come up. He had to run, and he couldn't take me with him or to your house. I was pissed, and we had another argument."

"I got to tell you, Greg, I think I agree with your uncle. In fact, I'm surprised he brought you to my house, knowing that Simon Boone had been killed."

"Well, yeah, we talked about that. I'm glad he changed his mind."

Bonnie patted Greg's shoulder. "Me, too. Let me guess, the call about me changed everything."

Greg nodded. "Uh huh. He figured he could look in on you, drop me off, and still make it to the other scene. You're right about Uncle Byron. He *was* kind of worried how I'd take seeing Simon Boone dead."

"Did you know Simon very well?"

Greg shook his head. "He was more Kyle's friend, and I knew Simon was getting weed from my pa. I never really liked Simon coming round. He was creepy in more ways than one."

"No kidding. I just spent the longest hour of my life thinking the little lunatic was going to kill me."

"Like I said, I'm glad he's dead."

Greg got a faraway look in his eyes, and Bonnie could tell he was replaying some scene involving his family. She began to feel guilty about interrogating the boy after all he'd been through.

"How you doing, bucko?"

He shrugged again. "All right, I guess. It's hard to say. You know, I've spent a lot of my life covering up for Ma and Pa and, in the last couple of years, Kyle. Couldn't really bring my friends around. Didn't know what sort of illegal crap we'd walk into. It was like . . ." Greg bit his lip, ". . . I was doing everything I could—getting good grades, playing sports, being on the student council—so that folks would think when they looked at me that was what the rest of my family was really like."

"The Good Child."

"What?"

"It's a clinical term in family counseling. One child takes it upon himself to be the ambassador for the family, the face the world sees. It puts tremendous strain on that child, always being freshly scrubbed, thinking their actions are the only thing that forestalls disaster."

"God, yeah, sometimes I just wanted to chuck it all."

"I can imagine."

"Since I was a little kid, I dreamed about being in a regular family. You know, go to church on Sunday, play catch with my dad, have enough money that we could go on vacations."

Bonnie made sure her eyes were glued on the road when Greg swiped at a tear.

"You want to hear something sick?" Greg turned in his seat to face her full. "As far back as I can remember, I wished Ma and Pa would just up and die, so me and Kyle could be adopted by some people who didn't lay around the house stoned all day."

"Oh Greg, don't."

A sound like an animal being wounded erupted from Greg's throat. "And I got my wish. First Mama to cancer, and now Pa and Kyle to that piece of shit, Simon."

Bonnie pulled onto the shoulder of the highway and turned off the engine. She opened her arms.

Greg fell against her, burying his face in her neck. He wailed, shivering in great racking sobs. Bonnie stroked the boy's back, offering wordless sympathy. She knew too much about the ache of loss to spout platitudes while the wounds were so fresh.

When the minutes had used themselves up, and Greg was ready, he lifted his head.

His man-child face was wet. "Sorry about that."

"About what?" She patted his damp cheek. "I didn't hear anything. Besides, can't a friend give a friend a hug without explaining the beegeebers out of everything?"

Hypatia whimpered from the backseat. Bonnie turned to see the dog sitting up. "Well, look who's back among the living. How's my girl?"

As if in answer, the dog moaned, then upchucked onto the backseat.

"Very articulate, Hypatia of Alexandria." Bonnie rolled down her window. "I would have settled for something not nearly so smelly, but that's just me."

After much debate, Bonnie agreed to let the young veterinarian keep Hypatia overnight for observation. The dog had a concussion. Her equilibrium was off. X-rays were needed. Consequently, she would experience digestive distress for the next twenty-four hours. The doctor would need to see how that would play out. She ushered Bonnie out the door with a promise to take good care of the golden retriever.

At the Subaru, Bonnie stood staring at the Aardvark Animal Clinic like she'd just left Hypatia in a concentration camp.

"She'll be okay. Missus P," Greg said.

"I know."

But it didn't feel like everything was going to be okay, and she didn't need Sigmund Freud to tell her why. This was the first time, since Ben died, that any of her animals wouldn't be with her at the house. She knew she was being silly, but there it was.

As Bonnie drove from the clinic, Greg kept staring at her.

"What?" she finally asked.

"You're pretty attached to that dog."

"My cat and three dogs are all the family I have left now that my husband's gone."

For the first time since he'd gotten in the car, Greg smiled. It was a pathetic, weak thing, but as far as Bonnie was concerned, it was something akin to a sunrise.

"Maybe I ought to get me a dog," Greg mused.

"You could do a lot worse."

"I got a lot worse. I got Uncle Byron."

Bonnie turned to see if Greg was kidding, but the stony look on his face told her otherwise. "I think it's time to tell me what's going on with you two."

"He's an asshole."

"Succinct, pithy, yet strangely uninformative. What say you elaborate without the use of pejoratives?"

Before Greg could open his mouth to reply, Bonnie added, "What happened last night?"

"We had a big fight." Greg squinted at her. "It goes back to Mama's funeral. He was an ass—" The boy frowned as if there was only one word to accurately describe Byron Hickman, and Bonnie was denying Greg access to it.

"Try 'difficult,'" Bonnie suggested.

"What?"

"Repeat after me. At the funeral, Uncle Byron was difficult."

"At the funeral, Uncle Byron was difficult."

"Now get on with your story."

"He wouldn't speak to Pa or to Kyle. All through Mama's sickness, Uncle Byron made no bones about how he thought the cancer was somehow Pa's fault."

"Didn't Byron's mother die of cancer?"

"Yeah, even the same kind. Mama told me it ran in the family. One of Grandma's sisters died of it, too."

"Did your mother ever bring up this point with Byron?"

Greg shrugged. "It wouldn't have done any good.

Uncle Byron just froze up whenever he got around Pa, or even if his name got mentioned. Had this crazy idea Pa corrupted Mama."

"Greg, I need to tell you that idea was pretty well accepted around the school the year your mother and father dropped out."

Greg raised his hands as if he was surrendering. "Look, I don't know about eighteen years ago, but I can tell you about most of my life. Mama was no saint. She matched Pa shot for shot, joint for joint, right up until the last. You want to know the thing that most drove Uncle Byron ape shit?"

"Who wouldn't?"

And since when did it become okay to curse around me? She decided to let it go for now, but to bring the behavior to a screeching halt if it continued.

"Pa brought her gifts and stuff, never shouted at her. He loved my mama, and here's the part that Uncle Byron could never get. She loved him back."

"You know, Byron not understanding their love doesn't prove him wrong. He could still make the point that Barty corrupted your mother."

Furthermore, Bonnie could see how his sister's choices would drive Byron crazy. Here was a young man, a police officer, whose sister and her husband chose a lifestyle that not only flaunted the law, but was a constant embarrassment to him. Every day he had to be torn between protecting his only sibling and doing his duty as a county law-enforcement officer. No wonder he resented and probably despised Barty.

"You'd think after eighteen years, Uncle Byron could get over it."

"What's time got to do with feelings? After your grandmother died, Byron might have felt it was up to him to rescue his only sister. After all, rescuing is what police-men are all about."

Greg sighed. "I suppose. Well, here's the deal. After Mom's funeral, Uncle Byron took me aside. He told me that I was the last one worth a damn, and if he could ever do anything for me, to give him a call."

"I admit that Byron's timing and tact could use a lit-tle work, but his heart sounded like it was in the right place. What did you tell him?"

"I told him to stick his offer where the sun didn't shine. God damn it—"

Bonnie gave him a warning look.

"Darn it. Where did he get off putting down my family?"

You could have been a little smoother, Byron. "Now you're living at your uncle's house."

"That's the problem. Last night, he started in on Pa and Kyle again. Said that they might still be alive if he'd have busted them like he should have."

Bonnie's Imp of the Perverse was screaming to give

answer to that premise, but every possible reply would only add fuel to the fire.

"Go on."

"You should have seen him, acting so smug. I got mad. Said some things I shouldn't have said. Finally I asked him, if he felt that way, why didn't he bust Pa and Kyle?"

Bonnie knew the answer before the boy could say it. "I would imagine it was the same reason your uncle came between you and those state troopers yesterday."

Greg nodded. "Yeah. Uncle Byron said he would have shut down Pa and Kyle long ago, if it wasn't for me. He couldn't predict what would happen once the wheels got set in motion, and he didn't want me to go down with Pa and Kyle."

"You believe him?"

"I don't know. One thing I do know. I don't like Uncle Byron, not even a little bit. And I don't think I'm going to change my mind anytime soon. And there's the problem."

"The problem?"

"He's asked me come live with him—like, forever."

The Bluffs were cold.

Bonnie reached up and took Greg's hand. He pulled her onto the mesa top. Once she stood beside him, Greg turned round and surveyed the flat expanse.

"What is this place?"

She felt the weight of the past twenty-four hours drop off like a pair of wet shoes. "You ever read Winnie the Pooh?"

Greg cocked his head and gave her a half smile. "Not recently."

"Winnie had a place he called his Thinking Spot. This one's mine." She checked her watch. "And until Byron gets back, I'm offering it to you."

Greg nodded appreciatively. "I like it."

"Want some help with that thinking?"

Greg took a deep breath as if he were taking in the whole of the Bluffs in one large gulp. A gust of wind blew across the mesa and ruffled his hair. Overhead a hawk shrieked.

"Would it be okay if I just took a look around—I mean, on my own?"

"Mi mesa, su mesa."

Without another word, Greg jammed his hands in his pants pockets and set off. Bonnie watched him for a dozen steps, then let her feet carry her to the far ridge. She stared down at the valley below, then at Pikes Peak in the distance. The red-tailed hawk sat atop a tall pine tree.

"I thought that was you," Bonnie whispered, feeling the grip of the unreal.

You'll always know where to find me, babe, she heard

in her mind.

"I got to tell you, Benjamin David, I'm not quite comfortable with the idea of talking to a bird-spirit."

Good. I never liked you comfortable. You always benefited from a little shaking up.

Bonnie rubbed her fingers across her lips, thinking she still wasn't sure if she might not be losing her sanity. "This is plenty strange, Ben."

She heard a chuckle in her head. *As strange as you having dinner tomorrow night with Trent Hendrickson?*

"I won't if it bothers you."

I'll have you know, missy. I'm above such considerations. I have evolved spiritually.

"You're a God damn bird, Benjamin. Don't make like you're some kind of archangel at the right hand of God."

Just be careful, Bon. There's things going on you don't see yet. The hawk lifted off the tree and spiraled down to the valley floor.

"What kind of cryptic bullshit was that?" Bonnie surprised herself with how loud she called out.

A hundred yards away, Greg looked back at her. She waved self-consciously.

Oh good, Pinkwater, make the youngster think you're loony. While you're at it, tell him your dead husband is at the base of that pine over yonder and is probably hunting wabbit.

Greg waved. No, she corrected herself, he was calling her over.

By the time she crossed to within a few feet of him, Greg was leaning far over the mesa's rim. A stiff breeze blew his hair out of his face.

"Come look."

"Be careful." She shuddered, thinking that's exactly what Ben had advised her. "You're too close to the edge."

Greg turned back to her and grinned. "You *got* to see this."

Bonnie inched her way to his side. The cold wind caught her full in the face, seeming to slice right into her bones. Her heart in her throat, she leaned over the edge. Below was something she'd seen only once or twice in coming to the Bluffs. An eagles' nest, big as a truck tire, sat perched on a rock shelf that looked too small to support it.

"Very cool," she said, and meant it.

"It looks new."

"I think you're right," Bonnie agreed.

The eagle family that built this abode had probably inhabited it just last summer. The small branches still hadn't come unraveled. Peeking out of snow, delicate feathers clung to the bowl of the nest. Bonnie could just picture the eaglets straining up to take some morsel from their father or mother. Now they were gone.

Life goes on.

Greg stepped back from the edge. "Think they'll be back?"

"Hard to say. Eagles and hawks have been known to come back to a nest again and again as long as they have a successful breeding, and no one disturbs the nest while they're gone."

"I'd like to see that."

"I'd like to see it with you. Maybe next summer."

"Maybe." He met her eyes. "I've been doing some thinking."

"Congratulations."

"I'm going to take Uncle Byron up on his offer."

"I thought you might."

Greg held his hands up. "I still don't like him. I may never like him. He kind of scares me."

"How so?"

"He's intense. It's like when I'm wrestling, except Uncle Byron is like that all the time. Am I making sense?"

"I think so. What made you decide to live with him then?"

"First, it would only be until I graduated, or at the outside, until the fall, when I went off to college."

"True."

"Then there's wrestling. If I go into some foster home in Colorado Springs, I'll have to go to school there, too. I'll end up wrestling for some other school, if I get to wrestle at all."

"I'm sure any program would welcome a state champion."

"Yeah, but I've wrestled for East Plains since the seventh grade. I want to bring home one more trophy before I go off to college."

"Then living in East Plains with your uncle makes sense."

Greg still looked dubious. "I suppose so. But he still scares me."

By the time they'd walked down the long path and across the neighbors' fields, Byron was waiting for them, leaning against Alice, The-Little-Subaru-That-Could.

Her former student looked exhausted.

"Finally. I thought you guys would never show. They'd find my frozen corpse stuck to this rusted-out Subaru."

"I'd like to see that," Greg said, then smiled to show he didn't mean it, not completely.

"I'll bet you would." Byron put his arm around Greg. "Buddy, I need a favor."

Greg gave Byron a suspicious glare. "Yeah?"

"Don't take this wrong, but I need to talk to Missus P in private. Then we'll go to dinner."

Bonnie expected Greg to get resentful, but he surprised her. He bobbed his head in agreement.

"How long do you need?"

"Maybe fifteen minutes."

"That's cool. I'll just take a walk up to the road." He pulled his collar tight on his throat. He'd only taken a handful of steps when he turned back. "I'm going to take you up on your offer."

Byron broke into a grin. "That's great! We'll celebrate tonight."

The two held each other's gaze for a moment, then Greg resumed his walk.

"Do I have you to thank?" Byron asked.

Bonnie shook her head. "He came up with it all on his own." She decided she'd keep the business about being scared to herself.

"What do you want to talk about?" She nodded toward the police tape that ran across her entryway and garage. "And where can we go?"

"We can go in. I called while I was waiting. They've already processed the scene and told me I could let you in the house."

"That's very comforting. I thought I might have to sleep at the school tonight."

Byron lifted the tape, and she ducked beneath.

Once inside, she scanned her house and immediately saw the bullet hole next to the hall. "Can I let the animals in? They haven't been fed all day."

"I don't think you should just yet."

Slowly Bonnie walked into the kitchen. At the base of the breakfast island, a dark pool of blood stained the linoleum. Bonnie's stomach lurched at the coppery smell.

Byron touched her elbow. "I'll help you clean it up. Then we need to talk."

She had just put the mop to the blood when Byron started in. "At nine forty-five this morning, deputies found the body of a young girl in the trunk of a car."

Bonnie leaned heavily onto the mop. She held her breath, waiting for the other shoe to fall.

"What do you know about a girl named Janice Flick?"

Bonnie's knees went to rubber, her mind shooting back to an image of a sallow-faced girl with oily hair.

"I don't have the math gene," Janice had said.

Bonnie remembered thinking she wanted to throttle the girl. "How did she die?"

"Do you really want to know?"

Bonnie wasn't sure if she did, but she heard herself ask again, "How did she die?"

"She was strangled."

A student strangled?

For a moment, Bonnie couldn't get her mind around it. In the last forty-eight hours she'd witnessed the aftermath of four deaths, but this news fell on her like an avalanche. Students weren't supposed to die. Everyone knew teenagers were ten feet tall and bulletproof.

Bullshit, Pinkwater. How many shocked parents have you tried to comfort after their darlings rolled their pickups or died in an accidental shooting? Except this was murder.

Robert Spiller

"She was a student in my last-hour block. She'd only been in the district about two weeks."

"What can you tell me about her?"

"She didn't have the math gene."

"What?"

"It's one of the last things she said to me."

Byron leaned close. "Did she say anything else?"

Bonnie let her brain kick into playback mode as frame by frame she evoked the images of that class. "Oh my God, she asked me to go to the bathroom."

"And that's significant because?"

"Janice was out of the room when Luther Devereaux was murdered. In fact, she never returned. I lost track of her in all the excitement."

Bonnie wasn't sure what reaction she expected from Byron, but a calm nod wasn't it.

"Interesting," he said.

She wanted to shake him. "Did you hear me? Janice was in the halls when the murder took place, and now she's dead."

"I heard you. I've got a different mystery, and Janice Flick is smack-dab at the center of that one, too."

As Bonnie waited on Byron, she thought she could hear her own heartbeat.

"The gun we took from your house this morning—the one Simon Boone had. It belonged to the Reverend Kevin J. Flick."

CHAPTER 11

"WHAT ABOUT REVEREND FLICK?" GREG STOOD IN THE
doorway, his collar hiked, his nose red.

Bonnie waited, hoping Byron would be the one to
break the news to the boy. When he didn't, she said,
"He's going to hear about the girl at school."

Byron looked, for all the world, like someone caught
between wanting to stonewall and run from the room. He
turned toward Greg. "Janice Flick, a girl at your school,
was found murdered this morning."

Greg's face went ashen. "I know her. She's the one
you told the story to."

Bonnie nodded. "Hypatia."

Greg seemed distracted, his eyes darting from Byron
to Bonnie. "The dog?"

"No, well, yes, the same name. I told Janice the story
of the original Hypatia, the fourth-century mathematician from Alexandria."

Robert Spiller

How the hell could you have been in the room and think the story was about my dog?

Greg pulled up a stool and sat at the breakfast island. "Now Janice is dead. And her father?"

Byron gave Bonnie a disapproving glance. "This is what I was trying to avoid. This sort of evidence shouldn't become common knowledge."

"You told me."

"Now I'm about to double my mistake. Greg, the gun Simon used belonged to Reverend Flick."

"Simon stole the gun from the Flicks and killed my father and brother?"

"I don't think so. When I questioned the reverend this morning, he went to his gun safe. Obviously, the pistol was gone, but the safe was locked. It wasn't broken into."

"He could have locked it after he took the gun out." Greg's voice went high, almost hysterical.

Byron reached across the island and gently laid a hand on Greg's wrist. "That would suggest the reverend had something to do with Barty and Kyle's deaths. At this point, all we know is that the safe was locked after the gun was removed."

"Why would the reverend want to hurt my father and brother?"

"Good question. Did Barty have any dealings with the Good Friday Temple?"

Greg shook his head. "Not that I know of. He wasn't

much for going to church."

"How about trouble with the Reverend Flick himself?"

Up until now, Bonnie felt as if Byron was tiptoeing around the topic of Janice, but now she could see where this line of questioning was going.

"What kind of trouble?" Greg asked.

Byron tugged at his ear. Again his face and voice communicated the fact he'd already revealed too much and was about to reveal more. "The reverend moved his family to East Plains, took the position of assistant pastor, because Janice had been caught up in drugs and gangs back in Denver."

She certainly had the appearance of someone who starts off each day with a cocaine cocktail. "So you think the good reverend may have murdered Greg's father because he was providing drugs to darling daughter?"

Bonnie realized she could have phrased the question a little more delicately, but decided what was done was done.

In for a penny.

"I did," Byron said, "but the pastor has an alibi for the entire day."

Let's just say it. "Soooo, someone else in the Flick household got into the safe."

"Someone else." Byron patted Greg's arm. "What do you know about Janice?"

"Janice?!" Greg shouted. "Now you think Janice killed my family?"

"I knew this was a mistake." Byron's face went hard.

"Settle down, Greg, and you, too, Byron. Good God, you're worse than two-year-olds." Bonnie gave the men a reproving glance. "Greg, your uncle has to consider all the possibilities."

Greg's chest was heaving, his eyes wild. "Why would Janice have anything against Pa or Kyle?"

Byron hesitated before he spoke, obviously not relishing his next question. "The girl had a history of drug problems. Your—"

"And Pa dealt drugs. It always comes back to that."

Byron nodded resignedly. "Your father dealt drugs. So what I need to know is, did he deal to Janice?"

"How the hell should I know?" Greg leapt from his stool. "Mister Devereaux, Simon, now Janice. Pa seems to have dealt to just about everybody in East Plains. But if you're asking if I ever saw Pa deal with Janice, the answer is no."

"That's what I'm asking."

"Like I told Missus Pinkwater, Pa and Kyle kept me out of their business. Hell, they could have sold to Janice." Greg shrugged. "I wouldn't have any idea unless she showed up at the front door."

A sudden thought brought Bonnie up short. *If the girl killed Barty and Kyle, then Greg is the obvious suspect for*

Janice's murder. Bonnie had no doubt this fact wasn't lost on Byron. "What did Reverend Flick have to say about Barty or Kyle?"

"He claims he never met either of them. Also claims Janice had licked her drug problems since moving to East Plains."

"How could he be so sure?"

"Flick is a single dad. He and Janice have been closer since moving here. They've bonded and all that."

Bonnie had trouble picturing the sullen girl bonding with anyone, let alone her preacher father.

Byron must have caught the skepticism in her face. "Flick says the girl was coming around, which brings up another sticky bit."

Greg cocked his head. "What?"

"Back in Denver, before Janice's difficulties, she and her father liked to go range and target shooting. They'd just started up again out at Rattlesnake's place."

In spite of the seriousness of the conversation, Bonnie felt a smile creeping onto her face. Rattlesnake was an extreme survivalist who maintained a shooting range out in the desert. He rode a tricked-out Harley with a diamond-back canopy that spit flames. For a price, out on his isolated range, you could fire anything from a tank to a rocket launcher. Bonnie had met Rattlesnake on several occasions out at the school. She genuinely liked the man and had more than once wanted to see his place for herself.

"So, Janice has been target shooting for a while?"

Byron nodded. "Since she was eight."

A look passed between Bonnie and Byron. *God damn, Mister Hickman. Are you thinking what I am?*

Whoever killed Barty and Kyle had known what he or she was doing. The dead pair had taken one shot each—to the heart.

Bonnie pushed the sushi tray across the table toward Byron. "Just try one without the fish. I don't eat raw fish any more than you do."

Byron stared at the proffered sushi as if Bonnie was offering Drano on a Ritz. "What is that stuff around the outside?"

"Seaweed."

"I don't do weeds."

"Come on, Uncle Byron." Using chopsticks, Greg picked up a compact ball of rice sporting a blanket of salmon. "Just slather the thing in soy sauce and wasabi. You won't taste anything but fire." The boy spread a generous smear of green goo on his sushi.

Byron curled his lip. "I'll have you know that in the day, I was known as *he-who-eats-habaneros-whole.*"

"Then this stuff should be no problem." Greg smiled at his uncle, a carny sizing up a rube. He took a large bite of his sushi, then licked his fingers.

Oh Hickman, you're being hoisted by your own testosterone petard.

"Give me one with the avocado in the middle."

Using chopsticks, Greg set the sushi on Byron's plate. The deputy covered the roll with wasabi, then poured on soy sauce.

"That's a lot of wasabi, Byron. Maybe you should—"

Byron popped the entire roll into his mouth. At first, nothing happened. He chewed the appetizer as if he was merely judging its texture. Then his eyes went wide. Deliberately, Byron reached for his beer. He up-ended the bottle.

Bonnie burst out laughing. "I tried to warn you."

The last of the beer drained from the bottle, Byron turned to Bonnie, tears in his eyes. "What? It wasn't all that hot."

Bonnie gave Greg a sidelong glance, and they shared a smile. "I must have been mistaken. You, Mister Hickman, are a man among men."

"Don't you forget it." Byron wiped at a tear.

The smile evaporated from Greg's face. "I don't want to spoil anybody's appetite, but if Janice did kill Pa and Kyle, then who killed Janice?"

The Sixty-Four-Thousand-Dollar Question.

Byron let the costly inquiry hang in the air while he wiped his mouth with his napkin. "Don't take this the wrong way, Greg, but you have the best motive."

"Me?!"

Bonnie took a firm rein on her Imp of the Perverse. No purpose in hell would be served by explaining the logic to the boy.

Instead, she asked Byron, "Assuming Janice did kill his father and brother, how would Greg even have known?"

Byron held up a silencing hand. "First things first. How well did you know the Flick girl, Greg?"

The young man still wore an incredulous expression as if he couldn't get his mind around the fact that anyone could suspect him. "We didn't exactly travel in the same circles—I mean, I was a jock, and she was a . . . whatever."

"A girl trying to find herself," Bonnie offered.

Byron worried his lower lip. "Fair enough. Can anyone verify your whereabouts yesterday?"

"All day? No."

"What about the list of people you talked to?" Bonnie pulled back the sleeve on Greg's left arm. No ink-smeared list of names emerged.

Surprise, surprise, Pinkwater, the boy bathes.

"What list?" Byron eyed Bonnie suspiciously.

"Don't have a cow, Uncle Byron. I just asked some people a few questions about Matt and Mister Devereaux."

Byron tossed down his napkin. "You had him investigating Luther Devereaux's murder?"

Heat rose into Bonnie's face. "I didn't—"

"No," Greg said in a calmer voice. "In fact, she told me not to get involved."

"Involved in what?" Byron's face lost none of its hard edge.

Enough of this shit.

She told Byron about the list of students out of class during fourth block. When she finished, Greg filled Byron in on what he learned from the people he talked to.

Several times Byron appeared as if he wanted to interrupt, but he kept his peace until Greg finished.

"Not bad." He gave each of them a disapproving stare. "Now hear this. Your investigation is over. Hell, Missus P, it almost got you killed . . . twice."

Before Bonnie could reply, Byron went on. "You know, that list doesn't cover everybody. There's also that business with the PE teacher saying no one was up in the loft besides Matt."

Uh oh. "I take it you haven't talked to Harvey Sylvester in the last twenty-four hours."

"I got a message from the office this morning that Mister Sylvester wanted to speak with me, but no. I was tied up all day with Flick and then with you. What's going on?"

"Harvey's about to change his story."

Byron gave her an up-from-under stare. "I thought he might. He had Missus Devereaux in his office, didn't he?"

"What?" Greg said.

Bonnie gave her former student a smile. "There's no flies on you, Deputy Hickman."

"Occasionally, we get things right. I talked to the Kramer boy." Byron narrowed his eyes at her. "You went to see Sylvester?"

She blanched. "This morning."

"You've been a busy queen bee. You know, Sylvester's little peccadillo doesn't get Matt off the hook."

Bonnie could see Byron's point. As a witness against Matt, Harvey was now discredited. However, that didn't negate the overwhelming evidence still stacked against the boy.

"It's a start." Byron patted her hand.

He placed his napkin back in his lap. "This is hardly dinner talk. And this is supposed to be a celebration of Greg coming to live with me. What say we gab about something else, anything to take our minds off this Devereaux business?"

For days Bonnie had been focused on clearing Matt. She had no clue about how to change tracks.

"How about a two-thousand-year-old murder instead?" Greg asked.

Bonnie rested her hand on her chin and peered at Greg. "Are we talking about Hypatia?"

"Yeah. Is all that stuff you said in class true?"

Bonnie gave Greg a quizzical glance. *Now you re-*

member the story, when an hour ago you thought it was about my dog. What's going on here, buster?

She decided to let it pass. "Mostly. The gory details of Hypatia's death were on the money, but like any story based in history, there's more to it."

"This is the Greek math lady who was murdered?" Byron settled himself in his seat. "I remember when you told my Algebra One class this story twenty years ago."

"Exactly. If it ain't broke, don't fix it." She nodded to Greg. "I was trying to make a point, and I might have oversimplified just a tad."

Greg didn't react to her admission. Like Byron, he made himself comfortable.

You still got it, Pinkwater.

"Okay. I need to take you back to fourth-century Alexandria. The religious climate of the city is in flux."

"Christians," Byron stated.

"Christians, indeed. It's been four centuries since the death of Christ. What was once a fledgling religion is now one of the most powerful forces in the Roman Empire. Since Constantine, it is the official religion. Christianity still has its problems, heresy and the like, but nobody's throwing Christians to the lions anymore."

"Was Hypatia a Christian?" Greg sat up, his face intent.

"Hardly. You might say she played for the opposing team. She belonged to a sect whose members were called Neoplatonists."

"Like in Plato?" Greg asked.

"Like in Plato. The Neoplatonists believed in the ideals of Plato. A man could better himself by striving for the ideal in politics and compassion with his fellow men. Even if one doesn't achieve these standards, the striving alone would improve the human race."

"As opposed to Christianity," Byron said, "which claims we are a fallen race and need the hand of God to achieve redemption."

Bonnie gave her former student a questioning stare. She'd always assumed the young man shared the religious convictions of the majority of East Plains.

Byron must have read the expression on her face. "Don't get me wrong. I think we really do need a helping hand from the Man upstairs."

"Anyway." Greg waved his hand impatiently.

"Anyway, your uncle's right. What was brewing in Alexandria was a major difference in religious perspective. And for Hypatia, the problem was even more pronounced. She wasn't just a follower of Neoplatonism, she was the leading teacher."

"Oh shit," Greg whispered.

"Watch your mouth," Byron said, but kept his attention focused on Bonnie.

"When Hypatia was a little girl, her father had warned her, *All formal dogmatic religions are fallacious and must never be accepted by self-respecting persons as final.*

A CALCULATED DEMISE

You can imagine this sort of attitude didn't sit well with the fourth-century Christian community."

Byron chuckled. "It wouldn't sit well with Christians today."

"Well, couple this with the fact that she held symposiums on Neoplatonism almost daily at her home or the famous library, and you can see there was a storm brewing. From all historical evidence, it was a tempest whose ferocity Hypatia underestimated."

"What about her followers?" Greg spoke as if this ancient woman was in the next room and not dead for the past sixteen centuries. "Didn't any of them warn her?"

"If they did, she didn't listen. If anything, in the last months of her life, she became even more vocal, more public, which led to her undoing."

"She caught the notice of someone powerful," Byron said as if this was a foregone conclusion.

Damn, Mister Hickman, you continue to surprise me. "Have you ever heard of Saint Cyril?"

"Can't say that I have. Then again, I'm not Catholic."

"Saint Cyril was one of the first Catholic saints, an eventual pope. At this time, he was Patriarch of the Alexandrian Christian community. Almost immediately upon being installed, he began a systematic program of oppression against any whom he considered heretics. This included Jews—he burned their synagogues. As for pagans, he treated them with open contempt."

"Hypatia would be a tasty target," Byron said.

"You bet. One day, early in his rule, as Cyril was strolling about his religious fiefdom, he noticed a crowd gathered at a private residence."

"Hypatia's?" Greg sounded like an eager contestant on *Jeopardy*.

Bonnie nodded. "She was involved in a Socratic dialogue with a large number of her followers. Cyril was struck with her beauty and eloquence. He went back to his church and declared Hypatia dangerous."

"Uh oh," Greg said.

"Uh oh is right. Most scholars believe Cyril inflamed a rabid maniac named Peter the Reader. A short time later, this same lunatic abducted Hypatia. He and his followers murdered her."

"And that was that." Byron shook his head in disgust.

"Almost. Apocryphal legend has it that as she was being consumed by the flames, Hypatia looked down from her pyre, and like Christ, forgave her murderers."

By the time Byron had brought Bonnie back to her house, it was past nine. Greg was fast asleep in the backseat.

"So, where do you go from here?" Bonnie stood outside the Mustang, leaning on the open door.

"Home," Byron said wearily.

"I mean with the investigation, smart-ass."

"I'll talk to Harvey Sylvester and Missus Devereaux —try to figure out the connection, if there is any, between a man stabbed in a wrestling loft, two shot out on the plains, and a girl strangled in her car."

"So you think there is a connection?"

Byron yawned, his eyes going soft. "I don't know, Missus P. Pinning down Janice Flick's whereabouts in the last minutes of fourth block would be a good start. Did anyone see the girl anywhere near the loft? Or with anyone?"

Rubbing his eyes, Greg sat up in the backseat. "I could help."

"No," Bonnie and Byron said together.

Greg shrugged. "Suit yourself."

The boy may as well have said, "I'm going to do what I want."

Bonnie made to walk away, then turned back. "Greg, I'm going to see Matthew tomorrow. Do you have anything you want me to tell him?"

A pained cast came over Greg's face. "Tell him to hang in there, and that I'm thinking about him. That we're doing everything we can to get him out of there. Tell him I'm sorry about his brother."

Byron leaned across the passenger seat. "What time are you going?"

"Whenever morning visiting hours are, why?"

"I'd like to come."

Bonnie knew she'd have to consider the offer. On the one hand, Byron was the enemy. He'd arrested Matt, would try to collect further evidence to prove Matt guilty. On the other, her former student seemed to be keeping an open mind.

"Call me. I'll let you know."

"I'll do that." Byron put the Mustang in gear, spun out of the drive and up the hill.

Bonnie watched him disappear into the night before she went into her home. Euclid, Hopper, and Lovelace sat by the front door. Bonnie scratched both dogs across their backs before scooping the cat into her arms.

"Mama's home."

While she opened cans and shoveled food into bowls, the image of Luther Devereaux surfaced in her mind—the dead staring eyes, the pool of blood, the carving knife stained red.

Luther, you big derriere, the problem is that so many people hated your guts.

The image of the knife auditioned once again across the stage of her mind. This time the letters *EP* were prominent on the handle.

"East Plains," she said aloud. "One of Hattie's carving knives."

Bonnie debated all of thirty seconds before she reached for the phone. The phone rang once, then a familiar voice came on the line.

"Caulfields'."

"Hattie, it's Bonnie Pinkwater."

"Damn woman, we're getting to be regular phone buddies."

"You know better than that. There's nothing regular about either one of us."

"Ain't that the truth. What can I do you for?"

Bonnie hesitated, thinking how best to begin. Hattie was very protective of her tiny kitchen realm.

"I had a few questions about the knife that was used on Luther. Could we get together on Monday?"

The phone was silent a moment before Hattie answered. "Is it important? You know the police talked to me already?"

"I think it's very important."

Hattie sighed. "If it was anybody else, I'd tell 'em to shove it, but seeing as it's you, how about tomorrow instead?"

Hattie's candor never failed to put Bonnie at ease. A few years back, Bonnie had nursed Hattie's daughter, Melissa, through Algebra Two. Since then, Hattie treated Bonnie like royalty.

"I suppose I could come out to your house." Bonnie winced, thinking of the drive to Punkin Center—even farther east than East Plains.

"To hell with that. I'll be out at school tomorrow. Got to put together next month's menu. How does eleven tickle your fancy?"

CHAPTER 12

To proclaim Hattie Caulfield a big woman was akin to suggesting that a five-hundred-pound bag of flour makes a nice-sized biscuit.

Once upon being asked how much she weighed—by an undoubtedly suicidal student teacher—Hattie shot him a withering glare, then sweetly replied, "Three." At six foot four, she was undoubtedly the largest woman in East Plains.

Her method of management could best be described as an iron fist in a clear plastic serving glove. Like a chained bear, she was often seen ranging up and down the serving line, admonishing her staff and giving the evil eye to any student who had the temerity to belittle school food.

Only Lloyd and Hattie possessed keys to Hattie's kitchen domain, so Bonnie was forced to knock. "Hattie, it's me, Bonnie Pinkwater."

Usually, Hattie's expression resembled the carved

stone of some grim monument, but the face that greeted
Bonnie was anything but grim. The giant woman gave
Bonnie a gap-toothed smile.

In a voice made gravelly by years of smoking unfil-
tered cigarettes, she exclaimed, "Hey, math lady! Come
on in."

Ten years earlier, Hattie's girl, Melissa, had struggled
with Algebra Two. Bonnie had taken the girl under her
wing. Melissa had earned an A-minus, and Hattie had
proclaimed Bonnie a miracle worker without peer and a
lifelong friend.

Hattie stepped aside.

Bonnie stared down the serving line and across the
stainless-steel prep tables. Hanging like sentinels on a
rail above the tables, spatulas and knives dangled from
leather thongs. A conspicuous gap in the array bore mute
testimony to a missing knife, most likely the very imple-
ment that brought an abrupt and violent end to Luther
Devereaux.

Her footfalls echoing on the tile floor, Bonnie felt
like a tourist visiting a foreign land. In her twenty-eight
years of teaching at East Plains, her duties rarely brought
her into the inner sanctum of Hattie's culinary realm.

The big woman ushered Bonnie into a miniscule office. "Sit yourself down."

With surprising grace, Hattie lowered her considerable bulk onto a rolling chair behind a gray teacher's desk.

Bonnie took the only remaining seat, a padded gray chair at the end of the desk. A tan filing cabinet completed the spartan furnishings.

"What can I do for you, my dear?" Hattie leaned forward, resting her chins on her beefy hand.

No point beating about the bush.

"I don't think Matthew Boone murdered Mister Devereaux, and I need your help." Bonnie stared unblinking into Hattie's heavily lidded eyes.

"Of course, he didn't." Hattie slammed the flat of her hand down on the desk. "That boy wouldn't swat a fly if it was tickling his Adam's apple. What can I do to help?"

Bless you, Hattie.

"Right now, I'm wondering about that knife."

Hattie winced. "I still can't believe someone used one of my carvers. You got no idea how careful I am with the large knives."

"When was the last time you know for sure the knife was here?"

Hattie didn't hesitate. "Tuesday. We do all the hard inventory on Tuesday, nonperishables, implements, and the like."

"About thirty hours, from Tuesday morning to Wednesday afternoon. Any chance of finding out who had access to the knives during that window?"

Hattie rose and pulled a black three-ring binder from the filing cabinet. "Like I told you yesterday, anybody else asks, I tell 'em to shove it. Truth is, my dear, ain't nobody comes in and out of this kitchen, I don't know about it."

Hattie opened the folder and ruffled through the pages. "Actually, the time is even more closed down. I didn't do inventory until I sent everyone home on Tuesday."

"And no one got into the kitchen Tuesday after you took inventory?"

Hattie gave Bonnie an up-from-under look and an accompanying frown.

Bonnie blanched. "Okay, stupid question, but I had to ask. Let's start with Tuesday."

"Tuesday was crazy. Had the senior-citizen luncheon that day."

Every month, the senior citizens from all over the plains arrived in Silver Key vans. They came to the high school for a free meal and a get-together. Lloyd and Hattie devised the event under the auspices of making the school a community center. The concept caught fire.

In an area as large as East Plains, many senior citizens—especially those who no longer drove—were isolated on their remote farms and ranches. Once a month, they could laugh at old jokes, glad-hand their cronies, and talk freely about a time nobody but their generation seemed to care about anymore.

"Who hosted the dinner?" Bonnie asked.

"The student council, and they did a terrific job. Every STUCO member was assigned to three or four senior citizens. Made those folks feel special—carried their trays, refilled their glasses, even sang a ninetieth-birthday song to the Longette twins."

Geez Louise, ninety. "What other students worked on Tuesday?"

"You mean, besides Matt?"

It was Bonnie's turn to give the jaundiced eye. "Yes, besides Matt."

"All last week we enjoyed the esteemed services of Kip Hendrickson, Esquire. Puke face that he is."

"What trouble did Kip get into last week?"

"Funny you should ask. A run-in with the late great Mister Luther Devereaux. Some business to do with wrestling."

Probably the same hassle that brought Trent Hendrickson down to see Lloyd. "Do you know what happened?"

"You kidding? That kid bitched continuous the whole time he was supposed to be scrubbing pots." Hattie whispered, "Asshole," under her breath. "Anyway, according to Kip, Luther was unfair at the week-before's wrestle-off. Kip claims he pinned some other meathead, and for some reason Luther didn't count it. Kip didn't get to wrestle that weekend. I believe the charming young man had words with Luther, got up hard into his face. As a result, Kip's young behind ended up in in-school suspension."

In-school suspendees invariably did menial labor, the kitchen a favorite of Lloyd's.

Alarms went off in Bonnie's cranium. She reached beneath her chair and retrieved her fanny pack. She hauled out the absent-student list from Friday. Sure enough, eleven names up from the bottom was Kip Hendrickson. The boy had been called out of class by Lloyd at two thirty-five.

Bonnie pictured the spoiled rotten Kip stalking around the kitchen, furious with the idea of having to do menial labor, furious with taking orders, but especially furious with Luther Devereaux for putting Kip's thin rear end on kitchen duty to begin with. In her mind's eye, Bonnie saw Kip take down the carving knife and stash it in his leather jacket.

Why in God's name Kip would be wearing a leather jacket while on kitchen duty was beside the point. Hoodlums wore leather jackets. Murdering hoodlums most assuredly did.

"You didn't by any chance see Kip looking suspicious near the carvers?"

Hattie shrugged. "As much as I would like to swear the little shit is Satan's own thief, I really can't. It's crazy in here at lunch, and I'm the head cat herder. I have to say I didn't see Kip up to no good."

Hattie's answer didn't cool Bonnie's enthusiasm. Kip—as the cops on TV were fond of saying—looked good for the knife theft. To boot, Bonnie would be having dinner with Kip's horndog father. With a little luck, and a lot of finesse, maybe she could pick what Trent passed off as a brain.

She and Hattie spent the next ten minutes perusing Wednesday's temporary staff. Besides Matt, Kip was the only student worker. Bonnie just couldn't see any of the adult staff harboring enough of a grudge against Luther to slice his throat. Besides, they would attract too much attention going up to the wrestling loft.

As Hattie closed the binder, she leaned in again. "Heard you got your butt in a wringer with The Divine Pain in the Ass."

Bonnie pursed her lips and nodded. "I just don't know when to shut up. Now Divine wants to see me Monday morning bright and early."

Hattie made kissing noises. "Just give that lime-green heinie a big smooch and don't look back. And whatever you do, don't go venting your spleen on Mister Potato Head. Not a good career move."

"I know. I promised Lloyd I'd be good."

Hattie stood. "Keep that promise. You're too good a math teacher to lose."

"Hattie, I'm not going to lose my job. Just a little slap on the wrist."

"So says you. Scuttlebutt in the community is that some of East Plains's fairest and finest are pissed off at you, and Divine is doing some ass kissing of his own. Just watch your back, girl."

Now Bonnie *was* getting afraid. What sort of non-sense was Divine brewing up? God damn the man. Why couldn't he catch some virulent disease and drown in erupting sores?

Hattie waved a hand in front of Bonnie's face. "Earth to Bonnie."

The big woman smiled mischievously like she had read Bonnie's mind. "You know, people like Divine always get theirs in the end. And with a target that big and that lime green, Divine is sure to get his paddled someday."

Bonnie unlocked her classroom with a thousand thoughts screaming for attention. Matthew. Kip. Divine. Trent. All demanding an audition, their faces floated across the stage of her mind. Bonnie sat down at her desk and tried to impose some order on the chaos.

She'd come away from Hattie with copies of the personnel sheets from Tuesday and Wednesday.

She went to the blackboard and drew two large, intersecting circles—a Venn diagram. She refused to let her brain get sidetracked into the dozen or so facts she knew about the mathematician John Venn.

One circle she titled *Out of Class*. The other became *Kitchen Help*.

She tapped the fish-shaped intersection between the

Robert Spiller

circles. "Whoever killed Luther lives right here, having both means and opportunity."

She quieted the not-so-still voice that suggested one person could have stolen the knife and a second person did the actual killing.

"Too complicated."

Bonnie drug out two student desks to the front of the room and spread the lists out on top. She moved from the desks to the board and back again transcribing names into the circles.

Kip, STUCO, and Matthew all entered the *Kitchen Help* circle. The *Out of Class* circle was crowded with names by the time she finished, but only Matt and Kip were in the center intersection.

"It's Kip. It's got to be."

The words hadn't fully escaped Bonnie's lips when she heard a noise at her classroom door. Superintendent Xavier Divine, arms folded across his chest, lime-green corduroys gleaming, stood in her doorway.

"What does Kip have to be?" Divine's lips curled in a smirk, a bald-headed cat munching on a canary.

He damn well knows something nasty, and he's dying to slap me with it.

Divine crossed the room, gesturing toward the blackboard. "This is more of the nonsense that put you and the school in hot water to begin with, isn't it?"

Bonnie bit back one sarcastic retort after another.

Remember, you promised Lloyd. "I was just doing some harmless speculating."

Divine pulled a closed metallic tube from his breast pocket. He depressed a button on the tube and the upper third flipped open revealing a pencil-thin pair of reading glasses. With a flourish, Divine jammed the glasses onto his unremarkable face.

"These names, am I correct in assuming you've obtained them by enlisting other staff members in your crusade for Matthew Boone?"

"The boy is innocent."

"And you've determined this by your superhuman powers of mathematical deduction?"

Bonnie wanted to slap religion into the man. Again she ignored her Imp of the Perverse, which was now screaming for her to say something scathing.

"The boy is gentle, incapable of the violence implicit in Luther's death."

"Implicit," Divine said, as if hearing the word for the first time. "And the police obviously are incapable of arriving at this implicit truth without your assistance."

Maybe. "I never said that."

Divine held up a silencing finger. "No. What you said—in front of a class full of impressionable students—was that the murderer was still at large."

"That's not true."

"Oh? So at least a half-dozen parents called me and

lied? Is this some sort of conspiracy against you, Missus Pinkwater? Because if it is, we need to nip this blatant character assassination in the bud."

Bonnie opened her mouth to answer Divine's sarcasm, but the man cut her off. "All of this is irrelevant. Come Monday, you will apologize to each of your classes for your reprehensible behavior. Next, I will provide you with a list of parents. You will call and apologize to them for filling their children's minds with nonsense when you should have been filling their young brains with equations . . ." Divine waved his pudgy hands as if mathematics was of no consequence. ". . . and whatever.

"Lastly, you will discontinue your involvement in matters best left to the police. I'm talking immediately."

To emphasize his point, Divine grabbed an eraser and expunged a swath across the Venn diagram. He offered a cold smile.

"I trust we understand one another."

His hand was on the doorknob when Bonnie said, "Just a God damn minute, Humpty Dumpty."

"You called him Humpty Dumpty?"

Byron kept his eyes on the road, but Bonnie could tell he wanted to stare at the crazy woman in the passenger seat of his Mustang.

Bonnie reddened. "I only wish I had stopped there. Once the floodgates were opened, I couldn't hold back."

She shook her head ruefully. "There were a lot of sentences that started with *Where do you get off* and others that ended with *You got another thing coming*. It felt good at the time, but I broke my promise to Lloyd. And that feels horrible."

"What did Divine do?"

Bonnie could still see the superintendent's bloated face. "Swelled up like a lime-green toad. I didn't really give him an opening to speak, and all that bile backed up into his jowls."

Byron chuckled. "I'm going to assume that things ended on a less-than-friendly note."

"I'm glad you find this amusing, youngster. 'Cause I got a bad feeling. The man had malevolent intent written all over him when he stormed out."

"What did he say?"

"Nada. He just waddled into the hall, slamming the door behind him."

Byron inhaled sharply. "Sounds ugly. Any chance of the superintendent forgiving and forgetting?"

It was Bonnie's turn to chuckle. "The Divine Pain in the Ass? Not bloody likely."

"I remember something you used to say to me all the time back in Algebra One, when I got into trouble."

Bonnie's mind traveled back to a simpler time. The

young Mr. Hickman was constantly in Dutch with the powers that be.

"Are you talking about the end of the world as we know it?" Bonnie asked.

"Something like that. You always told me, 'Chin up, boyo. With any luck we'll have thermonuclear war before sundown, and none of this will come to pass.'"

"None of this will come to pass," Bonnie said wistfully.

The smile on Byron's face evaporated. "You sure you're up to this visit?"

She nodded. "Matthew's been in that jail for over three days. He's scared, and he's alone. My problems are nothing compared to his."

Byron looked as if he might reply, but he kept his silence. Bonnie stared at her former student, glad of his company. When she'd left Xavier Divine, she was shaking—angry at Divine, terrified for what the superintendent might do with the ammunition she'd just given him, and despondent for letting the man get to her the way he had. Instead of waiting for Byron's call, she'd gotten ahold of him.

He'd answered like he was waiting for her call and was parked at her house when she arrived home.

"Want to hear a theory concerning Luther's murder?" Bonnie asked.

"I'm all ears."

She made a show of studying his face. "I wouldn't go

that far. Couldn't be more than 80 percent."

Byron shook his head. "You going to tell me that theory or just make cruel jokes at my expense?"

She built the case against Kip in layers, first mentioning the altercation with Luther. She brought in the tight security in Hattie's kitchen and the hard inventory. She ended with the personnel ledger and the Venn diagram.

"Kip was the only student worker who had both opportunity and means."

"Didn't Matt have the same opportunity and means?"

"Well, yes."

Byron glanced Bonnie's way. "Missus P, Kip wasn't found hunched over Luther Devereaux's dead body. Kip's fingerprints aren't on the murder weapon. No one saw Kip going to or leaving from the wrestling loft."

"Someone might have."

"Who?"

"Matthew Boone."

Matt stared from Bonnie to Byron, his puffy eyes darting first to one then other. His nose and eyes were red. He'd been crying.

Bonnie didn't want to think what might be happening with this child-man. A county jail could be a cruel place for someone as naïve and damaged as Matt.

Dear God, I hope his parents were smart enough not to inflict the knowledge of Simon's death on the boy. He's got more than enough trouble on his plate without that added sorrow.

She kept her face open, confident. "Matthew, do you remember Deputy Hickman?"

Matt's lips formed into a tight crease. He squinted at Byron. "You read me my rights."

"That's right, Matt. And I need to warn you again. Anything you say now can be used against you."

Tears welled in Matt's eyes. "I want to go home!" he bellowed.

The guard who'd been standing several feet behind Matt stepped forward, but Byron held up a restraining hand. The two men exchanged looks before the guard returned to his original post.

"Matthew, listen to me." Bonnie placed a hand on the Plexiglas. "We're doing everything we can to get you out of here, but now we need your help."

Matt sniffed. "My help?"

"Yep," Byron said. "We need to know everybody you saw from when you left Missus Pinkwater's class to when Mister Sylvester found you."

Matt gazed helplessly at Bonnie as if the task assigned him was overwhelming. From the look on his face, she could tell they'd be lucky if the boy could remember his name right now.

She turned to Byron. "Let's try a different approach."

Bonnie took a deep breath and put as much Mister Rogers in her voice as she could. "Matt, I'm going to name some people. If you saw them at all, either in the loft, on the steps down to the gym, in the gym itself, or even in the hallway when you were getting Mister Devereaux's water, I want you to tell us as much as you can. Do you think you could do that?"

Matt fidgeted in his seat. "I'll try."

"Good boy." *Ease the boy into it, Pinkwater.* "Before we start, Greg says hi. He wanted me to tell you that he thinks about you every day."

Matt noticeably relaxed. A tentative smile crept onto his face. "I didn't see Greg in the loft, or on the steps, or in the gym, or in the hallway."

By the end of his assertion, Bonnie recognized the cadence from *Green Eggs and Ham.*

Bonnie smiled. *Not with a fox, not on a box. I do not like them, Sam I am.*

From the corner of her eye, Bonnie noticed Byron looking dubious at this line of questioning. An annoyed part of her wanted to ask him if he had a better idea, but she was afraid of upsetting Matt. She gave her former student what she hoped was a barely perceptible shake of the head.

Go with the flow, Byron.

"That's good, Matt," she said. "You didn't see Greg.

Are you ready for someone else?"

"Uh huh." Matt smiled, clearly enjoying what he perceived as a game.

"Do you know Janice Flick?"

Matt nodded furiously. "The girl who dresses in black. I saw her."

"Where?" Byron asked.

Matt's cautious look told Bonnie he wasn't sure if the game permitted him to answer Byron.

"It's okay," Bonnie said.

"She was at the back of the gym. I saw her when I came down for water."

"What was she doing?" Byron had gotten into the spirit of the exercise. His voice had lost its earlier urgency.

"Just standing there, watching the sevies play dodgeball."

That little shit. She was supposed to be going to the bathroom. "Was she still there when you came back with the water?"

"Yep. Still there."

"Do you know Mister Devereaux's wife?"

Matt nodded enthusiastically. "She's pretty, but I didn't see her, not in the loft, not on the steps, not in the gym, not in the hall."

"Fair enough, Matt-I-am."

The boy chuckled. "That's me. Matt-I-am."

"That's you, all right. Here's another. He's on the

wrestling team. Kip Hendrickson."

"Him I saw. He was in the hall."

Bonnie took a moment to get control of her voice. "Where in the hall?"

"Just outside the gym."

Bonnie resisted the urge to pump a fist in the air.

For the next ten minutes, she and Byron took turns naming everyone who was either out of class from two thirty to three or who had access to the knife. Bonnie considered the continued exercise futile. She'd found out all she needed to know.

"My head hurts," Matt said finally. "I don't want to play anymore."

"I don't want to play anymore, either," Bonnie said.

Byron nodded. "You've been a big help, Matt."

"But I can't go home yet, can I?"

"Not yet, buddy."

Matt mirrored Byron's solemn expression. "I'd better go back. Thanks for coming, Missus Pinkwater." He stood.

The guard spoke on a walkie-talkie clipped to his shoulder, and a steel door slid open. A moment later, Matthew Boone was gone.

Bonnie turned to her former student and was about to speak when he stopped her.

"I know what you're going to say. Kip Hendrickson was in the right place at the right time."

"Wrong, Mister Know-It-All. I was going to mention Janice." She could see Byron had come to the same conclusion she had.

He leaned back in his chair. "If she didn't murder Luther Devereaux herself, she was at the back of the gym when Luther was killed. She was in a perfect position to see the murderer go up and be there when he came back down."

Bonnie reached the final conclusion. "And for that she had to die."

CHAPTER 13

HYPATIA LOOKED SO PATHETIC, BONNIE WANTED TO cry. Besides being bandaged and shaved, the big dog sported a plastic cone around her neck.

She peered up at her mistress. Her melancholy spoke where she could not. "Do you see what this woman has done to me? Could my humiliation be any more complete?"

Bonnie squatted down and gave Hypatia's snout a kiss. "It's only temporary, sweetie. And if anybody could look good in a plastic cone, it's you."

Doctor Zelda Wickette handed Bonnie a tube and a roll of bandages. "Antibiotic, like Neosporin. Just slather it onto the wound and cover the whole thing with a new bandage. Once a day should be enough. She has to wear the cone for at least a week. Keep her away from the rest of your dogs. They'll want to lick at the bandage."

"I'll keep the others in the dog run."

"Groovy."

Bonnie suppressed a smile. She long suspected the woman spent far too much time around animals. Now she seemed to have shot back in time to the sixties.

"Groovy, it is." Bonnie paid and led her injured soldier out to Alice, The-Little-Subaru-That-Could. "Let's get you home, cutie pie."

Twenty minutes later, Bonnie was opening her front door. *Thank God, I left the other dogs ensconced in the run.* Without even thinking, she scooped up Euclid. Bonnie rubbed her face in the cat's soft fur, inhaling the rough smell of him. She brought Euclid down face-to-face with Hypatia.

"Look who's come home."

The cat snuffled as if to say, "Nice cone, dog breath."

The kitchen phone rang.

Bonnie set Euclid down. "I'll be right back, you two."

She grabbed the receiver on the fourth ring. "City Dump."

"Pretty lame, Pinkwater," Trent Hendrickson said.

"It takes one to know one." About to begin the oh-so-mature name-calling, Bonnie remembered the information she needed from Trent. "Where am I taking my big strong hero for dinner?"

"You choose."

"Do you know Savino's in Old Colorado City?"

"I can find it. Should I pick you up?"

"I just brought Hypatia back from the vet. I'd like to

spend some time with her. Do you mind if I meet you at the restaurant—say in about an hour and a half?" Bonnie used her best Suzie Sunshine voice coupled with a smile she hoped Trent could feel through the phone line.

"I'll be there with bells on," Trent said.

The big rancher hoisted his foot onto the table. Bonnie's bowl of vegetarian chili rattled, and some of its precious contents sloshed onto the burgundy-colored tablecloth. She could feel the stares of Savino's patrons burning holes in her back.

Trent stroked the shanks of his boots. "Nile crocodile lowers and black-cherry goatskin uppers. Smooth as a baby's butt. Go ahead, touch 'em."

Kill me, God. Kill me now.

Bonnie made an effort not to let her smile flag. After all, the big orangutan was already talking. With any luck, she could steer the conversation to Kip. She stroked the boot and had to admit there was something of a baby's butt in the feel.

"Very much the infant."

"Lucchese. The finest boot makers this side of boot hill." Trent laughed at his own joke.

Bonnie inwardly cringed at what she was expected to do next. "How much did they cost, Trent?" Shamelessly, she once again let Suzie Sunshine out of her cage.

By now, Bonnie was inured to the routine. She'd had to make the cost inquiry when Trent introduced her to the fascinating world of bolo ties—his being a turquoise-and-silver number from a Hopi craftsman in New Mexico. Cost three hundred and seventy-five dollars.

Then came the lizard-hide belt with the sterling-silver conchs—three hundred dollars. Which led directly to the suit jacket with an ostrich-skin yoke—seven hundred dollars.

"Twelve hundred smackers." He lowered his leg to the floor. "But you know those babies aren't the most expensive shit-kickers in my closet. That honor goes to a hornback alligator pair, uppers and lowers."

Bonnie geared herself up. "How much were those, Trent?" *Gag me with a hornback.*

"Thirty-eight hundred dollars."

Trent pronounced the number as if just the price alone would assure him entry into her bedchamber. He offered what he must have considered his aw-shucks-I'm-just-a-little-ol'-filthy-rich-country-boy smile.

Bonnie held his gaze for as long as she could stand it, then demurely turned her attention to her food. *Enough already with the fashion show.*

No such luck.

"You ready for the pièce de résistance?"

"Who wouldn't be?"

Trent gave her a quizzical glance, probably to ascertain if she was putting him on.

Bonnie's gaze and smile never faltered.

The rancher hesitated only a moment longer, then removed his white cowboy hat. He set it on Bonnie's head. The hat fell unceremoniously across her forehead and ears.

As I long suspected, the man has a watermelon head.

Like an old hand, she used her thumb to push the brim out of her eyes. "I'll bet this is one expensive hat."

"To truly appreciate this little beauty, I need to tutor you in the ways of the Xs."

In spite of herself, Bonnie's interest piqued. "As in algebra?"

Trent guffawed. "Not algebra, and not George Strait's exes, either."

When Bonnie didn't react, Trent started singing. "All my exes live in Texas."

"I don't—"

"That's why I hang my hat in Tennessee."

Bonnie tugged on her ear, fighting down a giggle. "Xs in Tennessee?"

"Forget it." He reached across the table, taking Bonnie's hands in his.

What's this?

"Okay, here's how it works," Trent said. "Xs are a unit of quality. The more Xs you got, the better the hat."

He stopped with the obvious intent of giving Bonnie time to digest the explanation up to that point.

Got it, Einstein. More Xs, more value. "Go on."

"Your average cowboy hat might run four to six Xs; an excellent hat, one hundred. Now you're getting into some serious coin."

Bonnie wondered if it was time to ask the magic question, but Trent removed the white hat from her head and cradled it in both his meaty paws.

"Now this little honey here." He slowly rotated the hat so she could see front, back, and sides, even tilting it so she could see the inside.

"Good-looking hat."

"Chinchilla and beaver." He winked at her. "Had to order it special from San Antonio."

Showtime, Bonnie. "How much does a chinchilla-and-beaver cowboy hat cost, Trent?"

The rancher waved aside the question. "I'll tell you in a minute. First, guess how many Xs this sweetheart is listed as."

With no basis for comparison, Bonnie took a stab. "Three hundred."

"Nice try, cutie. One thousand."

Cutie?

Bonnie didn't linger overlong on Trent's uncalled-for familiarity. She found herself impressed. After all, ten to the third power was nothing to sneeze at.

"Wow."

"A thousand Xs. Chinchilla and beaver. Five thousand dollars." Trent elongated the last three words for effect.

Geez Louise, for that, you could have bought a hot tub, you schmuck. "My God. Don't tell me you have an even more expensive hat back at home."

Trent shook his head. "No, this baby is my primo. After they made this sweetheart, they broke the mold." He put the cowboy hat back on his head like he was donning a crown.

Angelica was right. You are one boring old fart.

The mathematician in Bonnie demanded she tally Trent's wardrobe. She whistled. "Not counting your jeans, socks, and underwear—you're not wearing mink underwear, are you?"

"No mink underwear."

"Good. Then not counting those, you have over seventy-five hundred dollars on your back, head, and feet. How does that make you feel?"

Trent didn't miss a beat. "How does it make you feel?"

Oh piss, the man thinks his ostrich-skin yoke makes me hot. "Let me get back with you on that one."

She pushed away her chili bowl. "You up for a change of subject?"

Trent flashed his pearly whites. "That all depends."

Step carefully, Pinkwater. He still thinks this is pillow talk. "Do you remember last Wednesday?"

Robert Spiller

Trent scratched his chin. "Last Wednesday. Last Wednesday. Wasn't there some business concerning a murder?"

Bonnie slapped Trent's arm. "Smart-ass. I was mostly wondering about something you said."

"Me?"

Bonnie took a deep breath before she dived in. "You came down to the school to see Lloyd." She almost said, "about Kip," and was glad she didn't. That would tip her hand unnecessarily.

Trent nodded. "I wanted to get to the bottom of some trouble between Luther and Kip."

Bingo.

"What kind of trouble?" She hoped she didn't sound too eager.

"Probably not news to you, but Luther Devereaux was a prick. He lorded over the kids on his wrestling team like a Saddam Hussein. Sometimes he went too far."

"Too far?"

"Okay, get this. Before practice on Monday, Kip and another boy were goofing around. You know, playing grab-ass the way teenage boys do. Devereaux went off on my boy."

Trent's jaw muscles clenched, as did his fists. "I'm talking major blowup, cuss words and all."

Bonnie had heard Luther was free with his expletives in practice and had become even more so as his retirement loomed.

"Anyway," Trent started in again, "right away, Kip's involved in a wrestle-off. My boy pinned his opponent, held him for way over the needed three seconds. Luther, just on a malicious whim, refused to count."

"That bastard."

"You bet. Anyway, Kip thinks he's got it whipped and let's up on the boy, who gets free. Luther counts it as a reversal. The other boy wins on points."

"What an asshole." *Don't overdo it, Pinkwater.* "Then what happened?"

Trent exhaled loudly. "Then Kip got mad, justifiably so. There was name-calling, and Kip got himself an in-school suspension. You know, where they got to do odd jobs around the school rather than cooling their heels at home."

"I'm familiar with the concept."

Trent reddened. "Of course, you are. Well, I came down to the school to set things right."

Unexpectedly, Bonnie felt a kinship with the late Luther Devereaux. Parents were always scheduling meetings with her to *set things right*. She fought back a grin, thinking of a fantasy response she'd concocted for parents who felt a constant urge to *set things right*.

In her fantasy, at the beginning of every school year, Lloyd would hand out four cards to each staff member—similar to the *Get Out of Jail Free* cards in Monopoly. Except, these cards were to be played whenever a teacher was unable or unwilling to listen to one more parent complaint. When the annoyance level reached maximum, the teacher could lay down one of her cards. At this point an appropriate retort might be, "Up yours!" or "Oh my, look at the time," or Bonnie's favorite, straight from *Just Shoot Me*: "You're boring, and I have legs. So long."

Bonnie let none of this reverie change her expression. "How did Kip do with his punishment this week?"

"He was a bear to live with, slamming doors, playing his music too loud—the usual crap."

"How about Wednesday? How was his mood then?"

"He was . . . wait a minute." Trent squinted at her malevolently. "What's with all the questions about Kip, and now Wednesday? You don't think Kip had anything to do with Luther's death, do you?"

Bonnie tried to answer immediately, tried to tell him, "Of course not. Don't be absurd." The lie stuck in the back of her throat.

When five seconds of silence stretched into ten, Trent's expression told Bonnie he had the answer to his question.

"I'd heard that you were trying to find some way of proving that idiot Matthew Boone's innocence. I never thought you'd try to pin this on Kip." Trent's lips compressed into a tight line. "I saved your life, lady."

Bonnie felt heat and color rise up from her neck. "I'm sorry."

"You know where you can stick your sorry." Trent

rose as if he meant to bolt, then sat back down. He pointed a menacing finger at Bonnie. "Kip was nowhere near that loft when Luther was killed."

Before she could stop herself, Bonnie blurted out, "He was spotted in the hall outside the gym during fourth block."

"He was coming from his fourth-block class to the office. Lloyd called him down."

Bonnie knew Kip had English with Mister Glick during fourth block. If he was called to the office, Kip's path of least resistance might conceivably take him past the gym.

Trent rose again. "Lloyd called Kip out of class over the intercom, and two minutes later, my boy had his keister plopped down in Lloyd's overstuffed chair. If you don't believe me, bitch, check with Lloyd yourself." The big rancher turned on his heels and stormed out of the restaurant.

Bonnie returned home to chaos. Hypatia met her at the door in full-bark mode. An unholy din was coming from the dog run. The phone was ringing.

"Settle down, everybody. Mommy already feels like ten pounds of bird droppings." Hypatia stopped barking, but didn't relinquish her agitated state.

The house feels wrong.

Bonnie didn't have time to dwell on the anomaly. She raced to the kitchen.

"Pinkwaters."

"Bon, it's me." Lloyd's deep baritone came out of the receiver. "We need to talk."

Bonnie blanched. "I know. I screwed up again. Divine just knows how to push my buttons."

"We'll talk about him in a minute." Lloyd sighed a bone-weary sigh. "I just got off the horn with Trent."

"The man is quick. He just abandoned me at Savino's."

"Where you all but accused his boy of killing Luther Devereaux."

Bonnie considered splitting enough hairs to deny culpability, but she just didn't have it in her to play games with Lloyd. "In essence."

"This is getting out of hand, Bon. I've always loved your passion for your students, but this Matthew Boone thing has clouded your judgment."

Hanging in the air was the unspoken accusation of a promise broken.

"What do you want me to say, Lloyd? I believed Kip had motive, opportunity, and means to murder Luther Devereaux. I acted on that premise."

"Then here it is. Trent told you Kip was in my office two minutes after being hailed. I checked the time on his pass myself. He took less than two minutes. I would say that wipes out your premise of opportunity, wouldn't you say?"

Bonnie tried to picture Kip, after being spotted by Matt in the hall, racing up the stairs, stabbing Luther to death, racing back down, and still making it to the main office in under two minutes. And that didn't even address the matter of the blood. The boy was an athlete, but he wasn't a magician.

"Two minutes isn't enough time," she admitted.

"At least we agree on something. I mollified Trent, told him you weren't yourself lately because of this Matt Boone thing."

Bonnie wanted to scream out, "It's not a thing! An innocent boy is being accused of murder!" But she didn't see the good it would do, and so she kept her silence.

"Do you want me to call Trent?"

"God, no, at least not tonight. The man wants no part of you right now. He'd probably hang up."

"So, what's the plan?"

"As far as Trent is concerned, I just wanted to fill you in on the lay of the land. Superintendent Divine is another story. You didn't keep your promise."

Bonnie's heart sank. "No, I didn't, boss. Divine played me like a cheap guitar."

"You called him Humpty Dumpty."

"Now that was probably unwise on my part. Is there any way to repair the damage?"

The line went quiet for ten seconds. "I don't think so. The school board has agreed to Divine's request for an impromptu session tomorrow night. Your presence is mandatory."

Piss, piss, piss. "I'm going to assume I'm also the focus of the agenda."

"You *are* the agenda. What got into you, Bon?"

Bonnie considered Divine's arrogance, his demands, and the way he'd smiled when he ordered her to apologize. None of it excused the breaking of a promise. "Stupidity."

"Amen. Now, listen. I tested the water with Cal Upton."

Cal was the president of the East Plains School Board. Bonnie didn't hold out much hope Cal would be on her side. He and Divine were deacons in the same church.

"And?"

"And he is very disturbed that a member of my staff would be so disrespectful to a superior. You know he's voiced concerns about your outbursts in the past?"

The superintendent and now the president of the school board—Houston, I believe we have a problem. "I know. Did he say what Xavier is demanding?"

"Cal played his cards pretty close to the vest, but he did say the meeting would be open to the public. Calls are going out to all the parents who complained."

"This just keeps getting better and better."

"It's time to let this Matt Boone thing go, Bon. If you apologize for your imprudent remarks—"

"Imprudent!"

"Enough, Bonnie. I'm trying to save your job here. Get down off your high horse."

Lloyd's reprimand shocked Bonnie. She couldn't remember the last time her old friend had sounded so severe.

Lloyd sighed again. "Trust me on this one. Divine is out for blood. You have to apologize to him, to the incensed parents, to the board. Admit to a lapse in judgment and throw yourself on their mercy. Can you do that . . . for my sake, and for yours?"

Bonnie didn't have an ounce of fight left in her. "I can do that."

"Good. The meeting is at seven. Don't be late." He hung up.

Bonnie returned the phone to its receiver. She had a ringing in her ears, and a bad taste in her mouth. Divine would crucify her even if she apologized, but apologize she would. She owed Lloyd at least that much.

A knock sounded on her front door. When she opened it, Pansy Boone stared back at her.

CHAPTER 14

"Pansy?"

Mrs. Boone's gray pigtails framed a rosy-cheeked face. She offered a smile that was more an apology than a greeting. Bonnie could easily see Matthew and Simon represented in that long-suffering countenance.

"Can I come in, Missus Pinkwater? I desperately need to speak with you."

Bonnie looked past the woman into the drive. An unfamiliar car was parked by the front step.

She borrowed a car to get here. This should be good.

Bonnie stepped aside to let Pansy enter. "I'm sorry about Simon."

Pansy nodded gravely. "I long suspected Simon would end up the way he did. He was an excitable boy."

Lady, Warren Zevon was an excitable boy. Simon was a homicidal dwarf. "I'm sorry nonetheless."

"Thank you, but I'm not here to talk about Simon. I haven't much time. Frank doesn't know I'm here."

Bonnie suspected as much. Frank Boone would never deem to cross her threshold and would no doubt forbid his submissive wife, as well. Pansy's presence at Bonnie's house bordered on outright defiance. The woman must be undergoing an out-of-body experience.

"Can I get you anything?" Bonnie shut the door.

Pansy Boone's demeanor changed back to that of the docile wife—eyes lowered, hands placed one over the other, covering herself as if she were naked. She shook her head. "I promised Sarah Bezel I'd return her car pretty quick. She needs to get to work."

"All right. Then let's get right to it. What's on your mind?"

"Superintendent Divine came by this afternoon."

That news caught Bonnie by surprise. The Divine Pain in the Ass would be gathering allies, but Bonnie didn't think the Boones could be counted among them. After all, Matthew was their son, and Divine was pressuring her to quit helping him.

"What did the superintendent want?"

"You've heard about the school-board meeting tomorrow evening?"

"Principal Whittaker called me not five minutes ago."

Pansy's gaze darted about the room as if she expected her husband to jump out from behind the sofa and scold her. "I overheard Frank and Superintendent Divine talking. He asked my husband to come to the meeting, to speak out against you."

Once again, Bonnie couldn't fathom Divine's strategy. Surely, Frank didn't hate Bonnie so much that he'd side with the egghead, go against the best interests of Matthew.

"Go on."

"I'm not sure if you're aware that Frank means to run for the school board. The superintendent has promised to support him. Lately, those two have been thick as thieves."

That's all I need, the man whose family jewels I once suggested needed amputating being on the board.

"Did Frank agree to help Divine?"

Pansy nodded, looking embarrassed.

"Frank means to ask the board to censure me for helping his son?"

Pansy licked her lips. "My Frank is a great man. God has spoken to him, has spoken directly through him."

Bonnie's bullshit alarm was screaming. *Just shut up, Pinkwater. Get the info first, then slap the woman silly.*

"When Matt was arrested," Pansy continued, "Frank and I prayed. I was scared for my boy. I couldn't see how he could have done such a terrible thing. Matt's always been so gentle."

"And what did the Almighty tell your husband?" Bonnie made no effort to keep the contempt out of her voice.

Slowly, Pansy's eyes lifted to meet Bonnie's. "Matt's being arrested was God's will. That all things work together for good for those who love the Lord, and this was no exception. Because of his retardation, Matt would never go to prison and would end up in a hospital where doctors would take care of him."

You son of a bitch, Frank Boone. "Did God also inform your husband as to whether Matt actually did anything to make him deserve all this beneficence?"

Red crept up Pansy's neck into her cheeks. "I believed Frank just wanted what was best for our boy."

Bonnie's hand trembled with the desire to smack some sense into the woman. "Why the hell are you here, Pansy?"

Pansy took several rapid breaths. Evidently, she needed to steel herself to answer Bonnie's question. "After hearing Frank speak with Superintendent Divine, I don't believe that anymore. My husband seems willing to sell Matthew for a mess of pottage."

Bonnie recognized the biblical reference. One of a hundred-thousand facts she had stored away in the file cabinet she called a mind. Pansy was referring to Esau's selling his birthright to his brother, Jacob, for a meal. Not a stellar moment for either of the two patriarchs. If Bonnie wasn't mistaken, the woman was calling Frank a rat fink.

I couldn't agree more.

"Superintendent Divine said Monday's meeting would put a halt to your meddling. When I heard that, I knew I needed to speak with you."

"Why?"

"I came to ask you not to give in, not to let them silence you. My boy needs you."

Pansy reached out a tentative hand.

Bonnie took it in hers. "Hold on one minute. First and foremost, Matthew needs you, Missus Boone."

Once again, Pansy inhaled deeply as if in preparation for some monumental decision. "I know."

"I wonder if you do. It took a lot of guts to come here. Now, are you prepared to buck your husband on this matter, to be strong for your boy?"

Pansy's hands went to her braids, the tangible symbol of her subservience. At first, she merely stroked the long plaits, then her raw-boned hands clutched each in a tight fist. "I'll do whatever's necessary." Her eyes flashed in anger.

God damn, woman, I believe you mean it. Bonnie mentally apologized to Lloyd. If this woman meant to swim upstream against a lifetime of being a doormat, there was no way Bonnie could abandon her. Or her son.

"What can I do, Missus Pinkwater?"

"Two things come to mind. First, go home and give your husband hell for choosing a seat on the school board over his own flesh and blood. Be firm. Get him to change his mind about helping Divine."

Pansy blanched. "What if he refuses?"

Bonnie could almost see the confrontation playing in the woman's mind. She pulled Pansy close, put an arm around her shoulder. "How many children do you have?"

"Thirteen. The youngest is nine months."

"I think it would be fair to say your husband is not adverse to your marriage bed, if you get my meaning."

Pansy reddened, a sly smile tickling the corners of her mouth. "Are you suggesting I refuse my husband?"

"Yes, ma'am. I'm saying you cut him off at the knees, if he doesn't come around. We're talking long term."

For the first time in Bonnie's memory, Pansy Boone laughed. "I'll do it. What else?"

"I sure could use some friendly faces at that meeting. I wouldn't put it past Divine to keep the damn thing secret from anyone he wouldn't want there."

"Hattie would come."

Bonnie pictured the larger-than-life cook shouting down some of East Plains's so-called fairest and finest. "Now you're talking. Pack the hall with anyone willing to give up an evening."

"I'll call everybody I know. What are you going to do?"

Good question. "I'm thinking I'd better figure out who really murdered Luther Devereaux."

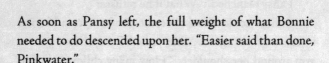

As soon as Pansy left, the full weight of what Bonnie needed to do descended upon her. "Easier said than done, Pinkwater."

She slumped down onto the carpet, back against the couch, arm around Hypatia's cone. "Mommy's quite a ways up shit creek, darling. No paddle in sight. If you've got any pull with the doggy gods, I could use the help."

Hypatia made an attempt to lick Bonnie's face, but merely poked her with the cone.

"Nice try, but I appreciate the intention."

Bonnie squirreled an arm around behind, digging her hand under the couch until she found what she was looking for. She kept a small whiteboard with an attached dry-eraser pen in the living room in case she had a brainstorm for some new pedagogy or a mind teaser to challenge her kids.

She replicated the Venn diagram. As before, she labeled the left circle *Out of Class* and the right *Kitchen Staff*. She filled in the names inhabiting the twin circles and the fish-shaped region between. Once again, the only two names plopped squarely in the intersection were Matthew and Kip. For obvious reasons, she didn't want to implicate Matthew, and Kip had an alibi.

Bonnie turned to look at Hypatia. "Miss Cone Head,

we seem to have come to an impasse. I could really use that celestial canine inspiration right about now."

Then she noticed the abbreviated word STUCO. "An aggregate. There's no telling how many children this actually represents. For all we know, any number of folks from the student council could find themselves sitting in the belly of the fish." Bonnie stabbed a finger at the word, smudging it.

Hypatia yawned.

"I'll overlook the commentary. Luckily, I know someone who can fill in the blanks."

She stretched as she stood. By the time she reached the phone next to the microwave, she'd dredged up Byron Hickman's number from her memory. Greg answered on the second ring.

"Just the man. I need your help."

"Missus P? Sure thing, what's up?"

"Hattie Caulfield told me the senior-citizen luncheon was last week. Is that right?"

A silence intervened before Greg answered. "Wow. Seems like a million years ago, but she's right. What about it?"

"I need the list of the student-council members who worked the luncheon."

"Okaaaay. Hold on. I think I got the names in my backpack. Be right back."

Bonnie was humming the tune of "Werewolves of

London" when Greg got back on the line.

"I love that song. Whatever happened to that guy?"

"He died. So it goes. Whatcha got?"

For the next three minutes, Greg rattled off names. By the time he reached the end of the list, two names— one a girl called to the counselor, and another an eighth grader whose parents came for him—joined Kip and Matt in the intersection of the diagram.

"Hey, what's this all about?"

"I'll tell you later, when I know more. How you holding up?"

"Not too bad. Uncle Byron and I lined up the funeral home. We're looking at coffins tomorrow."

Bonnie sighed. *You poor baby.* "So, you're taking tomorrow off?"

"Just the morning. I got elementary wrestling right after school. A dozen fourth and fifth graders are counting on me."

"You sure that's a good idea? Everybody would understand if you needed to postpone the practice or bag it altogether."

"Nope. I want to do this. Besides, Uncle Byron is lending me Grandpa's old Chevy truck. As soon we get out of the funeral home, I can burn my butt right to school. I should be back by lunch."

Bonnie put a face to Greg's grandfather, Byron's father— freckled cheeks, white bushy eyebrows, farmer's tan under a wide-brimmed straw hat. "How is your grandfather?"

"He looked good at the senior luncheon. He talked a lot about Grandma. He misses her."

"Tell him I said hello the next time you see him. If you need anything, let me know."

"You're not going to tell me what you're up to?"

"Nope. See ya." She hung up.

Bonnie stared down at the two additional names, a boy and a girl. She knew both children—one of the advantages of teaching in a school as small as East Plains. The girl was in Geometry, and Bonnie had known the boy's family since his older brother had been in Math Analysis.

She'd check with the counselor and the office to make sure neither child had an opportunity to sidle up to the loft and slice one odious wrestling coach's throat. But she didn't hold out much hope. She couldn't imagine either child murdering Luther. Then again, considering the extreme violence done upon Luther, Bonnie was having a hard time imagining anyone with enough rage or grievance to commit such an act.

She was missing something. She felt it like an itch beneath her skin. And time was running out.

Before going to her classroom Monday morning, Bonnie visited Counselor Freddy Davenport.

"Bonnie Pinkwater, as I live and draw labored breath." Freddy swiveled to regard Bonnie in the doorway of his small office. His rolling chair creaked imploringly. His sausage fingers laced across his prodigious stomach.

A lollipop protruded from between thick lips.

"How you doing, Freddy?" Bonnie never could be in Freddy Davenport's presence without feeling blessed.

He'd come to East Plains by way of the Colorado Springs Probation Office, deciding to save children before they ended up in the criminal-justice system. The man obviously loved what he did, regardless of the fact he'd probably keel over from a heart attack or stroke sometime in the near future.

Bonnie considered his hiring a major coup for the school.

Freddy removed his lollipop and waved it like a baton. "Can't complain, dear lady. As the saying goes, my plate is full."

I would imagine you could say that about any plate you've been in contact with. "I need some info, Freddy."

"I have no moment but to await upon your pleasure. How may I be of assistance?"

Bonnie shut the door behind her. "Last Wednesday, a girl, Clarissa James, came to see you at the end of the day."

Freddy tapped the lollipop against his lips. "I believe you're right, but you know I can't tell you anything we talked about. As I'm fond of saying—"

"I know. You live or die by the confidences you keep. I don't need any of that. What I'm really after is times."

"I don't understand."

"What time did she get here, and what time did she leave?"

Freddy brightened. "That I can help you with."

With effort, Freddy pushed himself upright. He waddled over to a beige filing cabinet positively littered with candy and wrappers—Tootsie Rolls, Jolly Ranchers, Milk Duds, several boxes of Raisinettes, a half-eaten Milky Way.

Bonnie could only wince as she imagined the man's cholesterol and blood pressure. *Hell, for all I know, Freddy could live to be a hundred while the rest of us tofu-eaters get bird flu.*

Freddy reached into a drawer and extracted a manila folder. "Here we are, Clarissa James." He ran a pudgy finger down the page.

"Came to see me just before two thirty. There's no departure time listed, but as I recall, we left together." He frowned. "That nasty business with Luther. Clarissa and I went to the gym to see what all the fuss was about."

"You're sure about what time she got here?"

Freddy gave her an up-from-under look. "Very sure. The girl was distraught, had wanted to see me earlier in the day, but I was otherwise occupied. She came to my office while I was still with another student. Had to cool her heels in the hall. Truth be told, she stood framed in that tiny aperture . . ." Freddy pointed to a narrow wire-and-glass window about halfway up the door, ". . . until my two o'clock got nervous and took his leave."

"That's disappointing."

Freddy eased himself back into his chair. From the protests it made, the chair was planning imminent suicide. "Want to tell me what this is all about?"

She considered stonewalling the way she had with Greg, but maybe Freddy could be of help. "It's Matthew Boone."

Freddy nodded knowingly. "Luther could be devastatingly brutal when the mood struck him. Matt was often the focus of his cruelty."

"I don't think Matthew killed him."

Freddy sat up, which for him amounted to straightening his neck. "Do tell."

Bonnie shook her head. "I don't have anything concrete, but I know that boy. He wouldn't hurt a fly."

"People will surprise you, Bon. I could tell you tales of angelic children who cut relatives in half with shotguns because they felt they had no other choice. Ten-year-olds who left home in the morning and ended up strangling a classmate on the school bus. Sometimes people are caught in circumstances that squeeze them so tightly they explode."

"Not Matthew."

"I hope you're right. I like that boy. On what I assume is a related note, I heard about your trouble with

Mister Dumpty."

Bonnie flushed. "You know what I called him?"

"Apropos, if you ask me. Oh, don't look so surprised. You've been in this school district long enough to know secrets have an abysmally short life expectancy and rumors fly on the wings of eagles. I, for one, intend to make my presence felt at tonight's board meeting."

Bonnie leaned over and gave the huge man a hug. "You're a sweetie."

"It takes one to know one."

Checking on Charles Sweringer, the eighth-grade student-council member, proved to be an exercise in duplicity. With Lloyd's office not four feet away and Bonnie's promise of compliance still fresh on her lips, she hinted to Lloyd there might be some hanky-panky going on in the boy's bathroom. Luckily, Vice Principal Murphy was otherwise occupied with another problem, so Lloyd was forced to investigate himself. As soon as Lloyd had departed, Bonnie swooped down on Doris, the office secretary.

"Doris, I need your help."

"I heard about your trouble with the superintendent. What were you thinking, dear girl?"

Bonnie cast an anxious glance toward the door, knowing full well Lloyd would return any minute. "I promise to give you a blow-by-blow soon, but right now I'm in a bit of a time crunch."

"I'll hold you to it. What's the problem?"

With an economy of words that would bring a smile to a copy editor, Bonnie laid out her inquiry. When she finished, Doris typed a scant dozen keystrokes and finished with a flourished tap of the ENTER key.

"Follow me."

Bonnie did precisely that. From the back of the teacher's lounge, a printer spit out a single sheet of paper. Doris handed the sheet to Bonnie.

Bonnie kissed Doris on the cheek. "Thank you, Doris."

"No problem, dear girl. That's an updated list. In light of Wednesday's horror, it includes any students who were out of class for any reason, including release by classroom teachers or even aides." Doris turned to leave the lounge, then embraced Bonnie. "I'll see you at the meeting tonight."

Was I the last to find out about this meeting? Bonnie scuttled out of the office before Lloyd could come back.

On the way to her room, still ten minutes early for her first-block class, Bonnie perused the paper. With every step, her spirits fell in proportion. When Charles Frederick Sweringer and his parents exited East Plains Junior/Senior High for an orthodontist appointment in Colorado Springs, Luther Devereaux had fifteen minutes yet to live.

CHAPTER 15

WES OLIHEISER WAS WAITING AT HER ROOM. "GOT A minute?"

Wondering what was on his mind, Bonnie peered up at the tall boy. The usual mischievous smirk had vanished. He looked positively grim.

"Come on in."

Wes wheeled on her as soon as the door closed. "I'm really sorry for getting you in trouble."

The boy's jaw muscles worked, and Bonnie could see him fighting back tears.

"Of all my teachers, you've always been my favorite, and now, because of my big mouth, they're going to fire you."

Bonnie stared at Wes, her throat dry. *The little shit has a heart after all.* "Who says they're going to fire me?"

"My folks. They're pretty mad at you. Divine called them. They're coming to the meeting tonight."

Is anybody staying home? The board should be selling

tickets.

She held Wes at arm's length. "I'm touched, Wes. I really am. But don't get yourself in trouble over me."

Wes sniffled. "Screw my folks. They didn't listen when I tried to explain how things really are."

Bonnie's first inclination was to lay into the boy for disrespecting his parents. *But what the hell, they're supporting Divine. Screw them, indeed.* "And how are things, as Wes Oliheiser sees the world?"

"You were just trying to give Matt a chance, and I ran my mouth when I should have chilled."

A fair assessment. "Are you thinking all the trouble I'm in is because of you?"

"Isn't it?"

She gave his chest a push. "I'll have you know, young man, I was getting myself in trouble before you were born. I'm perfectly capable of any number of impetuous actions, rash judgments, foolish remarks, and taking downright idiotic stands without the help of one Wesley Marvin Oliheiser. I'm a grown woman, you know?"

The first inklings of the Oliheiser smirk returned to the boy's face. "Way past grown, I'd say."

"And proud of it, smart aleck. What you see before you is the accumulated wisdom of a life well spent." She held up her right index finger. "However, now that we are mutually baring our souls, I recognize in you a failing that I, too, share. Have you ever heard of the Imp of the Perverse?"

Wes squinted at Bonnie to see if he was being put on. "Are you calling me a pervert?"

"I wouldn't be the first, I'm sure, but no. The term comes from a short story by Edgar Allen Poe. In the story, a man commits the perfect crime, a murder. All he has to do is keep his trap shut, and he's home free."

"But he can't do it."

"Nope. He ends up shouting out the deed on a crowded street corner. Sound like something you'd do?"

"I don't know about the murder part."

Bonnie gave the boy a hard stare. "You know what I mean. Sometimes our mouths are very unruly companions."

"Now that sounds like the Bible."

"There's probably a few good things in there, as well. I'll tell you what. Assuming I don't get my skinny rear end canned, what say you and I make a pact?"

"What kind of pact?"

"An Imp-of-the-Perverse pact." She elevated the pinkie of her left hand. "This will be our signal. If you see me getting ready to blurt out some nonsense I've got no business saying, just hold up Mister Pinkie."

The patented Oliheiser grin returned in full force.

Bonnie slapped his arm. "I know what you're thinking, mister. Half the fun is getting me to say outrageous things."

"Well, yeah. Most of them don't get you in deep caca,

but the pact thingee is a good idea. Does it go both ways?"

"Absolutely. That's the way pacts work." She extended her pinkie. "Deal?"

He hooked his little finger to hers. "Deal."

"Now, go sit down." With an imperious gesture, she pointed to his seat in the back of the room. "Don't give tonight's meeting another thought. Everything's going to be okay."

The boy nodded and took his seat.

Okay, Pinkwater, you convinced him. Now do the same for yourself.

The morning, then the afternoon raced by, as if being chased by dragons. Bonnie watched as the last of her fourth-block Algebra One class lined up to file out. She glanced at the clock as she had done a hundred times that day—three thirty. The meeting was in three and a half hours. She still had no idea what she intended to do beyond taking an unsupported and likely suicidal stand.

Divine's going to have me for dinner, and I tied the bib around his neck. God damn the man.

Perversely, an irrelevant thought having nothing to do with her problem refused to give her peace until she promised it free run across her synapses.

"You okay, Missus P?"

Greg Hansen had somehow crossed the room unob-
served and now stood at the opposite side of her desk.

Good God, Pinkwater, you are riding the Oblivion Express.

She dredged up a smile. "Depends on how you define 'okay.' I still have all my teeth, and I'm not troubled
by the heartbreak of psoriasis. Truth is, I was just thinking about Hypatia."

Bonnie saw Greg gear up to respond. Before he
could speak, she added, "The Greek mathematician, not
the dog."

"You're never going to let me live that down, are you?
I figured you meant the woman. What about her?"

Bonnie nodded toward the clock. "You got the time?
I thought you had elementary wrestling."

He shrugged. "The little shrimps will take at least
fifteen minutes to dress out. What about Hypatia?"

"I went to see Counselor Davenport this morning
about . . ." once again she felt a definite reticence to share
". . . just some stuff."

*Why the clam routine, Pinkwater? If anybody can be
trusted, it's this boy.* And yet she made no effort to clue
Greg in.

He leaned onto the desktop. "The same stuff you
wouldn't tell me about yesterday."

She reddened. "Pretty much."

He let ten, then twenty seconds pass, obviously hoping
she'd crack. When she didn't, he sighed. "Anyway . . ."

"Anyway, we were talking about Matt, and I tell Mister Davenport I don't think Matt would ever commit such a heinous murder. The boy just doesn't have it in him."

"And this leads to a conversation about Hypatia?"

Bonnie waved him quiet. "I'm getting to that. No, it did not lead to a conversation about Hypatia. What it did lead to was Mister Davenport saying something I can't get out of my mind: *Sometimes people are caught in circumstances that squeeze them so tightly they explode.*"

Greg stared at her as if she had just revealed she intended to give up teaching and raise chinchillas. "And that led to a conversation about Hypatia?"

"Again, no. Bear with me. Since Sunday I've been thinking about the concept of between."

"Like folks being squeezed tight until they explode?"

She slapped his arm and stung her hand against his rock-hard bicep. "That's just one example, you rude child. *Between* is a deceptively simple, yet profound mathematical concept. It's important in the theory of limits and differentials. There is an actual theorem in Real Analysis called the Squeeze Theorem. On top of that, betweenness has geometric implications, as in midpoints of line segments, bisectors of angles, and points identified on a plane and in space."

Greg pulled back from the desk. "Don't slap me again, but does this have anything at all to do with a conversation about Hypatia?"

"Once and for all, there was no conversation between Mister Davenport and myself about Hypatia."

"Then call me stupid, but I don't understand."

"Okay, here's the thing, stupid. Mister Davenport's comment got me ruminating on another application of betweenness—intersections on Venn diagrams." She knew she was treading dangerously close to revealing her actual application of a Venn diagram, but there was nothing for it if she meant to continue.

And besides, what's the big deal if he does find out what I've been thinking?

"The intersecting circles?" Greg asked. "Like one circle is cats, and the other is animals without tails, so the middle section is cats without tails? This is sounding nuttier by the minute. Hypatia comes in here somewhere, right?"

She wanted to hit him again, but instead found herself smiling, as well. "Yes, Hypatia comes in here somewhere. Remember, I mentioned Hypatia made an enemy in Saint Cyril, the Christian Patriarch in Alexandria?"

"And he got some loony to kill her."

"Peter the Reader."

"Remind me, if I ever become a killer, to get a nickname that rhymes. I think it helps if you want to be taken seriously."

She gave the boy a sidelong glance, thinking he was in a good mood considering all he'd been through. "Anyway, once again, I might have oversimplified the story by implying there was a purely religious reason Hypatia was murdered."

"Don't tell me. Hypatia was a terrorist."

"In a way she was, although, like most terrorists, she didn't consider herself one. She was a dangerous person who unknowingly involved herself in the politics of her time."

"And it got her killed."

"It got her murdered."

Greg sat atop a student desk, settling in for the tale. "Go on."

"At the time, Alexandria was the seat for the prefect of the entire Roman Province of Egypt, an enlightened man named Orestes. Naturally, he was drawn to Hypatia."

"As in boyfriend-girlfriend?"

Bonnie shook her head. "Probably not. Hypatia didn't seem to have much use for such things. Let's just say they were friend-friends."

"Okay, friend-friends."

"Good boy. From all evidence, Hypatia didn't realize being friends with the prefect of Egypt carried with it certain risks."

"From Cyril?"

"Primarily, but from others, as well. A power struggle was brewing between—there's that term again—Cyril, as the religious leader of Alexandria, and Orestes, the political representative of Rome. Hypatia was caught in the middle between two very powerful men."

"Between again."

"You bet. Cyril was trying to sway the hearts and spirits of the citizens of Alexandria, and Orestes was trying to govern their bodies and minds. Hypatia, for all her intellect and mathematical acumen, didn't realize that by befriending one side, she was alienating the other. Or maybe she did and didn't care. But Orestes may have also imperiled her by hinting to Cyril that he was interested in the patriarch's Christian community."

"Why would he do that?"

"Why do politicians do anything? To be all things to all people. Although fifteen hundred years later, Abraham Lincoln would declaim the folly of attempting any such nonsense."

"But Orestes was just playing Cyril?"

Bonnie shrugged. "Who's to say? Orestes, like all Roman officials, was at least a nominal Christian. But I'm getting ahead of myself. The fact is, Cyril *believed* Orestes was serious about Christianity, and perception is everything. Cyril also believed something, or more precisely someone, was standing in the way of his ambition to truly enlist Orestes in his campaign for a Christian Alexandria."

"Hypatia."

"Give the boy a cigar. It was like a classic love triangle, another example of complex betweenness. We have Orestes, caught between his friendship with Hypatia and his fear of Cyril's growing power. Cyril, trapped between his own fear of Hypatia's persuasiveness and his need to proselytize Orestes. And Hypatia, blithely inhabiting this Venn intersection between two worlds destined to collide in Alexandria."

"Only one of the three ended up murdered."

Bonnie tugged on her ear. "Which brings us back to Mister Davenport's assertion. Sometimes people are squeezed so tightly they explode."

"And when Cyril was squeezed, he exploded all over Hypatia."

"I would imagine he felt he had no other choice, but we shouldn't lay all the blame on Cyril. After Hypatia's death, Orestes had the opportunity to investigate the murder and decided not to."

"What? She was his friend."

"Just another example of someone being squeezed. Orestes was charged to keep the peace in Egypt. Between pressure from Rome to keep a lid on growing unrest in Alexandria and the constant threat of the rabid elements of the Christian community, Orestes did nothing. The peace of the region outweighed the death of one extraordinary woman."

"So Orestes was two-faced and a coward and sacrificed Hypatia because he didn't have the guts to stand up for his friend even after she was murdered."

"The sad part is that none of it changed anything.

Orestes's efforts couldn't forestall the inevitable. Alexandria was doomed. Before long, open warfare broke out. Jews killing Christians. Synagogues being burned. Everyone against the pagans. In the end, the Library at Alexandria, the greatest library of the ancient world, became the last casualty in a political and religious conflict that consumed everything in its path."

After Greg went off to teach tiny humans how to grapple with one another, Bonnie felt even more confused. A tessellation of faces danced in and out of focus, each demanding their fleeting moment on the stage of her mind and each offering no solution how she could satisfy any of them.

Pansy Boone—"Don't let them silence you. My boy needs you."

Tell you the truth, Pansy, besides jutting out my jaw and telling Divine to suck lemons—which I'm fairly sure won't play all that nicely—I'm pretty well tapped out.

Lloyd Whittaker—"Apologize to Divine and the board. For my sake and yours."

The only person Bonnie felt like apologizing to was Lloyd himself. He deserved better than she intended to give him. He would probably make any number of guarantees to Divine and the board, then she would come along and blindside the lot of them. She could just picture the scene.

She'd approach the podium. A low hum would permeate the hall. All eyes would be on her, expecting a subdued and penitent homily.

"I'm sorry for the consternation I've caused in the community." She'd turn to Divine with a look of abject remorse.

"I'm sorry I called you a nursery-rhyme figure." *If I had my way, all the king's horses and all the king's men would leave your sorry ass in pieces.* "However, I will not repent of my position that Matthew Boone is innocent, and I intend to go on saying so to whomever will listen."

At that point, the shit would hit the rotary mechanism.

She cleared her mind of Divine and the meeting, only to have Freddy Davenport's portly frame take stage front and center. "Sometimes people are caught in circumstances that squeeze them so tightly they explode."

Somehow this statement had earlier brought to mind Hypatia, Cyril, and Orestes. Cyril's ambitions had impelled this supposed man of God to murder. He was caught between circumstances that gave him no choice.

Wait a minute.

Freddy had been talking about Matthew. Even a mild-mannered boy like Matthew could be forced by circumstances into committing murder.

Think, Bonnie. That statement would also be true if the

murderer was someone other than Matt.

Then there was the murder itself. Luther Devereaux wasn't just eliminated. The man was butchered. Whoever killed Luther brought both planning and passion to the crime. The killer hated Luther Devereaux.

And yet.

"And yet he could approach Luther without making the man suspicious," she said aloud.

Luther was going blind, but he wasn't deaf. He certainly heard his killer climbing the concrete-and-metal steps to the loft. The sons of bitches rang out with every step a person took. More than likely, Luther turned to see his murderer approach.

This fact made Matthew the perfect suspect. Luther would never consider Matthew a threat because the boy belonged there. His appearance in the loft was expected.

So the actual murderer needed the same advantage.

Betweenness was the key. The murderer inhabited the intersection between *Out of Class* and *Kitchen Staff.* Also, if Freddy was right, and the brutality of the crime seemed to bear that out, then the killer was caught, squeezed into circumstances where he or she felt there was no other choice.

Impelled to a crime of passion—like the story of Hypatia and Cyril.

What possible circumstances could make someone not just take the life of another, but also do it in such violent manner—become a homicidal maniac?

Cyril was driven by ambition. Ambition to rid Alexandria of pagans and Jews. Ambition to remake a city of the intellect into Augustine's City of God. Most of all, ambition to make an ally out of Rome's prefect, Orestes.

Hypatia died because she was an impediment to Cyril's ambitions.

Did Luther stand in the way of someone's ambitions?

In answering that question, Bonnie suddenly knew the answer to all the others.

CHAPTER 16

BONNIE'S LEGS FELT LIKE LEAD AS SHE CLIMBED THE steps to the loft. Long before she reached the top, she heard the excited voices of ten-year-olds. She had to listen a little closer to catch the lower strains of Greg's.

"Throw your legs over his. That's it. That's it. Use your weight. Make your opponent tire himself to get you off."

Bonnie cleared the top step.

Greg was kneeling next to a girl with her blond hair tied back. She was wrapped around a struggling dark-skinned boy.

Greg looked up. "Missus Pinkwater." The two words did little to hide the real question: What are you doing here?

"We need to talk." She barely got the words out, so dry was her throat.

Greg's face went hard and wary, but only for a moment.

He regained his composure, except for his eyes. They alone betrayed his uneasiness. He tapped the blond girl on the shoulder.

"Hey, guys. I need to speak in private to Missus Pinkwater. Why don't all of you take a water break?"

Amid a flurry of shouts and pushing, the dozen or so wrestlers vacated the loft. Once the last of their footfalls echoed on the gym floor, Bonnie said, "Luther never saw it coming, did he, Greg?"

The boy didn't miss a beat. "What are you talking about?"

His gaze challenged hers, daring her to prove what she so obviously suspected. The hint of a smile played at the corners of his mouth.

Bonnie felt herself grow cold with fury. She narrowed her eyes. "Don't wear that face with me, you little bastard. Forget about Luther, and I suspect you've already forgotten about Janice, but how could you do this to Matt?"

Greg's smile evaporated. Once, then twice, he opened his mouth to reply, then merely shook his head. He pushed past her. The last thing she heard as his feet clanged on the loft stairs was, "You wouldn't understand."

That's the problem, dear boy, I understand too well. You traded your future for his.

An eternity later, when the first of the ten-year-olds returned, Bonnie was hugging herself, still standing where Greg left her.

"What happened to Greg?" the blond girl asked.

Bonnie blinked back a stinging tear. "I wish I could tell you, honey."

In a fog, Bonnie navigated the steps down from the loft. She trudged the long hallway past the lockers. She needed to call Byron, clue him in on what had happened with Greg. And yet, with every passing locker, with every echo of her feet against the tiles, she couldn't bring herself to reach for the cell.

And you know damn well why, Pinkwater. Although right now you feel like God's perfect fool.

Bonnie had often told people she'd been teaching since the year rope was invented. In that time, she'd had students who kept alive the spark, made teaching gratifying. Some were fun. Some were brilliant. Some were more than a little creative in the mischief they perpetrated. The good ones reminded her of herself when she was a girl.

And then there was Greg.

Like no other student, he inhabited a place in her heart difficult to define. And yet, perhaps not so difficult.

Looking back, she realized there were times, many times, she wished Greg were her own child—the way he'd taken Matt under his wing, the hardships he'd endured being the good son, how easy it always had been to joke with him, to listen, to empathize. Just that afternoon, while she was telling him the final chapter of Hypatia's story, they'd almost completed each other's thoughts.

God damn it, the child could make me laugh.

And if the truth be told, in the months since Ben's death, she'd needed laughter.

Perhaps that was why it took her so long to arrive at the realization of Greg's guilt. She didn't want to see it. A part of her fought the logic, fought the consequences of coming to what now seemed an obvious conclusion. That same part was resisting the urge to call Byron.

She pulled the phone from her fanny pack just as she was approaching the front office.

Lloyd's sonorous drawl floated out. "She's the finest math teacher this school has ever known, twice nominated for Colorado Teacher of the Year, winning once."

The next voice Bonnie heard sent a chill up her spine and made Bonnie plaster herself against the outside wall.

"I'm sure all that's true," Divine countered. "And no one's asking for her resignation. At least not yet. However, and don't mistake me on this point, Principal Whittaker, if Missus Pinkwater doesn't apologize to myself, to the board, and to the good people of East Plains, I have Cal Upton's assurance she will be placed on administrative leave for an indefinite period of time."

"I have her word she'll apologize, Superintendent."

"And what about this business of Matt Boone?"

"Are you so sure you're right and she's wrong?"

"My God, man, listen to yourself. The boy was found with the knife in his hand, blood soaking his clothing. His own father believes in his guilt. Does Missus Pinkwater have even a shred of evidence that points the finger of culpability toward someone other than Matthew Boone?"

Divine's question brought Bonnie up so short she never heard Lloyd's answer.

What proof do you have, Pinkwater? For all your fancy-schmancy logic, all you have is a Venn diagram and the story of a long-dead female mathematician.

Even Greg's final words—"You wouldn't understand"—could be interpreted any number of ways.

Lloyd's voice brought her back to the present. "Missus Pinkwater intends to drop the entire affair. I give you my word."

"I wouldn't be so quick to hitch your wagon to that woman's star, Whittaker."

"I've known her and her late husband for twenty years. I'll take my chances."

"As you will."

Divine delivered the three-word phrase like a death sentence. Bonnie felt her breath catch in her chest. She hurried down the hall and out the front door.

Way to go, Pinkwater. Things couldn't be more bollixed, if you'd planned it.

As Bonnie drove away from the school, she fingered the cell phone's keypad, tapping at random numbers. Each time she filled the screen, she cleared the number and began again.

How could she tell Byron what she knew without sounding like a madwoman? Divine was right. She had no proof.

Before she could tell herself not to, she punched in Byron's work number. The phone rang four times. Byron's voice mail kicked in.

"You missed Deputy Byron Hickman. Leave me a message, and I'll get back to you."

Bonnie was about to hang up when she realized she was more than a little relieved not to be talking to an honest-to-God person. A message would suit her right down to her shoes. When the beep sounded, she squeezed in as much of her theory as time would allow. She even had the presence of mind to end with, "I know I'm right, Byron. Call me on my cell."

She closed out the connection.

That's it. He either believes me, or he doesn't.

At times like these, she most missed Ben. She wanted him to wrap her in those strong arms of his—wanted to smell him, feel the roughness of him against her face, bounce her reasoning off his excellent mind. She suspected this terrible longing was behind the illogical belief that Ben's spirit now inhabited an enigmatic red-tailed hawk currently sailing the winds above the Bluffs.

And what's that say about your mental state, Pinkwater?

Bonnie didn't give herself a chance to answer. She pulled off onto the shoulder of Highway 84. Alice, The-Little-Subaru-That-Could, slid to a tilting halt. Bonnie exited the car, slamming the door behind her. Although the wind bit with an icy insistence, she kept walking until a good hundred feet separated her from the vehicle.

She bent down and picked up a stone.

Bonnie let it fly, aiming at the crossbar of a telephone pole across the road and maybe forty feet distant. The stone thwacked the beam with a satisfying thud.

Bonnie snatched up another. With a grunt, she hurled the new stone at the opposite side of the crossbar. This time the little bugger missed by a good five feet.

You're getting rusty, Pinkwater. Was a time you could make that shot ten times out of ten.

Bonnie pegged another stone at the pole, and was rewarded with a hit. Again and again, she hurled rocks at the inoffensive telephone pole, sometimes true to the mark, sometimes wide of the beam. With each miss, she grew more determined and grunted louder in frustration.

Her back and shoulder began to ache. The last stone she hurled caused her to lose her balance. She landed hard on her rear end, then slid in a dusting of snow.

When Bonnie came to a stop, her hands were dirty and raw, her seat was damp, but more than that, it was sore. She'd slid across something, and now the damn thing was jammed into the base of her spine. She twisted sideways and extricated a palm-sized comma of a stone that had ripped a hole into her pants.

Angry at the stupidity of her situation, Bonnie made to toss the stone away. At the last instant, she took a second look. Although mostly gray, parallel streaks of brownish-red converged at one pointed end. An almost-perfect circle of black stared out of the coloration.

"An eye?"

The stone looked, for all the world, like the head of a hawk, a red-tailed hawk.

"Stop screwing with me, Benjamin." Again, Bonnie pulled back her arm with the intention of flinging the bloody thing into the next county. And again, she stopped herself.

"God damn you, Ben Pinkwater. You see what you've done? I'm getting as superstitious as you." She stuffed the stone into her coat pocket and struggled to her feet.

Bonnie waited, half-hoping, half-dreading the teasing voice of her dead husband would intrude the way it did on the Bluffs.

Nothing.

She couldn't remember when last she felt so alone.

Bonnie barely noticed the miles flying by as she drove home. Her mind was going like a roller coaster.

Greg was out there somewhere. *What would I do, if our roles were reversed? Where would I go?*

His secret was revealed even if she was the only one who knew it. Not being an idiot, he'd have to assume she'd call Byron.

Bonnie crested the hill at the top of her drive and let Alice coast. Long before she reached the bottom, she heard the dogs. Something didn't feel right. Their yammering had a manic, frightened quality to it.

She tried to convince herself she was imagining things—just a case of overtaxed nerves. Still, as she approached her front door, she picked up the snow shovel. Her heart was pounding as she let herself in.

What she saw turned the pounding to a trip-hammer.

The house looked as if someone had lobbed in a hand grenade. Upturned furniture, many pieces splintered, sat in a trail of ashes from the fireplace. Drawers were pulled out and their contents strewn about the kitchen and dining room. A carving knife stood erect, plunged into the butcher-block cutting board. Bonnie dropped the shovel

Robert Spiller

and pulled out the knife. She clutched the blade to her
chest and stepped into the dining room.

BITCH was scrawled in lipstick across the clear
panes of the china hutch. A lipstick arrow pointed to her
small dry-eraser board behind the glass.

*MEET ME AT THE EAGLE'S NEST.
I'VE GOT THE DOG, NOT THE WOMAN.
DON'T BRING THE POLICE.*

A meow from beneath the family-room couch made
Bonnie jump. Euclid poked out his small black head
and meowed again. The cat shivered. Still clutching the
knife, Bonnie scooped Euclid into her arms.

She rubbed her face into the cat's soft fur. "The son
of a bitch has Hypatia," she whispered.

The cat meowed once more.

Bonnie could only imagine Greg's state of mind as he
rampaged through her home.

God damn it, if that murderous bastard hurts Hypatia . . .

Bonnie didn't let herself finish the thought.

You're going to be okay, baby.

Bonnie slipped the carving knife into her coat pocket.
It thumped against the hawk stone.

"Sure could use some supernatural assistance on this
one, Benjamin. I feel like I'm about to go out on the high
wire without a net."

258

The wind picked up and the sun went down as Bonnie crested the top of the mesa. Across the flat expanse, Greg stood, holding Hypatia on a leash. The wind whipped at Greg's blond hair and black Windbreaker. He turned to face her full, struggling with the dog in one hand and a rifle in the other.

"I knew you'd come!" he shouted. "What was it you told me? The animals are your family now."

Hypatia lurched toward Bonnie, and Greg pulled back hard on the leash.

The dog yelped.

Hang in there, baby. Mama's going to figure a way out of this. "What is it you want, Greg?"

"Right now, I want you to come a little closer." The boy motioned with the rifle. "We need to talk."

She came within twenty feet.

"Close enough," Greg said. "Now take off your fanny pack and turn out your pockets."

She dropped the pack and let the hawk stone and the knife clatter to the ground.

Greg nodded appreciatively. "Pick up the knife."

Idiot, Pinkwater. Did you really expect to get close enough to this homicidal boy to do damage with a kitchen knife?

She bent and retrieved the knife.

"Now toss it to me. And don't do anything cute,

Missus P. I'm not in the mood."

Underhanded, she tossed the knife. It landed at Greg's feet, and with a swipe of his leg, he kicked it over the rim.

"You've complicated my life."

Bonnie tried to keep a rising anxiety out of her voice. "How about if I uncomplicate it? I'll just take my dog, and we'll call it even."

A smile, the same cocky grin he'd worn in the loft, appeared on Greg's face. "That's what I've always liked about you, Missus P. You never let things get you too far down." He craned his neck to peer over the rim.

"You know what's down there?"

Bonnie let her gaze travel the mesa and come back to the spot where Greg stood. "I'm thinking the eagles' nest."

"And below that, about a hundred feet of nothing. This here dog probably doesn't know how to fly, does she?"

Bonnie felt her knees grow weak. "Don't, Greg."

"No? So here's what we're going to do. You're going to tell me everything. How you figured out about me and Luther. Who you've told. Everything."

Before she could speak, he added, "And if I think you're not being straight with me, Hypatia—the dog, not the Greek lady—takes a flying leap."

And I'll be next. I'll get to live as long as I have his attention. Make the story a good one, Scheherazade.

"Hypatia led me to you."

She waited for Greg to make the joke about the dog, but Bonnie could tell from the grim set of the boy's face, the time for joking was past. He nodded for her to continue.

"Hypatia was murdered because she was in the way of Cyril's ambition. The Patriarch believed Hypatia was thwarting his plans. She was murdered horribly. So was Luther Devereaux."

Bonnie paused to let the effect of her words sink in, but if she expected remorse from Greg, she never got it. His face was unreadable.

"Go on."

"I asked myself, whose ambitions, whose dreams, had Luther Devereaux been trampling underfoot?" She met Greg's eyes with hers. "Luther wasn't going to let you get out of East Plains, get away from Barty and Kyle, was he?"

Greg shook his head. "No." The word shot from his lips like it was fire.

Bonnie stared at this once-precious boy and could see the strain he'd been under—staying close to herself and Byron, keeping track of everything they learned, interviewing everyone who'd talk to him on the off chance someone had seen him come down from the loft or in the company of Janice.

No wonder he'd been so distracted. If I'd been keeping so many balls in the air, I'd have trouble remembering my derriere, let alone keep straight a dog and a Greek woman with the same name.

"Luther was getting marijuana. You were his mule."

Greg nodded his head.

"Why, Greg? You told me time and again, you wanted no part of your father's business."

"Mister Devereaux was helping me get out of East Plains." The boy drew a long shuddering breath. "And he was going blind."

"You felt sorry for him?"

Greg turned away momentarily. When he looked back, his cheeks were red, and not just from the wind. "There was also Missus Devereaux."

Bonnie thought she might be sick. If he wasn't already dead, Bonnie felt she would have killed Luther herself. And she'd bury Angelica in the same grave.

Greg nodded. "Then a few weeks ago, Mister Devereaux told me he needed me to keep getting the weed even after graduation. He wanted me to wrestle at a local school—Greeley or Adams State."

"Why didn't you just refuse?"

Greg's eyes went flinty. "The bastard had pictures."

"Of you and Angelica?"

"Of me delivering weed, of taking money. I'd already been accepted into the University of Iowa, had all the finances worked out. They even said I had a good chance at a scholarship if I took state next month."

"So Luther Devereaux was squeezing you."

Greg looked up as if he hadn't heard. "What?"

"Forget it. When did you decide to steal the knife?"

"I was going to use one of Kyle's knives, but I didn't want it traced back to our . . . How did you figure it was me who took the knife?"

"You told me."

"Excuse me?"

"When I called you to get the list of STUCO names who worked the senior-citizen luncheon, you failed to include yourself on the list. I wondered about that."

"Maybe I wasn't at the dinner."

Bonnie gave him a rueful smile. "We both know that's not true, Greg. You said you talked to your grandfather at the luncheon, said you talked about how much he missed your grandmother."

"Shit. Sounds like I talked too much."

"Sounds like it. Anyway, once I placed you at the luncheon, you were a perfect fit in the belly of the Venn-diagram fish."

"Come again?"

"We talked about it, you and me, part of our discussion of betweeness. The circles were titled *Kitchen Help the Day the Knife Disappeared* and *Out of Class between 2:30 and 3:00.*" Bonnie stopped her ruminations as a new revelation struck her.

"Your father and brother were at the school to prevent you from killing Luther, weren't they?"

"They were too late."

Bonnie felt light-headed. "Because I let you out of class before the end of the day. They would have been on time, if it wasn't for me."

A grin spread across Greg's face. "I hadn't thought of it like that. I guess I have you to thank for making everything work out the way it did."

At that moment, Bonnie couldn't see anything in the ghoulish face before her of the Greg she'd held dear all these years. That boy had ceased to exist. She groped for the first thing she could think of to wipe away the devilish grin.

"Does that include being spotted by Janice Flick?"

Greg's knuckles went white on the barrel of the rifle.

Pinkwater, when are you going to learn to keep your mouth shut?

"She said she would never tell," Greg said. "And I believed her."

"She was crazy, Greg."

"Tell me something I don't know. Just after Janice told me she knew I'd killed Luther, she said not to worry. Damn girl loved me from the first day she got to East Plains."

Bonnie tried to picture the pair arm in arm—the sallow-faced girl with the oily hair and the boy Adonis, already the lover of a grown woman. Janice was doomed from the get-go.

"I thought I could make it work without having to

kill her. Besides, I kind of liked Janice. She was a good listener."

I'll bet. The girl probably hung on your every word.

"So you told her things. Like how you dreamed of being adopted by a normal family. Maybe how you sometimes wished Kyle and Barty were dead."

Greg's shoulders slumped. His eyes refused to meet hers. "Like I said, she was a good listener."

"So what happened?"

"On Friday morning, she drove me out to my house."

"Barty and Kyle were in the barn?"

Greg nodded. "They had just come down from the greenhouse and were pissed I'd brought a stranger over. There was yelling and pointing, and before I knew it, Janice pulled out a pistol. You got to know, I had nothing to do with the murder of my brother and Pa."

Bonnie wanted to challenge Greg's assertion, to tell him he had everything to do with their deaths. Instead, for the sake of her own survival, she threw him a bone. "I know."

"Just like that, before I could do anything, they were dead."

"What happened then?"

"I thought she was going to kill me, too. All I could think about was saving my own ass." The boy let loose with a wail. "I'm no different from that Orestes guy not standing up for Hypatia!"

"But you did strangle Janice."

The wind gusted. Greg teetered near the edge of the cliff. "It's funny. I was kind of numb, not mad or anything. I just knew she had to die. So after she put the gun away, I squeezed her . . . and squeezed her . . . and squeezed her."

With each repetition, Greg's voice went huskier, his eyes wider. "The rest was easy. I tossed the gun near Pa and Kyle and carried Janice's body to her car. I had plenty of time to stash the car and get back to school."

"And Simon did you the favor of stealing the gun."

Greg offered a half smile. "What can I say? For a while, things just kept going my way. Until you."

The look Greg gave her, half-malice, half-sympathy, made Bonnie's head swim. "I've told Byron, you know?"

Greg sighed. "There ain't nothing I can do about that. I'm sorry, Missus P."

One-handed, he raised the rifle to his shoulder.

CHAPTER 17

THE CELL PHONE RANG.

Muffled by the fanny pack and the howling wind, the ring still sliced into the silence of the moment.

Hypatia whimpered inside her cone.

The phone rang again.

"That would be your uncle." Bonnie stared down the barrel of the rifle, waiting for Greg to pull the trigger.

Again, the phone rang.

In the high wind, the rifle wavered in Greg's hand. "Don't even think about it."

Bonnie waited for a fourth ring, but it never came.

"See," Greg said. "No more Uncle Byron."

Be smart, Bonnie. Don't let this boy use you for target practice. "Doesn't matter. Even as we speak, my voice mail is kicking it."

"And?"

"I changed my voice-mail message. By now, Byron

knows I came here to meet you." Bonnie felt as if she were standing back and watching the lie manufacture itself.

Too bad you didn't think of that brainstorm for real, Pinkwater. At least for the moment, he's not blowing your head off.

"You're bluffing." Greg lowered the barrel ever so slightly.

"Do I look like I'm bluffing? Too much has happened for you to contemplate any more killing."

"Shut up and let me think."

That's the last thing I'm going to do.

"You may have gotten away with murder up until now, but you'll never pull this one off." She pointed her thumb back over her shoulder. "Trashing my house was your first big mistake. I'm betting you weren't as careful down there as you were in the wrestling loft or the barn— probably left something that'll point a large hairy finger right at Greg Hansen."

"I said, shut up." He fired over her head.

The deafening noise shook Bonnie down to her marrow. *Screw this.* Her Imp of the Perverse snatched the helm. She couldn't be quiet now if her life depended on it, which it probably did.

In for a penny.

"Then there's that goofy business with the dry-eraser note."

Greg's face drained of color.

"Let's see if I can remember the wit and wisdom of one Gregory Hansen, Esquire. *I've got the dog, not the lady.*"

Greg looked as if he might get sick.

Bonnie couldn't resist driving home the coffin nail. "You think good ol' Uncle Byron's forgotten that bit of confusion? I'm betting not."

She tapped her Mickey Mouse watch. "If you left right now, you could probably make it down to my house in time to meet him. Save Byron the trouble of coming up here and arresting your homicidal rear end."

The boy sighed—air escaping an overfilled balloon. The lines of anxiety, which a moment before had been mapping his face, smoothed out. He chuckled. "I'm screwed."

Bonnie's neck hair stood on end. Nothing of hysteria lived in the statement or the laughter—too much serenity and acceptance. The boy had made a decision, and Bonnie Pinkwater was sure she wasn't going to like it.

She took a step backward and stumbled over the hawk stone.

"Missus P, you know, you can be a real bitch."

Oh shit.

"I would be the first to admit that's something I could use a workshop on."

Greg's expression remained blank. "In the back of my mind, I guess I figured this would turn out badly. Looks like neither one of us will be around to see if the eagles come back."

He sighted down the rifle. "I promise not to shoot the dog."

"Hypatia!" Bonnie screamed.

The retriever lurched. The rifle jerked wildly. A shot sailed wide.

Bonnie snatched up the hawk stone at her feet.

Greg shook free of the dog. He leveled the rifle for his second shot.

Grunting, she let the stone fly.

The missile caught the boy in the bridge of the nose. He dropped the rifle and staggered backward.

As his heels crossed the rim of the cliff, Greg Hansen windmilled. Saving himself was now a lost cause. He had already made too large a commitment to momentum and gravity.

Greg and Bonnie shared a glance. Then, with a gurgling scream that cut through the wind's howl, the boy fell out of sight.

Abruptly, the scream halted.

Bonnie ran past her dog to the edge of the mesa. Clinging with one hand on the crumbling eagles' nest and one on its ledge, Greg Hansen stared wide-eyed up at her. Crimson poured from his ruined nose.

"Don't let me fall, Missus P. I don't want to die!"

Bonnie entertained the tempting thought of doing just that, letting the treacherous man-child fall.

"Please, I'm begging you."

With a sound of snapping twigs, the eagles' nest disintegrated. Greg's right hand sprang free. He made a frantic stab at the ledge, only to have the rock crumble. Again, he grabbed the ledge, and this time his hold was secure.

But not for long. That damn rock looks like it just wants to break apart. "Don't you fall, you little son of a bitch."

Bonnie unbuckled Hypatia's leash and lowered it.

The dog growled.

"I know, but I can't just let him die without doing something."

"Can you hold my weight?" Greg asked.

She shifted into a sitting position and braced her feet against a pair of rocks. "I don't think you have a lot of options here. I'm all you got."

Greg tightened his grip on the ledge with one hand and reached up with the other. His face went red, and his eyes protruded. Bonnie almost toppled forward as the leash went taut. She tilted back.

"Get onto the eagles' ledge. Hurry!"

The leash bit into her hand.

"I'm up," Greg croaked. "Now what?"

Bonnie wrapped the leash around her forearm. *Now we're connected, Mister Hansen. You tumble into the valley, you've got a good chance of taking me with you.*

She inched forward until she saw Greg's upturned face. "The two of us are going to have to pull this last bit off together. And I do mean pull. You ready?"

"Why are you doing this, Missus P? Why didn't you just let me fall?"

Good question.

"Maybe I'm just stupid, but I remember once knowing a Greg Hansen worth saving. Now, shut up and get ready. I'm going to count to three. One."

Bonnie felt a renewed tug on the leash as Greg moved up the strap.

"Two."

She leaned back and braced her feet against the rocks.

"Three. Climb, you little bastard." Bonnie strained against the leash. First one hand, then the other, then his head appeared at the rim.

Oh shit. Not ten inches from where the boy was rising lay the rifle.

Bonnie released the strap and scrambled for the weapon. Even as Greg was hoisting himself onto the mesa, he reached for the gun.

She snatched it from his grasp. "I don't think so, Greg."

The blood on his face and the feral look in his eyes made Bonnie scuttle back, all the while clutching on the rifle. She aimed at the boy whose life she'd just saved.

Greg regarded her, his face betraying nothing of gratitude. He tried to rise, his arms trembling, his face red.

"I need you to stay put, youngster."

Greg shook his head. "I won't go to prison."

He strained and pushed himself onto his knees. "I don't think you want to kill me, Missus P."

Bonnie raised the rifle and squeezed off a shot. Gravel exploded to Greg's left.

Hypatia started and rushed to Bonnie's side.

"Sorry, baby." Bonnie fed another round into the chamber. "You may be right, Greg. I may not want to kill you, but if you move again, I'll make you wish I had."

She reached for her fanny pack and dug out the cell phone.

When the helicopter landed on the mesa, all lights and whipping wind, Bonnie thought her face might crack from smiling. Or maybe from the cold.

It had been an uneasy forty-five minutes. Greg had threatened and cajoled, tried to reason with her, and in the end, cursed her for saving his life only to send him off to the living hell of prison.

She finally shut him up by reminding him prison was the fate he'd willingly thrust upon an innocent Matthew Boone. After that, Greg merely glared at her. And there they sat as darkness enveloped the mesa.

The door to the helicopter slid open. Byron Hickman stepped gingerly down.

"Uncle Byron!" Greg shouted. "You got to believe—"

"Shut your mouth." Byron wheeled.

His hand closed into a fist, and for a moment Bonnie thought Byron might strike his nephew. "We'll talk later, but for right now, put a sock in it."

He flipped Greg onto his back and cuffed his hands together.

Byron turned to Bonnie. "You okay?"

She nodded.

"I'll take Dad's rifle."

Bonnie loosened her grip. Byron took the weapon and helped her stand.

"When I got your first message," Byron said, "I went back to the evidence from Janice's gun. The CSI guys had pulled a few whole prints and a partial. The full prints belonged to either Janice or Simon, but we couldn't find a match for the partial until your call."

"Greg?"

"Yeah." Byron's face was a stony mask. "I'm really sorry about all this, Missus P."

Bonnie took hold of Byron's shoulder. "Not your fault. You warned me about getting too close to the case."

He thumped the side of his head. "I should have followed the evidence better. I can't help thinking I would have seen Greg's part in all this if he wasn't my nephew."

"Then he fooled us both. What happens now?"

"We all take a helicopter ride." He frowned at his nephew.

Bonnie stared at Deputy Byron Hickman, thinking she wasn't the only one who'd undergone world-shaking changes in the last few hours. When Byron woke that morning, he'd had a family. Taking in Greg, he'd saved part of the sister he'd lost. Now he'd have to arrest that same boy—to say nothing of burying a brother-in-law and nephew.

It had been a hell of a day. Bonnie checked her Mickey Mouse watch.

"Shit."

Byron's head snapped back around. "What is it?"

"I'm going to be late for my own hanging."

Bonnie's first helicopter ride made her grateful she'd not eaten dinner. Ten minutes after take off, the chopper was falling from the sky and preparing to land in the field beyond the administration building. Hypatia gulped again and again, like she might get sick.

Don't do it, baby. Mommy would be right behind you.

Hypatia's claws scratched against the helicopter's deck, and the retriever squirmed in Bonnie's arms. She tightened her hold.

Just get this thing on the ground.

When Byron had suggested they drop her off at the school, it had seemed like a good idea. Almost immediately,

Robert Spiller

she changed her mind. Since then, she hadn't had time to voice any objections to a gut-wrenching night flight across the inky blackness of East Plains.

The searchlight of the helicopter revealed a landscape of cars. *Dear God, it looks like everybody in East Plains decided my demise was too good to miss.*

With a decisive thump, the chopper settled down.

"You ready?" Byron asked.

Bonnie worked up what she hoped was a brave smile. "I was born ready, youngster."

Greg was handcuffed to a railing in the chopper. Bonnie let her gaze fall on the boy, but he refused to meet her eyes.

What a waste.

Byron slid open the door to the sound of a waiting crowd. They stood well away from the radius of the chopper's blades.

Hypatia barked.

"Hush, baby. Hopefully, they're friends."

Bonnie knew she'd spoken too soon when she spotted Cal Upton and The Divine Pain in the Ass. She helped a skittish Hypatia alight from the helicopter.

Byron poked his head from the chopper door. "Mister Upton!" he shouted. "Might I have a word with you?"

The tall man laid a palm on his chest as if he couldn't believe he was the one being hailed. He walked past Bonnie, giving her a quizzical stare.

Head down, Bonnie led Hypatia toward the warmth of the administration building. Like the Red Sea parting for Moses, the mob gave way.

The Divine Pain in the Ass looked positively apoplectic. "What's the meaning of this?"

"My car is in the shop." Bonnie had no desire to freeze another moment talking to a man who, if he had his druthers, would put her out of her job. She climbed the building's pair of steps.

Bonnie looked back and spotted Byron speaking with Cal Upton. The two men appeared to be shouting at one another, but the roar of the helicopter and the buzz of the crowd drowned out their voices. Divine stood paralyzed, obviously wanting to learn what Cal was hearing from Byron, yet also eyeing Bonnie with the look of a predator—an overweight, bald-headed predator in lime-green corduroys.

"Glad you could make it." Lloyd Whittaker ushered her into the warmth. He smiled and dug gnarled fingers into Hypatia's fur.

"Not half as glad as me."

"Not many folks would have thought to show up in a helicopter and to bring their dog. I suspect you've got a story to tell."

"You might say that." Impulsively, Bonnie embraced her principal. "Thanks for standing by me, boss."

Lloyd took her by the shoulders and studied her face.

Looking embarrassed, he cleared his throat. "You'd have done the same for me."

"I'd like to think I would."

Bonnie almost stumbled into Lloyd as something slapped her between the shoulder blades.

"You sure know how to make an entrance, Pinkwater." Hattie Caulfield's booming voice rose above the tumult of the overcrowded chamber. "You got half these stick-up-their-asses, pasty-faced, backstabbing Pollyannas ready to crap in their stretchy pants."

A tiny woman in a pink ski jacket shot Hattie a look that would have peeled paint. Hands on her hips, Hattie stared back until the woman looked away.

"Settle down, Caulfield," Bonnie said. "I'm trying to get out of trouble, not start a fight."

"Deary, you got a fight whether you want one or not." She pointed with her double chins toward the doorway.

Superintendent Divine minced his way into the chamber. "Ladies and gentlemen, now that Missus Pinkwater is here, we can proceed."

Like a king ascending his throne, Divine took his seat at the end of the school-board table. The other four board members appeared confused, but after a moment's hesitation took their seats, as well.

"Missus Pinkwater, please make your way to the podium."

In the center of the room, a battered wooden podium

faced the half-ellipse board table. On more than one occasion, Bonnie had stood at this focal point and faced either Cal or Divine. On every such occasion, she'd felt naked and exposed. Tonight, she would be naked, exposed, and in the company of a golden retriever wearing a cone.

Lloyd Whittaker raised his hand. "Superintendent, don't you think we should wait on Board President Upton before we proceed with the agenda?"

Shouting voices erupted throughout the room, both in support of Lloyd's suggestion and against it.

The Divine Pain in the Ass glared at the principal as if Lloyd had suggested they all take off their clothes and sing show tunes. "I'm sure Cal will be along shortly. Now, Missus Pinkwater, if you please."

Why the hell not?

Bonnie inched her way through the crowded room. She considered handing off Hypatia, but wasn't sure the dog would stand for it. Besides, she found Hypatia's company reassuring, cone and all.

On her way to the podium, Bonnie spotted Pansy Boone. The woman had a tight grip on her husband's arm. He looked sourly at Bonnie, but since that was his normal expression, she couldn't tell if Pansy had been successful in changing her husband's mind.

Trent Hendrickson leaned against a wall near the entrance. Sheepishly, he offered a weak smile, then to Bonnie's surprise, a thumbs-up.

She mouthed, "Thank you."

He mouthed back, "You owe me dinner."

Bonnie stopped at the podium and turned her attention to Superintendent Divine. She stared at the odious man, knowing it was petty but swearing she wouldn't be the first to speak.

"Missus Pinkwater, in the last five days, this community has endured a number of tragic incidents, which I, the board, and members of this same community believe have been exacerbated by your questionable behavior. While this school district was reeling from acts of extreme violence, you took it upon yourself to initiate rumors that have both disrupted classes and traumatized students."

Bonnie attempted to reply, but Divine cut her off with an upraised hand. "When confronted with your behavior, you responded with insults to my person."

Divine sat back in his chair, his hands folded across his ample belly. "I've been assured by your principal you plan to make a clean breast of everything and apologize to those you've offended."

A hand clasped Bonnie's shoulder.

Lloyd Whittaker had followed her to the podium. "Now hold on a blasted minute, Xavier."

Divine partially rose from his chair. "Principal Whittaker, you're out of order."

Bonnie turned to her lifelong friend. "It's all right, Lloyd."

"Not by a long shot is this anywhere close to all right." Lloyd Whittaker craned across her to speak into the microphone. "Is this how we do things now in East Plains? Railroad a respected teacher?"

He snatched the microphone from its gooseneck and faced the crowd. "Is it just me? Isn't anybody here curious why this woman showed up here tonight in a helicopter?"

"I believe I know something of that story." Cal Upton stood in the doorway. "Xavier, were you starting the meeting without me?"

A crimson flush enveloped Divine's egg-shaped dome. "I was just proceeding as we had agreed, Cal."

Cal Upton looked dubiously at his superintendent. "Thank you for your diligence, Superintendent. Do you mind if I take it from here?"

"Certainly not."

His voice quavered, and for a fleeting moment, Bonnie felt sorry for the man. The moment passed.

Screw him.

In long strides, the board president crossed the room. He folded himself into his seat at the center of the ellipse.

Bonnie took the microphone from Lloyd. "Mister Upton, may I speak?"

Cal Upton nodded. "By all means."

She inhaled deeply. "Mister Upton, board members, people of East Plains, nothing Superintendent Divine said is false. I did, indeed, challenge whether Matthew

Boone killed Luther Devereaux. What's more, I foolishly did it in my classroom. Like they say, hindsight is twenty-twenty, and if I had to do it again, I'd probably keep my mouth shut."

From the corner of her eye, Bonnie kept Divine in sight. The man had the uneasy appearance of someone who was waiting for the sky to fall.

Bonnie turned to face him. "As to the superintendent's assertion that when he confronted me, I hurled insults in his direction, I am guilty there, as well. Superintendent, you are well within your rights to demand an apology."

Divine appeared as if he wanted to add something to her homily, but she forged ahead. "Sir, let me say I deeply regret calling you Humpty Dumpty and beg your forgiveness."

Sniggers erupted throughout the room.

The superintendent bolted up from his seat, his face a deeper shade of scarlet. Cal Upton pulled him back down. The board president leaned across to his superintendent and whispered.

Bonnie switched off the mike and replaced it in its gooseneck. "What do you think he's telling Divine?" she asked Lloyd.

"If I had to guess, I'd say our good president is explaining that some days you eat the bear and some days the bear eats you. And this is one of those days when Xavier Divine is a late-night snack for a grizzly."

Cal Upton cleared his throat. He frowned at Bonnie. "I

think that apology is quite sufficient, Missus Pinkwater."

He looked out over the crowd. "Good people of East Plains, my tardiness was precipitated by an impromptu meeting with Deputy Byron Hickman. He informed me of recent events which, by their nature and gravity, necessitate an alteration of tonight's agenda."

For the next five minutes, Cal Upton related Bonnie's role in investigating the four murders. He ended with Bonnie's heroics on the Bluffs, painting what she considered to be a very generous portrait of her intelligence and bravery.

Bonnie's gaze fell upon Divine, and they locked eyes. A half smile told her she may have won this one, but the next time her derriere was out in the breeze he intended to punt it through the uprights.

Fair enough, Humpty, let the games begin.

Cal Upton stood. "Let me close by thanking one brave, and some might say, stubborn lady. Thanks to you, Missus Pinkwater, a killer was apprehended this evening."

He turned his attention to Pansy and Frank Boone. "Even more importantly, thanks to Missus Pinkwater, an innocent boy will be returned to the love of his family." Upton began to clap.

Heat crept into Bonnie's face.

At first, the crowd seemed unsure what they should do, then, as if most every man, woman, and child had been hardwired together, the room exploded into applause.

CHAPTER 18

BONNIE HAD FIRST NOTICED THE NESTING PAIR OF BALD eagles in early May. Since then she'd hiked up to the Bluffs every weekend. The eagles had repaired the nest and lined it with downy feathers. Just last weekend, Bonnie saw her first glimpse of an egg. This week, because the days were longer and the weather warmer, her hikes had been daily. Always careful not to freak out the birds, Bonnie had patiently sat near the rim, willing the eagles to forget she was there.

Thursday, her diligence had been rewarded. The mother eagle, while adjusting herself on the nest, had allowed Bonnie to spy the entire clutch—three eggs. If someone had forced Bonnie to explain why the sight had made her want to laugh right out loud, she'd have been at a loss. The simple fact was that this solitary nest of raptors and their ovoid offspring made her happy.

And what the hell, happy wasn't something in abun-

dance these days.

She'd come back this Friday afternoon, a woman on a mission. She meant to have a picture of these birds, this nest, and if the gods smiled, this clutch of eggs.

"Hold still, Hypatia." Bonnie tried to steady the camera.

The last thing she needed was a fidgety dog tugging at her leash. As Bonnie was leaving for the Bluffs, a not-so-still voice tried to tell her this might not be the ideal time to bring the dog.

Not that Bonnie really blamed the retriever. In the four months since the dognapping, Hypatia still whined whenever she and Bonnie hiked up to the overlook.

"You can't stay scared forever, sweetie. I know all about that."

To her credit, the dog didn't whimper, but kept her doggy thoughts to herself.

Bonnie took another step closer to the rim to get a better angle. She centered the nest in her viewfinder and took the first shot. She'd brought the digital so the process could be made as soundless as possible.

The mother eagle had spread her wings. The array of plumage filled the frame with a double triangle of red-brown, black, and white feathers—an eerie mixture of domesticity and wildness that took Bonnie's breath away.

Pinkwater scores. The crowd goes wild. National Geographic *clamors for a print.*

"Yeah, right," Bonnie whispered as she prepared for

the next shot.

Ben had always been the photographer in their family. Bonnie could count in the dozens the number of out-of-focus, misaligned, or headless photographs she'd taken of her husband. Most of the good shots she had of him had been taken by strangers.

"Mister, would you take a picture of my husband and me?"

Even the camera she now held had belonged to Ben. *Well, it's mine now.*

She heard a screech and looked up to spy the father returning, his wings bent back, his talons extended. Bonnie was sure the creature meant to rend her with those same talons. Teach her a thing or two about sticking her nose into family business where it wasn't welcome.

Hypatia barked at the incoming bird.

"Hush, sweetie." Bonnie stepped back, tripped, and sat down hard, but not before she snapped a picture of the eagle in flight.

She opened her eyes to see a now-quiet dog staring down at her. No angry daddy eagle in sight.

Her heart was beating double time when she allowed herself a viewing of the shot.

Not bad—eyes-closed, fall-on-your-butt photography, but what the hell.

The bird's tufted legs and talons seemed to be coming right out of the photo. It even captured the fierce amber glare in the eagle's eyes.

Bonnie scrambled to her hands and knees.

She brought her face close to the dog's snout. "If I let you go, do you promise to be good? I need one more."

Hypatia stared back, not promising anything.

"I guess that's as good as I'm going to get." She disconnected the umbilical and started crawling.

At the rim, Bonnie looked down and saw the changing of the guard. Twice before, she'd been there when the parents exchanged places. As the mother shifted aside to allow the father access, all three eggs were visible.

Ignoring the pain in her elbows, she braced herself, and captured the off-white ovoids in her viewfinder. She willed her hands to stop shaking.

Just take the damn thing, Pinkwater.

The camera whirred. There, pretty as you please, sat three not-so-tiny eggs electronically reproduced in a rectangle of light. Bonnie scooted back, the camera held high.

"Oh yeah, that's what I'm talking about!"

Hypatia was still where Bonnie had left her. "Good girl. Just one more thing to do."

Bonnie slipped the camera into her pocket, drew a long breath, and rose to her feet.

Three days after the dognapping, Bonnie had returned to the Bluffs to look for the hawk stone. No luck. She hadn't been able to find it anywhere. She'd also hoped to see the red-tailed hawk, but there again, nothing. Not then nor anytime since had the bird made an appearance.

Bonnie picked up Hypatia's leash and led the dog back to the massive boulder where she'd sat with Ben more times than she could count. She settled herself against the cold stone.

"I guess this is all about belief, Benjamin. I'm not really sure anymore what I believe, but this much I do know. I don't much want to keep coming here looking for some bird or spirit or whatever. It's just too hard. This was the place I shared with a man, flesh and blood, fingers and toes—my husband of thirty-three years. You died in a hospital room on Christmas Eve. I said good-bye."

A tear blurred her vision of the valley below and Pikes Peak beyond.

Hypatia licked her hand.

"Those times you bird-talked to me up here are starting to get fuzzy in my mind. I'm thinking before long I'll convince myself they were just the imaginings of a lonely woman. And lonely's okay. I can live with that. It's the price I'm willing to pay for all the good times."

She searched the sky, but no hawk challenged her assertions. "Anyway, this is good-bye again. And it's from a hell of a lot better spot than that smelly hospital room."

She stood upright and brushed off her blue jeans.

"You take care of yourself, Benjamin. Thanks for a half-billion smiles."

"Palm trees don't say graduation to me." Next to the dais, Bonnie set down her end of the artificial palm. An hour from now, twenty-eight teenagers would perform a solemn rite under the auspices of these same plastic fronds.

"Aren't these trees left over from the prom?" His face red, Freddy Davenport stood upright and sucked in a barrel of air.

"Waste not, want not. That's our superintendent's motto. Somehow they didn't seem so surreal a month ago." Bonnie massaged the small of her back trying to work out an ache.

Serves you right for volunteering your fifty-year-old back when Freddy could have commandeered any number of teenage spines. That's why God made juniors, Pinkwater.

She surveyed the fruits of her labor. Above her head, strings of paper gardenias festooned the otherwise-stark gym ceiling. These same gardenias encircled each of the four doorways leading into the gymnasium. The cinderblock walls sported posters of sugar-white sands, crashing waves, and hula girls. An artificial lei draped each of twenty-eight folding chairs.

A rustle made Bonnie turn.

Decked out in his black-and-purple graduation robe, Wes Oliheiser snatched a lei and hung it around his neck. Bare legs and hot-pink shower clogs protruded from beneath the robes. He clutched several sheets of paper in one hand.

"Hidey ho, Missus P, Mister Davenport. You both worked up a bit of a sweat this fine Sunday morning."

The sight of this free spirit pretending to be a man brought a reckless grin to Bonnie's face. "I'll have you know, you rude child, that women don't sweat. We glow."

"Then you're glowing all over the place." Wes hopped onto the dais and positioned himself behind the podium. He spread out the papers.

"Is that your speech?" Bonnie asked.

Wes was valedictorian. He probably would have been the second-place salutatorian behind Greg Hansen had not fate decided otherwise.

So it goes.

Freddy waved wearily. "I have to go change and do the final check on the diplomas. You kids be good."

Wes waited until Freddy exited the gym before he spoke. "Yeah, it's the speech. You want to hear it?"

The boy wore such a cockeyed look of mischief that Bonnie despaired. "Go ahead."

"Goat-head yourself. Here goes. Been a hell of a year—"

Bonnie held the pinkie of her left hand above her head. Since the day of their pact, Bonnie had resorted to the use of the pinkie signal only once before. True to his word, Wes had immediately brought to a halt the rant he'd been downloading on another senior boy.

Once again, he quit speaking at the signal.

Wes stepped from behind the podium. "This isn't my Imp taking over, Missus P." He waved the papers at her. "I know exactly what I'm doing."

"Does that include embarrassing your parents and Superintendent Divine?" She lowered her hand but kept the pinkie extended.

"You're going to have to trust me."

Bonnie studied the young man and knew he was right. Even if she had the inclination—which she didn't—with finals in the can, she'd already negotiated away most of her power. If Wes listened to her at all, it was out of pure courtesy.

"Fair enough," she said. "Then the answer to your first question is no. I'll wait to hear the speech along with everyone else."

"You sure? I think you'll like it."

"I'm sure I will, Wes. Just remember our pact."

"My Imp won't even make an appearance."

"Uh huh." Bonnie walked from the gym wondering, *How many times have I told that to someone myself?*

At her room, Bonnie locked her door and stripped down to her unmentionables. From a gym bag she brought out a large economy-sized container of baby wipes. What she really needed was a shower. Unfortunately, the girl's locker room was full of seniors changing into their robes.

This little camping trick of Ben's would have to suffice.

Ten minutes, some deodorant, and a little perfume later, Bonnie reached for her stockings.

With any luck, I won't smell too much like a newborn's bottom.

As she pulled on the slip, dress, and heels, an imagined orchestra played Bolero in the background. Just as the strings and horns reached their crescendo, Bonnie swung open her closet.

With the help of a lighted mirror, she put together her face.

That done, she checked her watch—a half hour to go.

Graduates would be gathering in the hall. Freddy Davenport would have already rolled in the diploma cart. Lloyd would be performing the tenth sound check that morning. Parents would be vying for advantageous camcorder seats in the gym's grandstands. Harvey Sylvester would be closing the betting book on which senior boy would be the first to shed a tear.

Bonnie smoothed out her dress and slung her fanny pack over her shoulder.

Showtime.

Bonnie hadn't been ensconced on her high metal bleacher seat two minutes when Trent Hendrickson plopped down beside her.

He tipped his black cowboy hat. "If it isn't the ever-vivacious Bonnie Pinkwater."

Bonnie sighed. Since the night of the board meeting, the man had been relentless. She'd felt obligated to offer a second dinner, and Trent had taken the gesture as open season.

"Hello, Trent. Should we cut to the chase? No, I don't want to sleep with you, not now, not anytime in the foreseeable future."

The rancher's smile never dimmed. "At least you didn't say never."

"You're hopeless."

"I prefer to think of myself as hopeful. Speaking of strange bedfellows." Trent pointed with his chin down to the gym floor.

Looking like a bear stuffed into a Western suit, Harvey Sylvester strode by.

"Yonder PE teacher is no longer Angelica Devereaux's boy toy."

In spite of herself, Bonnie turned toward the rancher. "And you know this how?"

"A certain school nurse cornered me last week—thought I might enjoy the news."

"I'll bet you both did."

Angelica and Harvey had been the topic of lounge gossip for the month after Greg Hansen's arrest. For a

Robert Spiller

while it looked as if Harvey might lose his job, and Angelica be brought up on charges of her own surrounding
her involvement with Greg. When the smoke cleared, a
severely worded reprimand was added to Harvey's file,
but he kept his job. As for Angelica, no charges were ever
filed. Bonnie suspected the widow cooperated big-time
with the police in exchange for her freedom.

Trent leaned in closer. "I even know who she replaced Grizzly Adams with." Once again he pointed with
his chin, this time toward the dais.

In folding chairs across the back sat Cal Upton,
Freddy Davenport, Lloyd Whittaker, and Xavier Divine.
Bonnie couldn't tell who Trent was indicating. Certainly
not Cal Upton—the man was a youth pastor at the First
Baptist Church. Hopefully not Lloyd or Freddy, since
both men were married.

"Divine?" she whispered.

Trent nodded. "Mister Dumpty himself."

Bonnie suppressed a giggle. She was having difficul-
ty picturing the rotund balding man keeping pace with
the oversexed Angelica. "I don't believe it."

"Believe it. I give him two months."

"Before she dumps him?"

"No, ma'am. Before his cholesterol-clogged arteries
explode."

This time Bonnie couldn't restrain herself. She and
Trent both laughed out loud, eliciting curious stares from

several onlookers.

The big rancher stood. "I've got to go. I'm supposed to be sitting with Kip's grandparents, and they just came in. Enjoy the show." He flashed his pearly whites and bounded to the floor.

He'd no sooner left than Byron Hickman approached, camcorder strapped to one hand.

"You two seemed to be having a good ol' time."

Bonnie patted the still-warm seat. "Join me, youngster, and don't read anything into that scene. Trent just told me a joke."

Byron looked as if he could use a good joke.

Bonnie hadn't seen much of him in the past few months. There'd been the funerals, of course, but she and her former student hadn't done much more than exchange pleasantries. As a relative of the accused, he'd been taken off the murder case. She heard he'd hired an expensive lawyer on Greg's behalf.

The few times she'd seen Byron, he'd seemed harried and preoccupied. Today was no exception.

He cleared his throat, looking embarrassed, as if he had something he needed to say and was trying to build up to saying it. "I'm going to tape Matt Boone when he marches in."

"That's nice." Bonnie felt like she was holding her breath waiting for the other shoe to fall.

"Matt came to see Greg last week."

"That Matt always was a forgiving boy. I never could see him holding a grudge." *Which is more than I'm inclined to do.*

"They talked about you."

Bonnie turned so she could look Byron dead in the eyes. "Just get on with it, youngster."

Byron ran a finger around the collar of his Western shirt. "Greg asked for you, asked if you would come see him."

There it was. "Did you tell him when they serve snow cones in hell?"

Byron reddened. "He apologized to Matt. He wants to apologize to you."

She took Byron's hands in hers. "Deputy Hickman, you're a nice man. I think it's wonderful you've stood by Greg all through this time, but hear this loud and clear. Greg Hansen is a murderer, a liar, a deceitful manipulator who played the two of us like a pair of hand puppets."

The fact that Byron nodded in agreement just egged Bonnie on. "He intended to let Matt go to prison for Luther's murder. God damn it, Byron. He's a monster. I want nothing to do with him." Her hands were shaking so badly she lost her grip on Byron.

"He would have killed me," she whispered.

Her former student pulled her into his arms. "I'm sorry. I promised I'd ask."

Byron released her, offered a weak smile, and stood. "You take care of yourself. Got to get down on the floor to catch the graduates coming in."

He stepped around an elderly couple who'd been making a valiant effort not to eavesdrop.

Damn, damn, damn. "Byron, wait."

She fished around in her fanny pack and came out with three photographs. "I took these the day before yesterday." She handed Byron the photos.

He ruffled through them. "These are from up on the Bluffs, aren't they? What are they, bald eagles?"

"Yes, to both questions." She waved him away. "No big deal. Just give them to Greg. He'll understand."

Byron held her gaze in his. "Thanks, Missus P."

The first strains of "Pomp and Circumstance" interrupted the moment.

"Get a move on, youngster. You wouldn't want to miss Matt strutting his stuff."

Wes Oliheiser adjusted the mike. He stared out over the double row of his classmates.

"Hell of a year."

Laughter erupted in the student ranks, although not much in the stands or on the dais. Lloyd and Freddy smiled.

Wes waited for the noise to die down before he began again.

"I don't think anybody is likely to forget the murders, so I'm not going to say much about them. There's been enough said anyway."

This time silence was the order of the day.

"I'm supposed to speak about the future and how this is the first day of the rest of our lives. So let me get that out of the way. From here we start the future, our real future, where we get to be grown-ups, get married, have babies, although . . ."

Wes made a show of staring at a senior girl who obviously sported a bulge beneath her robe. Bonnie couldn't be certain, but the girl appeared to make a familiar obscene hand gesture. Again, spontaneous laughter sprang up.

"Sorry, Amy. I couldn't resist. Where was I? Oh yeah, we have all of that to look forward to, but you know what? We would have gotten older even if we never went to East Plains High School." Wes stretched wide his arms. "What I want to talk about is what we're going to take with us from our time here. Which brings me back to my original statement—hell of a year."

He paused and looked toward where Bonnie was sitting. For a brief moment their eyes locked.

"If this last year taught us anything, it taught us not to jump to conclusions or onto bandwagons. There's a poster in Mister Davenport's office that reads, *What is popular isn't always right, and what is right isn't always popular*. I don't know about any of you, but in the last few months, it felt like that was written just for me.

"*What is popular isn't always right.* I can't speak for you guys, but I'm embarrassed about the bandwagon I jumped onto a few months back. So I'm going to take this opportunity to apologize to Matt Boone. Anybody who wants to join me is invited to do so." Wes turned back toward the four seated administrators. "That includes you guys."

He stepped from around the podium. Every senior boy and girl, including Matt, who simply looked confused, stood. The four seated men also rose to their feet, although Divine appeared reluctant.

"Matt," Wes began, "I just want to say I'm sorry for any trouble I caused you. My mouth sometimes gets away from me."

A red-faced Matt Boone shouted, "That's okay, Wes! I make mistakes, too!"

For the next few minutes, the seniors crowded around Matt, embracing him and offering their apologies. Several girls removed their leis and draped them around Matt's neck. One planted a kiss on his cheek. The lopsided smile that split the boy's face could have illuminated the entire auditorium.

Cal Upton stepped to the podium. "On behalf of the staff, administrators, and school board, I want to add my sentiments to those expressed by Mister Oliheiser."

A bit stiff and noncommittal, but better than nothing.

Too bad Cal didn't make Divine apologize. That would have been some sweet symmetry.

When the seniors had returned to their seats, Wes went back behind the podium. "Just one more thing we need to take from this place before we go to all those graduation parties. *What is right isn't always popular.* That's the tough one. Standing up for what we believe in. Taking the heat. Hanging strong when everyone is down on us. I learned a lot about that this year." Again, Wes glanced toward Bonnie.

She prayed he wouldn't single her out the way he had Matthew. To her relief, he looked back to his notes.

"Anyway, we could have done a lot worse than spend four years learning those two lessons at EPHS. For those and everything else you guys taught us, thanks."

To a round of applause, Wes stepped down from the dais.

As soon as the uproar died, Divine approached the mike. "Would Missus Pinkwater join me at the podium?"

Even though Bonnie had been expecting this moment for the last few hours, the invitation threw her into a panic. Now she wished she'd had time to take that shower.

As she weaved her way out of the stands, Divine continued, "We've arrived at the moment you've all been waiting for, the awarding of the diplomas. For the past few years, it has fallen upon myself to present the actual certificates to the class. However, one family has asked that Missus Pinkwater make a singular presentation."

When Bonnie reached the floor, she was met by Pansy Boone. Bonnie almost didn't recognize the woman.

"Your hair!"

Pansy's hair was no more than a shadow of its former glory. The woman's gray locks had been shorn, barely reaching her shoulders. "I had it done yesterday. Do you like it?"

Bonnie pulled Pansy into a hug. "I love it."

She held Pansy at arm's length to get a longer view. "What does Frank think?"

"He won't admit it, but I think he likes it, too. He brought me flowers last night."

"Pansies?"

"How did you know?"

From behind the podium, Divine cleared his throat.

"I've got to go. We'll talk after."

Bonnie climbed the stage, and Divine handed her a thick rectangle of purple and yellow, a diploma. Bonnie looked out over the students who had defined a significant portion of her last nine months.

"In my career, I've come to about a million of these events. I think Napoleon Bonaparte was in my first graduating class."

A polite smattering of laughter told her to get on with it.

"In all that time, I've never gotten the opportunity to

do what I get to do next." She paused to relish the moment. "Ladies and gentlemen, parents and loved ones, staff and board members, I give to you the class of 2004."

The walls reverberated with applause as everyone rose to their feet. For a full minute, whistles and ballyhoos echoed throughout the gym. Flashes, like tiny stars winking on, then off, exploded across the grandstands.

When the uproar faded to a workable level, Bonnie continued, "It is my privilege to present the first of the diplomas. Matthew Boone."

If it were possible, Matthew smiled even more broadly than before. His loose gait carried him to the foot of the podium.

Bonnie unwound the mike from its gooseneck and joined the boy. As she handed him his diploma, she reached up and turned the tassel on his mortarboard. "Matthew Boone will join the workforce almost immediately. Ladies and gentlemen, I give to you my newest colleague, a member in good standing of the East Plains' kitchen staff, Mister Matthew Boone."

Again, applause erupted across the gymnasium.

In the midst of the tumult, Frank Boone stepped forward and threw his arms around his diminutive son, knocking the mortarboard from his head. Bonnie stooped to retrieve it.

The elder Boone took it from her. "Thank you."

"My pleasure. By the way, I like your wife's haircut."

For the first time in Bonnie's photographic recollection, Frank Boone smiled. "Me, too."

Bonnie nodded at her long-term adversary and stepped past the trio. She suddenly felt exhausted and couldn't bring herself to climb back into the stands. Luckily, with her moment in the spotlight over, everyone's attention was focused on the stage and the remaining twenty-seven graduates. She slipped out of the gym.

Her intention had been to just take a breather, return in five, maybe ten minutes. However, once she found herself in the relative solitude of the hallway, her feet carried her to the front door and out into the parking lot. The June sun was warm on her face, but none of that warmth seemed to enter her psyche.

Get over it, Pinkwater. Nobody likes a crybaby.

Key in hand, she approached Alice, The-Little-Subaru-That-Could. When she opened the door, her breath caught in her throat.

On her driver's seat lay the hawk stone.

Bonnie stood there a long moment before the smile began to spread across her face. "God damn you, Benjamin Pinkwater."

Also available by Robert Spiller:

THE WITCH OF AGNESI

ISBN#1932815724
ISBN#9781932815726
Trade Paperback
US $9.99 / CDN $12.99
Mystery
www.rspiller.com

CHAPTER 1

THURSDAY WAS SHAPING UP INTO ONE OF those days that made Bonnie Pinkwater wish for a dart gun, the kind used to put rhinos, or in this case teenagers, to sleep. She brushed a gray tendril of hair from her forehead and held up her hands, palms toward her twenty-six student class, the signal for quiet. "One at a time."

Stephanie Templeton shook back her Barbie-doll tresses. "Just explaining to Morticia Addams here that The Witch of Agnesi doesn't have anything to do with witches."

The headache excavating the inside of Bonnie's cranium ratcheted to six on the Richter scale. Her finger twitched at the trigger of her fantasy pistol.

The other girl, Ali Griffith, opened her mouth to speak.

Stephanie cut her off. "It probably got its name because the curves look like witch's hats."

"Play nice, Stephanie. No name calling." Bonnie pointed with her chin toward the other girl. "Your turn."

Ali bristled.

Straight, jet-black, shoulder-length hair, black eye shadow, nail polish and lipstick, Ali—short for Alexandria—bristled better than most. Her dark eyes flashed, and she looked every centimeter the witch she claimed to be. It was easy to believe she might turn a sneering debutant into a spotted salamander.

Ali's ebony lips curled in disgust. "I never claimed The Witch of Agnesi had anything to do with the craft. I just said it seemed a weird name for a curve. Then this, this . . ." Her mouth formed around a B-word.

Bonnie was sure the word in question had nothing to do with Beelzebub. Though she agreed with Ali's unspoken assessment, she gave the girl a warning look nonetheless.

I'm getting too old for this shit.

Red-faced, Ali waved her hand at Stephanie and drew a long breath. "When I told Stephanie, she pulled a Cruella DeVille on me."

Stephanie huffed.

Ali shot her a threatening glare.

Time to take a nap, ladies.

A pair of well-aimed darts from Bonnie's fantasy pistol sent the two arguing girls into the arms of Orpheus. They slumped across their desks, hands dangling each to a side, a look of angelic peace glowing on their unlined faces.

From the hip, no less.

Unfortunately, the real Ali and Stephanie remained painfully awake.

The wall clock showed ten minutes until the end of first period.

Not likely to get more done anyway. "All right, I meant to work with some of the actual math of the curve today and save the story until tomorrow, but what the heck."

Several students settled themselves into their seats, giving Bonnie the vague fear that in her impending senility she'd become one of those teachers who could be distracted into wasting time. To quell a guilty conscience, she wrote both the Cartesian and parametric representations of the Witch of Agnesi equation on the board then drew the corresponding graph.

"As a matter of fact, you two, each of your points is well taken." She pointed to the Cartesian representation. "This implicitly defined equation and its corresponding curve have nothing to do with witchcraft, *per se*. However, how The Witch of Agnesi got its name makes an interesting tale."

The door to her classroom burst open. Edmund Sheridan, a tall Asian boy with blond-tinted spiked hair lurched into the room. "Missus P, Jesse Poole's beating the crap out of Peyton Newlin."

The roar of hallway commotion echoed into the classroom. Bonnie fixed a hand on Edmund's shoulder. "Go get Principal Whittaker."

"He's not in the school."

"Check the Ad-building." She let go of Edmund's shoulder then turned to her class. "Ali, you're in charge until I get back. Call down to the office on the intercom. Tell them what's happening."

When Bonnie saw Edmund still standing in the doorway she shoved him. "Get going. Take the back hallway."

She legged it out of the classroom. At the far end of the gymnasium/library hallway, past yellow lockers lining both sides, a raucous crowd screamed derision and encouragement.

What the hell, don't their teachers wonder where they are?

Opening and closing her mouth like an oxygen-starved goldfish, the new librarian, a twenty-something blonde who looked maybe fifteen, gazed out of her wire-glass window at

3

the chaos in the hall.

Bonnie shook her head and strode toward the uproar. I'm definitely too old for this. Grappling shoulders and pulling herself through, she worked her way into the deafening crowd. "All right!" she bellowed. "Step aside."

Jesse Poole, a bull-necked, teenaged Neanderthal with a glistening bald head sat astride the chest of a bloodied Peyton Newlin.

Bonnie grabbed Jesse's arm.

His meaty paw shoved her back.

She lost her footing and fell into the crowd, her beige wool skirt flying high across her chest. A bolt of pain lanced between her eyes as her headache notched to Richter seven. She rejected assistance and struggled to her feet. Smoothing down her skirt, she shouted, "Mister Poole, stand up immediately!"

A silence fell over the crowd. *All right, that's more like it.*

Jesse stood. Chest heaving, fists balled at his sides, he faced her. Tears poured from his red and swollen eyes. Rivulets of sweat streamed down his shaved head. He locked eyes with Bonnie for an eternal moment then advanced, stopping an arm's length in front of her.

Not liking this much.

"You don't know shit." He brushed past her and pushed through the crowd. "None of you know shit!" he screamed. Waving his hands as if fending off a swarm of gnats only he could see, he lumbered, hunched over for a few more steps. Then with a loping gait, he ran toward the back door and slammed through it.

No way did Bonnie consider challenging him. The

satisfaction of control she'd felt moments before gave way to numbed shock. Jesse Poole was a force of nature when angered.

"Back off, people. Let me through." Principal Lloyd Whittaker's nasal voice rose above the crowd murmurs. A white handkerchief in his hand, he knelt and wiped at the blood pouring from Peyton's nose.

As Bonnie approached, Lloyd looked up.

"I was over at Admin speaking with the superintendent. What happened?"

She spread wide her hands. "Jesse Poole—at it again." With a tilt of her head she pointed back the way Jesse had run.

"What did happen, Peyton?" Lloyd helped the boy to his feet.

"I didn't fight back." Peyton took Lloyd's kerchief and held it under a still bleeding nose. He peered at Bonnie over the cloth's reddening folds.

At four-foot-ten, his blond crew-cut rose only to the height of her chin.

"We'll talk about this in my office." Lloyd took him by the elbow. "Ladies and gentlemen," he shouted. "This is over. Anyone still in the hall when the late bell rings better have a pass."

He hurried the boy toward his office. "What was he doing out of class?"

I'm thinking he spent a portion of his time getting his tiny ass kicked.

Bonnie scurried to catch up. "Peyton and Edmund Sheridan do Calculus independent study in the Library." She followed Lloyd and the boy through the main office and into the principal's smaller one.

Peyton gave his nose a last swipe and set the handkerchief onto Lloyd's desk. He fell into a burgundy overstuffed chair and looked up at Bonnie. "Don't let him keep me out of Knowledge Bowl." He thrust out a defiant and split lower lip. "That would be just bunk. I didn't do anything."

Despite his posturing, she saw the pleading in his eyes. But what could she do? If he participated in a fight, a suspension wouldn't be long behind, which in turn would wipe out any possibility of his competing that night. She tried to ignore the selfish voice that whispered—*without Peyton your Knowledge Bowl team will fare pretty much the same as Peyton did a minute ago with Jesse.*

"I'm afraid that's up to Principal Whittaker."

Peyton's face turned red to his hair line. "It wasn't really a fight. I didn't hit back, Mister Whittaker. Jesse, he just pounds on me for no good reason whenever he feels like it."

Lloyd gave the boy a hard stare and poked his head out the office door. "Doris, get the school nurse down here."

He shut the office door and sat behind his battered oak desk.

Bonnie pulled a gray-cushioned folding chair up next to Peyton.

Lloyd leaned toward the boy. "Whether you compete tonight depends on how much I like your answer to my next question. And don't even think of lying to me, son. What did you do to provoke Jesse Poole?"

Peyton folded his pipe-cleaner arms across his chest and slumped back into the deep chair. A storm of emotions played across his freckled face. "He'd been picking on me, taking my books, pushing me in the hall, calling me names. He's a stupid jerk, just jealous because he knows I've got more smarts than he'll ever have." His voice rose with every justification until the final words broke into a squeak.

Lloyd's expression never changed. "You haven't answered my question."

And you're beginning to annoy me, Bonnie thought.

"I was getting a drink from the fountain when Jesse kicked my feet out from under me. I fell into the fountain, hit my head." He touched a bump on his forehead. "I had water in my face, down the front of my pants. Jesse said I pissed myself."

"How did you respond?" Lloyd asked, not even trying to hide his impatience.

Peyton's glance darted from Lloyd up to Bonnie. "I was mad."

She'd just about had enough of this boy's equivocating. She laid a hand on his thin shoulder. "Stop stalling, Peyton. Tell Principal Whittaker what he wants to know."

"I said I bet his mother would be real proud of him, picking on a thirteen-year old."

Bonnie drew in a long breath.

Lloyd sat back in his chair, tapping the pads of his fingers together.

A knock sounded on the door and Marcie Englehart, the school nurse entered. A gaunt woman with grey-blond hair, she wore a flowered apron over a blue denim jumper. She glanced about the room, nodded to Bonnie and Lloyd and bent over Peyton. After prodding his nose and the bump on his forehead, she pulled a cotton swab from an apron pocket and dabbed at the split lip.

Peyton winced and squirmed beneath her ministrations.

Marcie unclipped a tiny flashlight from a belt loop. She steadied Peyton's head with a heavily veined hand and trained the flashlight first into one eye then the other. "I don't think he has a concussion, but that lip's going to need a stitch or two."

Peyton shook his head. "No stitches."

She shrugged bony shoulders. "Suit yourself."

Looking past the boy to Lloyd, she said, "Stitches are what I'd recommend, but I can rig a butterfly for the lip."

Lloyd stood and stared down at Peyton. "Young man, this is your third altercation in the last month. I'm inclined to pull you from the team just to catch your attention."

Bonnie sat up to speak.

Lloyd quieted her with an upraised hand. "However, unless I find out you lied about your part in this, you can compete tonight. You know I'll have to call your parents?"

Peyton's eyes went momentarily wide and he nodded. "I suppose."

"You suppose right. I know you were angry, but that was an unwise thing you said to Poole. Now go with Nurse Englehart while I talk to Missus Pinkwater."

In an expression which lasted no longer than a second, Marcie articulated the demand that Bonnie fill her in later. Then with a hand to his back, Marcie ushered the boy through the door and shut it behind her.

Lloyd waited until the door clicked shut. Leaning forward, he whispered, "Truth is, Bon, I don't much care for our resident genius. He's sneaky and manipulative. My gut tells me there's a lot more to this business between Poole and him than he's telling."

Bonnie eyed her long-time friend, unsure how she should reply.

On the one hand, she agreed with Lloyd's assessment of Peyton Newlin. The boy was easy to dislike. Aware of his intelligence, he rubbed people's noses in it. On more than one occasion she'd wanted to wipe the smirk from his face and let him know she was unimpressed with his cleverness.

Lately however, she'd developed a grudging affection for the little schmuck. Behind the arrogant posturing she saw an anxious kid hungry for approval.

"I hear you," she said. "And you're probably right. I've never seen Jesse Poole cry before, but he did today. No doubt, Peyton said more than he's admitting to."

Lloyd ran a callused hand down his face. "If I were Jesse I'd have beat the daylights out of Newlin myself. My mother's dying, and this arrogant pipsqueak used the situation to—"

"He's just thirteen, Lloyd."

He waved away her excuse as if it lent a foul smell to the room.

"Bon, this is a bad situation. Poole's going to come after Newlin. You be careful tonight. Everybody in the school knows Knowledge Bowl is at the Interfaith Academy. Jesse Poole's no exception."

For more information
about other great titles from
Medallion Press, visit

www.medallionpress.com